WINGS OF TORMENT

VICTORIA PAULEY

Contents

To the weirdo. The freak. The reject.
Normal is overrated.

Author's Note

I'm thrilled to finally share Wings of Torment with you. While this is not a dark romance, the characters in this series all need to overcome their own issues. Some of these issues may hit close to home so please read the list below before diving in.

-This book features an FMC who struggles to fit in. She's bullied and ridiculed for being different (not by the main love interests).

-Instances of prejudice between the different types of angels.

-Open door sex.

-Episodes of PTSD from past trauma with flashbacks of a witnessed death

-Mention of the prior death of a parent.

-A difficult relationship with family.

-Demons intent on harm

Silver City University Map

1

HAYLIEL

Everyone stares.

Professors. Students. Even my friends, though they at least look happy to see me.

I feel their approach, but I can't focus on them. I can't seem to focus on anything but the utter destruction around me. The familiar ring of trees that once circled this old well has changed. Broken stumps and uprooted trees surround me, and the few that appear nearly untouched now hold up the bloodied angels watching me.

How did this happen?

Footsteps crunch over the scattered ash circled around me, quickly drowned out by the frantic thump of my heart. I should be used to the stares by now, but at least then I knew what they were for. Now I'm stuck in a vortex of confusion, and it doesn't feel like I'll ever escape.

A hint of leather fills my nose, so I know Zeke is close. He grabs my arms, and our eyes lock. His are full of concern as he trails them over my face and down my body. I'm sure my eyes must be wide and unhinged, but that doesn't stop him from pulling me into an embrace.

When his arms envelop me, all I want to do is collapse. I hold on to him, whether for comfort or balance, I don't even know, but I feel safe here.

His husky voice vibrates through his chest, but I can't focus enough on the words to understand. Before I know it, I'm being pulled away by soft fingers.

"By the Archangels, Hayles. Are you alright?" Dina asks, pushing the hair from my face.

"Yeah. I think so."

No one buys it.

Raphael hugs me next, pressing a kiss to the top of my head, and then his words are in my mind. *You gave us quite the fright, sunshine.*

I squeeze him a little tighter, pushing my words at him with ease. *I'm just glad you're all okay.* Nothing can get to me as long as I stay entwined with him. I'm protected from the world.

He turns me around and presses me into another warm body, this one unfamiliar yet recognizable all the same. Theo. He's never held me like this before, or at all, really. But within the confines of his arms, I feel nurtured and cared for.

"Are you sure you're fine?" Theo asks, pulling back to look at me.

I nod but can't stop the question from surfacing in my mind. Am I? Can any of us really be fine after what just happened?

Then I notice the blood. Theo's clothes are covered in it. He and Dina have faded claw marks on their arms, and Raphael sports a rather gnarly looking gash on his thigh, but I can't tell the severity beneath all the dried, crusty blood. Zeke is the least bloodied, with only a torn uniform and dark droplets of what can only be demon blood splattered across it.

"Enough about me. Are you guys injured? This isn't all yours, is it?" I eye the impossible amount of blood coating Theo's shirt, my heart pounding as I wait for a response. Have I failed them? These angels who have become my closest friends, were they harmed while trying to protect me?

"No," he replies, clasping my hand in his and poking a hole in my ever-growing worry. "We're actually considered the lucky ones, compared to what we saw of the other students." His grimace paints enough of a picture for me to believe him and forces my mind back to the day of the assembly. After that incident, I knew whatever happened in his past had to have involved demons. If his trauma had risen again during the battle, who knows what might have happened to him?

"Breathe, sunshine. We're all a little banged up, but we'll live."

The knot that had formed in my chest while I hid beneath my wings loosens, and I can finally breathe a little easier. We survived. Sure, with a few scrapes and bruises, but we're here. We're still breathing. As much as I try to focus on that, I can't shake the confusion. How did we, and everyone else, defeat a horde of angry demons? Had the Guild finally shown up with their special swords? That would explain the pile of ash at my feet, but I don't recall seeing anyone in a Guild uniform except for Zeke in front of me. The last thing I remember is the awful snarls from the encroaching circle of horrid beasts while I hid.

"What happened here?" I try to keep my voice steady but fail miserably, the words coming out shaky and soft.

Zeke is the first to respond. "You don't know?"

I shake my head. "I just remember hiding with my wings like a coward until I heard you all call for me. Then I was just so fucking angry and worried that one or all of you would get hurt. Next thing I know, there's a blinding light and the demons are gone."

My words don't ease the confusion from their faces like I'd hoped.

"Babe," Dina says, her voice soft. "That blinding light came from you."

Her words hit me harder than any demon had. The light came from *me*? But that doesn't make sense.

I gaze around my circle of friends, then beyond them to the still-gawking group of angels. It's thinned out some, but enough remain to make me wary. Keeping my voice low, I ask, "What do you mean?"

Raphael steps closer, sensing my unease. "The moment your wings opened, light flashed. Almost like you held a tiny storm within your wings and, as soon as they unfurled, a thousand bolts of lightning escaped."

"Once it dissipated, all the demons were just ... gone. Turned to ash," Theo says, running a hand through his messy curls. "If I hadn't seen it for myself, I might not have believed it."

I sway a little on my feet, folding my arm across my stomach to stop the odd sensations roiling through me. Zeke's next words halt the breath in my lungs.

"Your wings have been different ever since."

My wings!

I remember now that Zeke said something earlier, but everything felt like a dream then. My now-golden wings glint beneath the fading light. With a flex of my muscles, I spread them wide and watch as the color shifts beneath the dying rays of the sun.

They're beautiful.

Shit. Is this why everyone is staring? One more thing for the other students to ridicule me for. I'm sure Harold the Herald will take great pleasure in writing about this in his next column.

Panic settles heavy in my chest as I stand on display, desperately wishing to be anywhere else. Maybe if I hide inside my wings again, they'll forget I'm even here.

Professor Castiel stands among the group of onlookers. We share one brief look before he jumps into action.

"Alright, students. Please head to the tower so we may assess each of you for injury." A few students don't move quickly enough, so he speaks a little louder. "This is not a request. Let's move."

"But what about them?" an unfamiliar student says, eyes trained on me.

"They are not your concern. Now go, or I'll haul you there myself."

After a few grumbled words, they take off toward the tower. Professor Castiel looks from me to my friends, and then back to me. For a moment, I think he wants to say something, but all he does is nod before turning on his heel and leaving us.

"Come on, Hayles," Dina says, pressing a hand to my shoulder.

I nod, immediately grateful for her presence, and follow her down the hill.

The professor might have forced some angels to leave, but they aren't the only ones on campus. There are more at the bottom of the hill, and as soon as they see me, their eyes grow wide. Shit. I regret not putting my wings away sooner. They're the cause of the mess I'm currently in. Hell, *every* mess I've ever been in. Those suckers need to go away, stat.

With a quick flex, my wings disappear beneath my skin, and I let out a little breath. Instead of feeling uncomfortable like I expected, my new wings seem to hum beneath my flesh like a long-lost friend. There's a sense of comfort within them that both startles and worries me.

Why can't I just be normal?

I follow Dina toward the front doors of the main hall with Raphael, Theo, and Zeke following along. With everything else going on, I hadn't realized how strange it was for Zeke to be here. Doesn't he hate Raphael and Theo, or is it just my supposed relationship with them he doesn't like?

Clearing my throat, I ask, "How'd you find me, anyway?"

"I followed him," Dina says, pointing to Zeke.

"And I was following them," he says, pointing to Raphael and Theo.

"I felt your distress, sunshine. Like a tug on our telepathic bond or something. I don't really know how to explain it, but fuck, I can't say I'm not grateful for whatever it was."

"Huh. Is that a thing?"

Dina loops her arm through mine. "If the bond is strong enough, it is."

I glance toward Zeke, but I don't find the icy stare I expect. Instead, the strange look that's been on his face from moments ago hasn't gone away. Relief, maybe? Shock?

"Hayliel!" Gagiel races toward us with a beaming smile.

"Are you guys alright?"

"For the most part. Are you?"

"Yeah. I was studying in my room the entire time and only caught the end." His cheeks redden a bit, but he presses on. "I saw them cornering you, and I was so fucking worried. But then you just erupted like a volcano and took them all out. What the hell was that?"

I consider lying, telling him it didn't happen. If it were any-one else, I probably would, but Gagiel has been nothing but kind to me, and oddly, I trust him.

"We don't know, actually. But if you could keep what you saw to yourself for now, I'd really appreciate it. There's a lot to figure out first." I glance around, glad to find that no one is paying much attention to us here. Healers focus on tending to the wounded while university staff snap photos of the damage.

"I get it. I won't say a word, but I just wanted to let you know I think you're amazing. Even before all of this"—he waves a hand through the air—"thanks to you, my friends are coming back to campus after the Archangels' Feast in a few weeks. Well, if this whole attack thing doesn't scare them off."

"Oh, that's great! I can't wait to meet them." Something settles in my throat, making it hard to swallow.

He pauses for a moment, then wraps his arms around me in a quick hug. "I'm really glad you're alright." It barely lasts a second before he takes off, leaving me dumbfounded.

What did I do to deserve his kindness? How can he be so confident in someone like me, especially now that I'm an even bigger freak?

Raphael touches my shoulder, jolting me out of my self-pity party and reminding me where I am. Surrounded by pain and destruction.

How many angels were harmed in this attack? And how long will it take for Silver City University to recoup from the destruction?

"In all our research, does anyone remember reading about gold wings?" Raph asks, unperturbed by the scene around us.

I shake my head and fall deeper into my despair. We had a hard enough time finding anything helpful about my gray wings. What are the chances we'll find something now?

"That's why we're going to the principal. Maybe he can help," Dina replies hopefully.

"Maybe." I hope the words come out in a far sunnier tone than my current disposition. As much as I try to adopt the optimism my parents showered me with as a child, I can't seem to muster any up. And as we approach the broken white doors of the main hall, I can't stop the swirling in my gut that tells me, for the second time in so few months, everything is going to change.

2

HAYLIEL

Somehow, there's no damage inside the main hall. In fact, the only real evidence of an attack at all is the broken front doors and a few drops of blood splattered on the floor.

We head left toward the principal's office, but find it empty, and the receptionist is gone as well.

"Did anyone see him during the attack?" Dina asks, but everyone shakes their head.

Dread settles in my gut as we turn to leave. Was he hurt? Did he even show up and attempt to protect the school he runs, or did he hide away and leave us to fend for ourselves? I didn't really get that vibe from him, but my thoughts are a mess right now, and as much as I want to believe he wouldn't do that, I can't. I learned enough about myself today to make me realize I don't even know who *I* am, so how can I possibly know anyone else?

Before we get too far from his office, the principal exits a classroom with a group of healers in tow. He looks more disheveled than I've ever seen him. "There you are! I was informed you'd come this way, but I feared I would be too late."

"Too late for what?"

"Come, come. Whatever it is you're doing will have to wait until you receive a clean bill of health."

"Actually, Principal Cael, we were hoping to speak with you," Dina tells him as we approach.

"Very well, but see the healers first. That's an order." He steps away almost immediately and doesn't hear my objection. I feel fine, and I'd really rather not be under a microscope right now. Instead of arguing that point, though, I follow my friends and the healers into the classroom where they have their supplies set up.

One healer directs Theo to sit on the desk, questioning him on where the blood came from and if he's feeling woozy before he explains it isn't his. Another healer pulls me aside and directs me to a seat of my own.

"There's no need to look me over, really. I feel fine, and the few cuts and bruises I have aren't bothering me. You should focus on someone else."

It appears I've gotten saddled with the most stubborn nurse imaginable because she barely acknowledges my words and taps the desk.

Her face settles into something like awe when I finally take a seat. "Aren't you the angel who single-handedly defeated those nasty demons? And did so in a way that no one here has seen before, might I add?" I can only stare at her in disbelief, but the look on my face must be enough confirmation because she continues. "Precisely. So I apologize, Miss Hayliel, but you are most certainly getting looked at."

She focuses on my cut thigh first, but because of our angelic healing, it's barely a scratch. After a thorough search, she asks if I feel any pain and when I tell her no, she almost lets me leave.

"Your hand is swollen," she says, picking it up and putting light pressure over the puffy, red area.

I wince. "Yeah. I was weaponless, so these had to do. Unfortunately, no one tells us how hard their fucking skulls are."

"I have a feeling there will be some new contingencies in place so this doesn't happen again, but you should all be proud of the way you handled things today. We were lucky they didn't carry anything that could permanently harm us. As for your hand, nothing's broken, only bruised. If this doesn't feel better in a few days, come to the infirmary, alright?"

"I will." Jumping off the desk, I walk to where Zeke, Theo, and Dina wait for Raphael to finish with the nurse. It sounds like his ribs took the same beating as my hand because he's given similar instructions for care.

Before we depart, one of the healers calls out to us. "If you see anyone in need of healing, please send them here."

"It might be good to take a walk around campus with a stretcher. We saw a few injured students near the fountain who wouldn't make the distance on their own," Raphael tells her.

"And over near Knowledge house as well," Theo adds.

"On it. Good job today, students. Come see us if you need anything."

We head back to Principal Cael's office, walking past the still-empty receptionist desk and toward the rather angry voice coming from his office.

"I do not care how busy they seem. They are our protectors, for what little that's worth today. If we cannot rely on them when we need it most, then I don't see why I'd continue to help train their future recruits. Now go inside and find someone with authority, and don't call me before you do."

I share a shocked look with the others. Is he talking about the Guild? He must be fucking furious to consider rescinding his offer of support, but he has a point. They're our only line of defense against, well, anything. And if they aren't available to protect us, how can we feel safe?

We wait a few minutes before knocking, not wanting him to think we were eavesdropping, but before we can all enter, he asks to speak with me alone. I can almost feel the unease coiling off my friends behind me, but I assure them it's fine and stand in front of his desk as the others leave, shutting the door on their way out.

"We find ourselves here again, Miss Hayliel. Though I do wish it was under different circumstances. I'm not sure if you caught my conversation earlier, but I assure you, the Guild will answer for their failure today. And, if what I've heard is correct, we have you to thank for our victory today. Is that true?"

My throat feels dry, but I attempt to swallow, anyway. Instead of answering, I avoid the question. "The school has a great deal of fine students, Principal Cael. Our triumph today wouldn't have been possible without them."

He smiles, face softening. "Yes, yes. That we do. So would it also be true that you've had a rather sudden and spectacular transformation? Gold wings, if what they're saying is to be believed."

The attack has barely ended, yet already rumors are flying. Why am I surprised? "I ... Yes. It appears so."

"May I see them?"

I hesitate, not really wanting to expose myself again to this man, but not entirely sure I have a choice. With his eyes on me, I take a deep breath and release my wings. Just like on my first day of class, fear flows through me as I wait for him to get angry and expel me. He might not have done so before, but what if he does now? With new wings and a supposed new ability that I don't even understand, where am I supposed to go?

But, like before, he doesn't look angry. The principal's eyes widen as he looks at me, and I can't help but glance over my shoulder. My wings are slightly larger than before, with beautiful golden feathers of different shades that seem to shimmer even beneath the unnatural light.

"My, my," Principal Cael says. "Do you mind?"

His hand hovers over the edge of my wings, waiting for me to give my approval. I nod, recalling the last time he did so and how quick and unobtrusive it was.

He runs a fingertip along one feather, then another. "Fascinating." He steps back. "Thank you, Miss Hayliel. You can put them away now and bring the others in."

I open the door to let my friends in while the principal gets comfortable behind his desk. Raphael shoots me a questioning gaze, but I only shake my head in response. *All good,* I reassure him through our mental bond.

"So, Miss Hayliel. Do you feel any different?"

Do I? The more I try to focus, the more I realize how tired I am. But that could be from the change in my wings just as much as surviving the attack. "I'm not sure ... Maybe? It's been a long day, so it's hard to say for sure."

"Of course. My apologies. Please let me know if you notice something over the next few days. Your transformation is quite astonishing and rather unheard of. I suggest you speak to Professor Uriel about this." He must see the look on my face because he quickly adds, "I understand your hesitation, but despite your unfortunate history, he's still the Wingology professor. I believe I saw him in his classroom earlier. You should head there now."

"We will. Thank you, Principal Cael."

Before we can leave, he says, "Please accept my deepest gratitude, and from the school as well, for your roles in today's event.

Rest assured, I'll be doing everything in my power to ensure the school is better protected in the future."

We're silent as we walk down the hall and up the stairs toward Professor Uriel's classroom on the second floor. I wish we didn't have to go see him. Fate has a sick fucking sense of humor to send me to him for information. The professor who not only humiliated me on my first day of class but who has also mentally tortured me ever since, like he had a bone to pick. It's not my fault I was born this way, and it sure as hell wasn't like I *tried* to offend him. I can only imagine what his reaction will be when he finds out I'm even stranger.

We find the door to his classroom closed, but from the small window built into it we can see inside. He looks annoyed, almost angry, as he stacks the books that had fallen off the shelf. At my knock, he turns, and when he catches sight of my face through the window, he scowls. *Just great.*

When he opens the door and notices that I'm not alone, his demeanor shifts. Asshole.

"Students, come in." He pulls the door wide, focusing on everyone except for me. "I'm surprised to find you lurking in the halls after the day we've had. Those horrible, aggressive beasts have caused quite a mess, haven't they?"

"Uh, yes. Of course. The school will have a lot of repairs to make, I'm afraid," I offer awkwardly. It looks like Theo wants to say more, but Raphael puts a hand on his arm to stop him. "Principal Cael sent me here to talk to you. Do you have a minute?"

His face scrunches up slightly, like it physically pains him to say yes. "Perhaps your friends can finish cleaning up those books while we talk."

Without waiting for a response, he steps away, and I follow. Oh goodie. More time alone with this joyful professor. Except I'm not alone. Zeke follows along beside me, and I let his presence bolster my confidence.

Noticing that we aren't alone, Professor Uriel laughs it off. "Ah! A Guild intern. Please send my gratitude to your superiors for their fine work today. Things would have been a lot worse had they not shown up and taken care of our little demon infestation."

Neither of us correct him. I'm not sure why Zeke doesn't, but I'm grateful for it. Rumors are bound to spread about what really happened on that hill, but I have zero intention of confirming those. Let them wonder. The change in my wings has already caused enough of a scene. I'd rather not add fuel to that fire.

Something shifts behind his eyes when we don't respond, and I wonder if he can feel the tension coiled tight around us. We already knew he wasn't on the battlefield, but does he know he's just given himself away?

Instead, he says, "So, what did Principal Cael want you to speak with me about?"

Here goes nothing. "Well, there's been a sudden development with my wings, and he thought you might know something that could help."

"I see. And what is this sudden development?"

Under his attentive gaze, I feel like an insect being examined beneath harsh light. Maybe this was a mistake. I can always go back to researching in the library, right?

A warm hand grips my palm. He doesn't say a word, but Zeke's long, nimble fingers entwined with mine is enough to break the spell I'd been trapped under.

"You'll be happy to know that my wings are no longer gray," I start.

"Oh?"

"But I'm afraid they still aren't exactly normal. Ever heard of gold wings before, Professor?"

His forced smile vanishes, turning into a frown. "Excuse me?" he asks incredulously.

Of course he'd make me repeat myself. What is it with this guy? "None of us really know what happened, but I have gold feathers now, I guess? The gray is completely gone."

"Hmm. Very strange indeed." His eyes flash with something unreadable before settling back into his signature look of un-happiness. "We've all been through a great ordeal today. I think it best if you go back to your dorms and focus on healing."

I share a look with Zeke, blown away by the obvious dis-missal. Yet I really shouldn't be. It was dumb of me to think he'd help at all.

Raphael, Theo, and Dina head over to us, having finished clearing the books from the floor. My voice doesn't seem to want to come out, so all I can do is stare at Professor Uriel and hope that maybe this was all some joke, but he continues to say nothing.

"Professor Uriel," Zeke says, his voice demanding every ounce of attention. "We came here for answers, not to be sent off to bed like errant children up past their bedtime. If you have any insight into what the change in Hayliel's wings mean, we, and I do include the principal in that, would appreciate the information."

The professor's face morphs into something ugly. Clearly he doesn't enjoy being talked to like that by a student, especially not one who appears to be my friend.

"I knew nothing when her wings were gray and I certainly don't know why her wings are now gold. There hasn't been a case of gold wings since before the Archangels saved us from the plight of God. How would—"

"So there *have* been golden-winged angels before?" Theo asks, his face contorting into an expression of confusion.

"What? No. What I mean is, this case is highly unusual and I don't have any answers for you. Now"—he checks his watch—"I have much left to do, and I will see you all when classes resume."

Striding past, he rushes out the door and leaves us with even more questions than we had before.

3

THEO

I hadn't liked that professor before, not after what he did to Hayliel on her first day, but now that asshole is even higher on my shit list.

What the fuck even was that?

My hand shakes a little as I play through the conversation. My gut tells me this guy wasn't heavily involved in protecting the school. He looked far too polished to have been fighting demons. The five of us had been in the thick of it, and only Ezekiel made it out unscathed. Somehow, I doubt Professor Uriel had the matching skill of a Guild intern.

My hands continue to tremble, so I tuck them into my pockets and hope the others haven't noticed. Now isn't the time to let my memories in, so I do my best to shove them down. I'll likely regret it later. Over the years, I've come to realize that ignoring it only means it will come back with even more force. But at least then I'll be alone.

Hayliel droops a little. Today can't have been easy on her. Not that it was easy on any of us, but she'd taken the brunt of it. A physical change like that was bound to be exhausting. Especially when no one seemed to know a damn thing about it.

Dina places a hand on her shoulder. "Why don't we head to my dorm room? We can talk more freely there and rest a little."

We leave the classroom, grateful to get away from the weird vibes left over from Professor Uriel. He's a teacher, for fuck's sake. He has a responsibility to his students, but with Hayliel, it seems he's more than ready to shirk them.

Pushing the back doors open, we step out into the fading sunlight. It dips below the tree line as twilight approaches. The fountain bubbles, just like it always does, but it no longer soothes me. Now, I can't seem to erase the image of those two wounded angels resting against a spout of muddled pink water. Like something from a nightmare. At least it runs clear again now.

One of the Fallen statues is broken, cleaved in two with deep claw marks etched across the usually unblemished surface. The depth of their infiltration is astonishing, but with no one here in a position to defend us, I suppose it could have been worse.

Instead of entering the front door, Dina motions for us to follow her around the left side and fly up to her balcony. No issues with me. I've dealt with enough shit today that I'll gladly avoid any extra interactions with angels outside of our little group.

Hayliel though ... She looks almost scared. Raph senses it too, and we both stop to talk to her.

"What is it, sunshine?"

She looks down at her feet, kicking an errant stone. "I'm kind of nervous about taking my wings out again. What if someone sees? What if they've faded back to gray? Or what if ..." She turns away from us, searching the distance for something, or maybe nothing at all. "What if I can't control whatever flash of light killed those demons and I end up hurting one of you?"

Turning to the others, I say, "Dina, Ezekiel, why don't you head up? We'll be there in a moment." I don't bother waiting for a reply — though I fully expect one from the Fallen house leader, who for some reason hasn't left yet — and instead stand directly behind Hayliel.

I don't say anything. Neither does she. And when Raph approaches, we only stare off into the distance with her.

After what seems like ages, but is probably only a few minutes, I whisper, "Everything is a bit scary, isn't it?"

"But you aren't alone, sunshine. You're never alone. Not with us."

She leans back into me, letting her head fall onto my chest while reaching out to grip Raph's hand. Still she says nothing.

I bask in the feel of her warm body pressed to mine, regardless of the circumstances that got us here. "If you aren't ready, that's alright. We'll be your wings, your feet, your arms. Whatever you need of us."

"Whenever you need it," Raph echoes.

"Thank you," she whispers, wiping a tear away.

Another beat passes before Raph and I move, shifting to stand on either side of her and letting our wings out.

Raphael takes her arm, instructing her to wrap them around our necks. "Hold on tight, baby."

With a few flaps of our wings, we're in the air. It's not like we have very far to go, but I shift my hold from her waist to her thigh so she's a little steadier between us.

When we land on the balcony, a thickly wedged boot props the door open, and Ezekiel and Dina are talking quietly.

Hayliel squeezes my hand, offering a quiet thanks before she moves toward Dina.

"Here." She tosses a handful of clothes at her. "I had Zeke use his key and grabbed you some clothes."

"You're a genius, babe. And these better not be skimpy, or I swear—"

Dina laughs, then fakes a pain in her chest. "You wound me!"

Hayliel's laugh echoes from the bathroom, and as if her happiness is somehow connected to all of us, a smile spreads across our faces. Even Ezekiel's, I notice, though when he catches me looking at him, it fades right back into a scowl.

Dina moves to the bed, propping herself up against the pillows while Raph and I grab a chair. There's a third chair, but Mr. Guild Intern must not enjoy comfort because he doesn't take it. Instead, he leans against the hard surface of the wall, his ever-present scowl plastered on his face.

When Hayliel emerges, looking much more comfortable than before, she curls up on the bed with Dina and lets out a long sigh.

No one talks, but the silence isn't awkward. There's too much that needs to be said, too many things to discuss that it's almost overwhelming.

Raphael finally breaks it, sitting forward to rest his elbows on his knees. "Anyone find it weird that both Principal Cael and Professor Uriel wanted to speak with Hayliel alone? What was it they wanted to say without us there?"

"It was pretty standard with the principal, at least from my experience. He wanted to see my wings for himself, just like he did on my first day when Professor Uriel brought me in for the supposed "prank." Both times he felt one of my feathers too, but other than seeming fascinated, he hasn't really said much."

"Girl. He touched one of your feathers?" Dina asks, looking horrified.

Hayliel's face scrunches up. "Yeah, but it didn't feel creepy. More like he was curious. I'm not sure if he knows more than he's letting on or he just really enjoys discovering new things, but nothing from him ever made me feel uncomfortable."

"Well, I guess that counts for something," I say, though I don't like the idea of her flashing her wings and getting felt up by anyone, especially an angel in a position of power. "And

Professor Uriel? It was obvious he wanted to get Hayliel alone by making us clean up. I'm glad Ezekiel stayed by your side."

The angel in question holds my gaze, and for a moment I think he might be about to smile, but he only nods once before looking away.

"That piece of shit changed his tune real fast when he realized I wasn't going anywhere. He even asked me to thank the Guild for all their hard work in removing the demons, which only leads me to believe that asshole did jack shit to protect the school or its students."

"I picked up on that, too!" Hayliel adds. "And he seemed way too pristine to have seen any action. I mean, take us, for example. Dina and I changed clothes and look how bedraggled we still are?"

Dina hits her gently with a pillow.

I nod, remembering how odd I thought it was when he mentioned the aggressive behavior of the demons. To someone unfamiliar with them, I guess maybe it wouldn't be clear just how unaggressive they were, at least compared to what they could have been, but I don't bother saying so. Instead, I focus on the entire reason we went to see him in the first place. "I think we can all agree he's a dick, but the principal sent you there for information. Did he give you anything helpful about what your wings mean?"

Ezekiel scoffs. "He gave us a whole lot of fuck all."

His words elicit a snort from me. "I think I somehow know *less* after talking to him. And did anyone else catch the weird vibes rolling off him? The way he skirted around my wings and then hightailed it out of there was suspicious as hell."

We're all silent as we consider the possibility that Professor Uriel knows more than he's letting on, but why would he keep it a secret? What would he have to gain by staying quiet? And how is it that the professor whose entire fucking job it is to teach students about our wings knows nothing? It doesn't make sense.

"Since no one else is going to say it, I will," Ezekiel says, standing straighter. "Something weird is going on, and it's not just with the professor."

"What do you mean?" Hayliel asks, looking concerned.

"Well, for starters, when I arrived on campus, I tried calling several members of the Guild, and not a single line was answered. Even my father didn't pick up. And did anyone else notice the demons seemed rather fixated on Hayliel? They practically flocked to her location, but why? Tie that in with the flash of light, scorched demons, and her new wings … none of it makes sense."

"You're right. This doesn't feel like a random attack." I hadn't known about the Guild, but it wasn't like them to not show up. Fuck, that's literally what they're there for. Our protection. So what the hell were they so busy doing? As for the demons focusing on Hayliel, I had my own thoughts on what that meant, but I need to dig more into it before I tell the others.

"It's true. And, babe," Dina says, her eyes trained on Hayliel. "I think you're somehow part of it."

We're all quiet, lost in our own thoughts. There are too many unanswered questions, too many unknowns. I fucking hate it. I hate not knowing the answer and not being able to help my friends. Maybe if I had paid more attention, I could have known this would happen. Maybe I could have prevented it somehow, protected more students instead of letting them down.

No. Now isn't the time to spiral down that particular rabbit hole. That's better saved for later when I'm alone in my room.

"If we can't rely on anyone else, why don't we work together? I don't know about any of you, but I can't just sit by and let this go," Dina says, her voice strong and sure.

At her words, Hayliel sits up straighter. "I sure as fuck can't either, but it's not as if we had any luck finding information on my wings before. What says this will be any different?"

"We know more now," I say, wanting to reassure her. "It's no longer just about your wings. There are far more things at play than we realized, and that could work out in our favor. I'll monitor the news for anything that doesn't add up with what we know."

Raph nods. "Dina and I will put our ears to the ground and see if anyone knows something they shouldn't."

There's a beat of silence before my gaze flicks to the brooding Fallen angel. His scowl deepens when he notices that we're all staring at him, waiting for him to agree.

Raph must grow tired of his bullshit because he says, "Why are you even here if you're not willing to help?"

Before Ezekiel can respond, Hayliel stands from the bed and walks toward him. "I think what Raphael means is, will you help us? The Guild might be able to offer more insight than we'd gather on our own."

Unperturbed by our watching, he only trails his grumpy-ass gaze over Hayliel. I can only glimpse her side profile, but even from here I can tell how much hopefulness he must see on her face.

"I'll consider it," he finally replies before taking one last look around the room, sending a curt nod to Dina, then escaping through the balcony doors.

No one bothers watching him leave. Instead, we turn back to the now-dejected angel still standing by the wall and staring unashamedly at the spot that Ezekiel just walked through.

My heart breaks at the pain I see on her face. Or maybe it's disappointment. Either way, it's not something I ever want to see there, and it takes every fiber of my being not to jump off the balcony and go find the asshole who made her feel this way. I don't do any of that, though. Not today. Instead, I get up and walk toward her with slow, even steps. "Are you alright?" I whisper, placing a hand on her arm.

"Hmm? Oh. Yeah. It's just been a long day."

Like a good friend, I only nod and pretend I believe her. Maybe someday she'll let us in on whatever's going on between her and the Fallen house leader, but until then, all I can do is support her.

There's a loud chirp before Principal Cael's voice echoes across campus. "Students of Silver City University. After the devastating events of today, we are postponing all scheduled midterms by one week. Classes will be on hold for two days, and the previous lockdown has been lifted. You may use this time to go home and visit your families if you wish, but we require that you notify us of your intentions. This is only so we can be aware of who is staying and who isn't. Myself and the rest of the staff at SCU offer you our deepest regrets, but I assure you we will not be taken by surprise again. Over the coming days, we will work to repair the damage, but please use caution when getting around. If a friend is missing, please notify us immediately. Thank you for defending our great school. It will not be forgotten."

Almost immediately, Dina's slate lights up. She reads the name flashing across the screen before letting out a loud sigh.

"Your dad?" Hayliel asks, seeming to know what that means.

"Yeah. Guess I better start packing," she replies, heading inside the closet to answer.

"We should let Dina pack. She's going to have her hands full for the next few days, I suspect. I'll just send her a message real quick." Hayliel finds her bag propped up against the wall, but what she pulls out of it doesn't look like a slate at all. "Shit. I must have landed on it when the assholes pulled me from the sky. Can I use one of yours?"

Raphael pulls his out at the same moment a call from his mother pops up. He swipes it away without a moment's hesitation and hands it to her. That's when I realize I don't have mine.

"Fuck. My slate must still be in the library. If my grandparents found out about the attack, they'll be worried sick." Panic wells within me. Have they been calling? What must they think happened to make me not respond? They're too old to be worrying about me, dammit.

Hayliel wraps me in a hug. "Go. Check in with your family. I'm going to head to the main hall and see about getting a replacement slate. I'll reach out as soon as I have one, okay? Please be safe."

I squeeze her tight, not really wanting to let go but knowing I have to. Raph and I share a look over the top of her head. Neither one of us wants her to be alone right now, especially not after the demons converged on her like a target.

"I'll go with you," Raph says to Hayliel. "Just in case."

"Alright. But can we head out the main doors this time? As much as I loved you both carrying me, I think it will draw more attention than I want to deal with right now." The cutest blush I've ever seen spreads across her face.

"You got it, sunshine. We'll be nothing but plain, boring Janes. Promise."

Broken pieces of wood lie near the front door — which is barely attached to the house at this point — but otherwise no structural damage done. It's strange that they wouldn't have attacked here. Demons have an innate ability to sense angels.

They'd have known how many students were hiding in their rooms, so why didn't they force themselves inside?

Outside, the air smells of chilly darkness, of dew forming on leaves and mixing with the tart scent of blood. I wave to my friends, promising them I'll check in once I've spoken to my grandparents, and then I take off into the air.

Today has revealed so many things and yet nothing at all. Everything we've been working toward feels like it's grown three times in size. It's not only about Hayliel's wings anymore. There's more at play. If our group can uncover some of the secrets everyone seems to be keeping, maybe we'll be able to protect ourselves.

But that means relying on angels like Ezekiel. He's a complete enigma. I felt his presence during the battle, felt him following Raph and me as we raced toward Hayliel, but why was he following us? And why did he stay? It's pointless to think about, not without answers or understanding what happened between him and Hayliel to make their friendship so strained.

Whatever it is, his indifference is clearly hurting her. If he can't get his shit together, then I guess I'll have to do it for him.

4

EZEKIEL

Work together. With those Pure assholes? Never.

But as I fly above Silver City, I wonder if maybe that's a lie. Saying yes means being close to Hayliel, and if I say no … something tells me it will put a divide between us that I'm not sure I'll ever be able to break down.

I'm flying high enough that the twinkling lights look like tiny candles and remind me of the colorful toy Mom always talked about playing with when she was a kid. Fuck, I miss her. What would she think about the attack? Would she have any nuggets of wisdom to impart that would help shed some light on what was actually happening? I know she would. Dad might too, but ever since Mom died, things have been strained between us. He loves me and is proud of me. There's no denying that, but it's like he just gave up on the rest.

It's late enough now that the merchant district is dark. No vendors selling their wares, completely oblivious to the chaos that just rained down on us at the school. I fly a little further, over the entertainment district and then the production district with their large manufacturing plants lit up like beacons. Fallen angels are worked to the bone, taken advantage of and not paid a fair wage because of our wing color. It's disgusting. This district is my least favorite, and I usually avoid flying over it because of how much it pisses me off, but I'm clearly not in my right mind tonight.

Too much has happened for me to think straight. I can't stop the niggling hole in the center of my chest as my mind replays the attack today. Hayliel, tucked beneath her wings while a group of demons closes in on her. Raphael, Theo, and I racing to save her, fully knowing we're all too fucking slow. It shouldn't scare me this much. I barely know her, and it's not like I've even given myself a real chance to get to know her better lately.

Now I'm just supposed to work with her and the Pure boys she's always with? Act like they aren't laughing behind my back at how foolish I was to think this angel would choose me? Watching them today made me sick. I didn't miss the fact that her bond was strong enough that the blond one sensed her fear from across campus. The blow hurt less than I know it would have if we hadn't just survived a horde of fucking demons, but still.

Seeing them all together, the way they fought to protect her, poked a hole in what I thought was a very sturdy understanding of Pures. They didn't treat her like shit, even before the golden wings. If I hadn't been so caught up in my pain and misgivings, maybe I'd have noticed.

Unfortunately, the best chance we have at finding answers is by working together.

This day fucking sucks.

In the distance, lights shine from the mountain which houses Guild HQ. It spans the length of Silver City, and when the sun first disappears for the night, it's like a wall of fire separating us from the Archangels. At this time, though, it's usually more of a burning ember. Not tonight. Despite it being so late, many of the lights, including those near the top, are still on. Who knows, maybe one day they'll expand so far along the mountain, the university falls will be dried up by the fire. Swallowed up, just like the lives of its members. But part of joining the Assassins' Guild is understanding that your time is no longer yours. It belongs to the Guild, and every single angel within Silver City.

But if that's true, why hadn't anyone answered my distress call? Why had no one showed up? This attack wasn't a coincidence. It wasn't happenstance or accidental. They planned it. Shouldn't we have caught on to their behavior? Sensed something?

My mind spins until I'm dizzy. Is there anyone within the Guild that I can trust? I always thought I could rely on some of them, like Lieutenant Azrael and my dad, but now I'm not so sure.

The same irritating thought races through my mind. *You can trust Hayliel.* But that also means trusting her friends, and that's not something I have any intention of doing.

I shake off the depressing thoughts and focus on the task at hand. I need to give a statement of events, and I need to find someone to take my ire out on for leaving us high and fucking dry.

There's a flurry of angels coming and going from the main doors, which is odd for this time of night. Not that we ever close our doors or have the day off, but tonight it seems like over half the Guild members have shown up.

With this many members on patrol, how in the fuck did no one answer my call? How is it that, with all of these fucking angels, no one came to our aid? With a deep breath, I shove down the rage threatening to bubble over. I can get pissed off later. Now, I have a job to do.

I land a few feet away from the doors, startling the guard there. That's not a good sign. If his superior found out that his reflexes were so shot, I don't think he'd be in for a good time. Not that I'll say anything, but it has me even more confused. Why do they have exhausted sentries on duty at all?

Another recruit holds the door for me, shooting me a small smile as we enter a room filled with chaos. Three receptionists sit behind desks against the wall, looking more worn out than I've ever seen them. Their slates ring incessantly, the shrill sound grating on my nerves.

What the fuck is going on?

Irene, a Guild receptionist with buzzed brown hair and a scowl that scares off most angels, spots me, and I give her a curt nod before heading up the flight of stairs to the left. Luckily, I don't need to bother any of them to get where I'm going. I just need to log some information and hopefully find Azrael so he can give me some fucking answers.

"Zeke."

My dad is exiting the door I just passed by. He looks surprised to see me, which I suppose makes sense. He knows I don't often work this late.

Dad looks me over with a neutral expression, and even though his face never changes, I can tell he's worried when he says, "Why is your uniform torn? Are you alright?"

A little burst of anger bubbles over before I can stop it. "I'm fine, though I would have appreciated some backup. Why the hell didn't you answer when I called?"

"I'm sorry, son. It's been absolute mayhem here since late morning. It would seem every angel in the city has seen a demon today."

If that many angels have seen demons, and I know for a fact that there were at least twenty at the university, just how many demons are there? Before I can ask for more details, Dad's slate pings and he throws me an apologetic look before answering.

"This is Lieutenant Kirach," he says, before a long pause. I can't hear what the person on the other side says, but whatever it is, Dad doesn't look so happy. "Are you sure? I investigated that area myself only last week." More silence. I step closer, hoping to hear anything from the angel on the other end of the call. "No, I agree. Better to be safe than sorry. I'm on my way."

Dad ends the call, looking far more weary than usual. "I'm sorry, I have to go." He places a hand on my shoulder, squeezing gently. "We'll talk about this more tomorrow, I promise."

I don't bother replying. He means well, and I can't fault him for that, yet sometimes I wish he had a normal job and could actually be there when I needed him. But I've spent my whole life wishing Mom was still alive, and that never got me shit. Wishes are for fools and little kids. None of it ever made a difference.

Continuing down the hall, I head toward the on-duty Lieutenant's office, but instead of finding Azrael behind the desk, it's Lieutenant Atlas. I've seen him a few times, but we've never worked together. Azrael typically handles the interns because of his knack for developing young minds or some shit.

"Intern Ezekiel. What are you doing here?"

Instead of answering his questions, I pop off with one of my own. "Why wasn't my call for help answered?"

He raises an eyebrow, steepling his fingers together on top of his desk. "It's been a very busy day. There have been quite a lot of calls and unfortunately, not all of them can be answered."

It takes all my strength not to roll my eyes. Shit. This would have been so much easier with Azrael. I take a calming breath, hoping the words come out less aggressive than I feel. "Yes, I heard. But I also called the number to that slate right there, and it doesn't seem to be ringing at all. So I'll ask again. Why wasn't my call for help answered?"

Well, that was a fail, but sometimes being polite only gets you walked on. I need answers, and for whatever reason, Lieutenant Atlas only wants to beat around the damn bush.

His eye twitches, which is the first sign that maybe I went a bit too far. "Mind your tone. I don't care that you're an Oren. You will respect your superiors. As for your call, one little intern wasn't a major concern today and so it was ignored."

I bite back the slew of insults I want to let out because I don't need to get even more on this asshole's bad side. "It wasn't just *one little intern* in trouble. Demons swarmed Silver City University, and the campus was far from prepared or protected."

This wipes the annoyed look off his face. "Were there any casualties?"

"I don't believe we sustained any deaths, but there were quite a few injured. More than our school healers can handle, I think."

He sighs, and a little color returns to his face. "I'll send a few extra from the Guild, and someone will be there shortly to perform a thorough investigation. If there's nothing more, I'll call this in."

I can't help the small bit of smug satisfaction that zips through me as I walk out. If Azrael had been here, I wouldn't have had to jump through hoops and prove my importance. He knows I don't bring up shit for no reason, and he can trust that when I bring up a problem, it's a fucking problem. At least now the wounded students will have better care and maybe, with someone examining the scene, they'll find something concrete to help us in whatever's coming.

Like discovering what the fuck the demons were after.

I walk over to the open space set up for interns, which has the unfair nickname of the *infant bullpen*. I sit down at my desk, unlock the slate there, and begin detailing events. It's quiet, which should help me focus, but I can't keep my mind on task.

What the hell is going on here? Lieutenant Atlas mentioned a bigger concern, but what was it? Does it relate to the influx of calls received to the main line, or what my dad mentioned about every angel in the city thinking they saw a demon? There are too many variables, and it's starting to piss me off.

Before I can spiral out of control, I make a mental note to dive deeper into this and check the call logs. Maybe I'll discover something helpful there, but for now I need to get this report done. As much as I don't want to admit it, there are angels at the university relying on me. Wounded students, scared students, and even the students I can't seem to escape from.

Regardless of my distaste for Raphael and Theo, something about what happened today, both at the Guild and the school, doesn't smell right. I'm not enough of an idiot to let those feelings stand in the way of justice.

And whatever complicated shit lies between Hayliel and me, I won't let that get in the way of digging up the truth.

5

HAYLIEL

How is it that this great university has three separate libraries, yet not a single one holds anything remotely useful? I press the tips of my fingers to my eyes, hoping it'll help me miraculously find something when I'm done. It doesn't.

Since the attack a few days ago, there's been a flurry of activity at school. Between frightened students heading home to their families and both school and Guild nurses working endlessly on the physical and emotional toll the battle had on us, things have been rather frenzied here. It's partly why Raphael, Theo, and I have kept holed up in the house libraries. Easier to pretend things aren't so fucked up. And easier to avoid the heavy stares of the other students.

I've kept my wings locked up tight, part of me hoping students will just forget and move on. Avoidance sounds like exactly what I need. Even Gagiel had reached out, making sure I was alright, but ultimately asking if the rumors were true. It's not that I don't trust him, but ... I'm not just the color of my wings and I'm tired of others treating me like I am. Am I being overly sensitive? Yes. Gagiel is so kind. There's no way he'd have meant to make me feel that way, yet the feelings are there all the same.

We didn't miss the fact that the Guild had sent someone over to assess the damage and gather any additional information about the attack. I saw him once, outside the Power house window. He looked nothing like Zeke does in his uniform. In fact, the new lieutenant made Zeke look like a fucking rainbow in comparison.

Over the past few days, Zeke has made himself scarce, but I have to assume he's the reason the Guild is here. Maybe he's agreed to help us after all.

Despite the lockdown being lifted, no one from our friend group cared to leave, and as much as I wanted to see my family, I haven't told them about the change. Try as I might, I can't seem to figure out why I'm so nervous. Mom and Dad are my biggest supporters. Through every ounce of trouble I experienced growing up, they were there for me. Even when I fucked up. Even when I let the bullies win or stooped to their level. So why am I hesitating? Theo says it's because I'm tired of feeling like I only bring problems, and that, at least from his perspective, if I can find out something factual and true about my wings, then maybe I can present them with a solution too.

I denied it at first, but the more I think about it, the more I realize he's right.

Theo stayed on campus for a similar reason, or at least that's what he said. He's more helpful here than at home, but something tells me it's more than that. He let it slip that home is with his grandparents, and even though I'm desperate for more of that story, I don't feel comfortable prying.

Raphael's excuse for staying was obvious, though I'm pretty sure he's going to have major consequences because of it. If I try, I can still hear the shriek his mother made through the phone when he explained he'd be remaining on campus. It's one thing to visit home when that place brings you comfort, but when all it does is add more weight on your shoulders, it's not a place you want to be anymore. We've been through enough shit lately that we don't need any more. We need a break.

Unfortunately, Dina hadn't been so lucky. Her dad was furious that she'd been put in danger like that and, according to the messages I received from her over the last two days, he's even considering pulling her from the university. She's fighting it though, and it sounds like she's at least convinced him not to do anything for now. Thank the Archangels for that. Hopefully she'll share more about what finally made him agree when she's back on campus later this evening.

I glance over at the large stack of books on the cart beside us. The bottom portion is our discard pile, holding the books we've already been through. Those don't have a single useful item. The top rack is the books we haven't been through yet, and as much as I'd like to think they hold new information, I'm beginning to doubt we'll find anything at all.

It helps that we have more to look for now. Before, our focus was super specific: gray wings. Now we're looking for any mention of golden ones, color-changing wings, and whatever the power was that killed those demons. With all of that to go on, it shouldn't be so hard, right?

Raphael slams the book shut, causing a student sitting in another section of the library to jump. "This is fucking painful," he admits, pushing the book away from him. "What I want to know is, are there truly no books to be found, or did someone get rid of them all?"

I grimace. "Well, if they got rid of some harmless words on a page, I'd hate to know what they'd do to me if they found out what happened during the attack."

Theo frowns, not liking that prospect one bit, and Raphael puts a hand on my arm. "I won't give that possibility even a single thought, sunshine."

Holding tight to his comfort, I follow his lead and force the thoughts from my mind. They don't deserve to take up even an ounce of space there.

"I know! Why don't we go somewhere? Classes are back in swing tomorrow, and we haven't done anything to blow off a little steam." Raphael beams, his smile so infectious that I can't help but join him.

"Yes. A thousand times, yes."

Theo shuts his own book, perking up at the change in topic. "What did you have in mind?"

Raphael practically bounces in his seat. "I thought we could stay close, keep it old school and not use our wings to get around, but that means we have to stay nearby. There's a market not too far from here that we could check out. Whimsical Wares, I think it's called."

My stomach drops all the way to the floor, and I let out a little frustrated groan before dropping my head into my hands.

"What's wrong?" Theo asks. "Have you been?"

I mumble out a reply, not really wanting to explain to these two very Pure angels why I can't go, but knowing that I have to.

"Huh? Did you catch that, Raph?"

"Not quite. Can you try again, sweetheart? Maybe this time without the hand over your mouth."

My face flames, but I drop my hands to find both Raphael and Theo watching me with different expressions lining their faces. Theo looks concerned, but Raph only looks playful, like he knows how to get me talking.

"Whimsical Wares is Pure only. I snuck in once, and it didn't really go so well." The memory of being chased, of barely escaping without getting caught, slips through my mind. Would they let me in with gold wings, or would they punish me for even trying?

"That's so fucking shitty." Theo looks angry, and it takes a minute for me to realize that he's mad on my behalf. My heart flutters at the thought of this Pure angel feeling so strongly against his own kind.

"Yeah, fuck that place," Raphael adds. "It's almost lunch. Why don't we walk around and see what sparks our interest? Today is about relaxing and having fun. Anything that threatens those plans can fuck right off."

My grin grows so big it hurts. "I love that! And at this point, anything is better than staring at the same old books and hoping for different words to appear on the page. It feels like I'm going insane."

"Well, if you are, we're coming too. Might as well throw us all in the same straight jacket." Raphael kisses my cheek before dancing away with the cart of books.

Theo cleans up our workstation while I email the principal, letting him know of our departure. They might have lifted the lockdown, but we're supposed to notify the school of our comings and goings as a way for them to track who's on campus at any given time. At least we *can* leave, though, and with everything that's happened, I can understand why they're doing it. By the time Raphael is back, we're ready to head out. It's weird leaving the campus and walking through the gate I haven't even stepped toward since arriving. Has it only been a month since the school year began? So much has happened that it feels far longer. Have I really only known Raphael and Theo for such a short time? When did my relationship with these angels change, morphing into something I'm not sure I could live without?

After the attack, it seemed like maybe I'd get there with Zeke too, but the space between us shifts like the ocean tides, ebbing and flowing so rapidly that sometimes it feels as if I'll drown.

We walk down familiar streets, making our way toward the merchant district and ignoring all signs of Whimsical Wares. Despite knowing this area, it feels somehow new with these two angels at my side.

"Have you guys ever just wandered the streets like this?" I ask them, spreading my arms wide before closing my eyes, in love with the freedom of this moment. I feel their gazes on me, and I can't stop the surge of something hot and potent from spreading through my limbs. When I finally open my eyes again, Theo is watching me with a familiar heat in his eyes.

He smiles. "Not in this district, but Raph and I were always escaping the confines of our homes and exploring the housing district. If we were fast enough, we could usually make it to where the housing district meets the entertainment district. We found this old park not maintained or visited by anyone else. The structure was rusted and broken, but it's where we went to get away."

His expression shifts near the end of his story, turning darker and almost painful. I'm desperate to ask him about it, but I stay silent, not wanting to ruin the mood. It's not the first time I've seen a flash of it cross his handsome face. Maybe in time he'll open up to me about it.

"Oh yeah. Theo and I were little hellions. We were both running from something, in our own ways, but we always had each other. Day or night, it didn't matter. If we needed one another, we risked the wrath of our families to show up." Raphael nudges into Theo as we turn down an unfamiliar side street. Their friendship reminds me of what Dina and I share, and I wonder what she'll think of our little outing.

A gust of wind hits me in the face, bringing with it the delicious scent of pastries, coffee, and freshly baked bread. "Oh, fuck." The words come out more of a moan than I intended, but holy shit. My stomach rumbles, reminding me just how hungry I am.

The scents come from a restaurant up ahead with a cute patio out front, complete with umbrellas to block the sun and cozy-looking chairs. It's quaint, homey, and exactly where I want to have lunch. My joy blossoms further when I find a sign that says *Everyone Has To Eat, Just Take a Seat.*

Another group of angels approaches from across the street, eyeing the last empty table on the patio. Raphael grabs my hand and sprints toward it, pulling a chair out for me. I don't miss the unsatisfied mutter from the other group, but at this moment, I can't find it in me to care.

Theo adjusts the umbrella to block just enough of the sun that it doesn't blind us, but still lets us bask in the warmth. The perfect day.

As I read the menu, I salivate. Fucking hell. The prices aren't wildly expensive, and it's not like I've spent much of the money my parents sent me to school with. If I'm mindful of spending,

I should be able to get through this meal without embarrassing myself.

The waitress comes over to take our order, her eyes widening as Raphael and Theo list off item after item. Maybe it shouldn't surprise me, given how much they usually eat at school, but that doesn't cost money. This does. Just how well off are they?

When the waitress turns to me with pen and slate in hand, I mumble off my measly order consisting of a sandwich, side salad, and a peach smoothie. She walks away, looking almost annoyed, but I can't be bothered to care. I won't let a damn thing ruin today.

It's not long before the food arrives and our table is overflowing with sandwiches, soups, cheeses, and a platter of different sweets.

"Help yourself to anything that interests you," Raphael says between bites of buttered bread. "We have more than enough for the three of us."

"I dunno ..." Part of me wants to say no. If I eat some, I'll feel shitty without paying and there's zero chance my budget will cover even a third of this. But the call from that warm, flaky bread is too loud to ignore.

"Then let me decide for you. Try this." Raphael shoves the bread forward, hovering just in front of my mouth and I'm lost in the aroma. I bite into it with a moan, my eyes rolling back into my head because fuck, that's good.

"Thanks, guys. You're welcome to try some of mine, too. I think they even make their own seasoned croutons."

We eat the rest in silence, and I end up trying a bite of almost everything they ordered. By the time we make it through the food, I'm beyond full and wishing I wore something a little more flexible. This was worth it, though.

Theo excuses himself, heading off to find a bathroom and leaving Raphael and me alone.

"By the Archangels, this might be my new favorite spot," he says before stealing another gulp of my peach smoothie. "Of all the things you tried, which did you like best?"

I pick a chocolate chip up off his plate and chew it while I think. "Damn. There's an entire list of top contenders, but if you're really going to make me choose, then I think it would be the sandwich I had. The baguette was cooked perfectly, and it's like they just *knew* how much of a sauce girl I am. What about you?"

He hums, smiling at me like I'm the center of his entire fucking world and making my heart squeeze.

"This is going to sound lame, but the chocolate chip oatcake took first place for me. If I could eat one of those every day, I'd die a happy man." He leans back in his chair, looking like the cat who got the cream just as Theo joins us.

"What was your favorite part of lunch, Theo?" I ask him.

"Hmm."

Before he can answer, the waitress comes back to take the rest of our empty dishes. She drops a couple candies on the table, but no bill before saying, "Thanks for stopping by. Enjoy the rest of your day."

"Wait. We haven't paid yet."

"Oh, it's no problem, Miss. The young gentleman took care of the bill inside. You're good to go."

I glance at Theo, who's suddenly looking anywhere but at me.

"Theo ..." I start, but Raphael threads his fingers through mine and pulls me up from my chair. It's only when we're a few feet from the café that I stop walking. "You didn't have to pay for me. I could have covered myself."

"You both could have covered your own. I know that. But I'd just eaten what was quite possibly the best gourmet grilled cheese I've ever had, so when I saw the waitress on my way back to the table I just decided to pay. That's all."

I laugh, trying to let the old thoughts of being someone's charity case seep from my mind. "That's great, but I'm still paying you back."

"Whatever you want, firefly."

Our eyes lock for a long moment, and the tension I'd just been feeling floats away. His nickname for me plays on repeat, sinking into my soul and warming me from the inside out. I want to ask him what it means, and if it has anything to do with the random ray of light that apparently shot out of me during the attack, but part of me doesn't want to know, so I stay quiet.

We keep walking, turning down random side streets with no real destination in mind. The food settles in my belly and the heavy feeling of overeating leaves as we enter a busy street lined with shops.

Ignoring the businesses selling food, we pass by a few sophisticated places with *Pure Only* signs in the windows. I expect to feel embarrassed, or like a burden, but Raphael and Theo don't even seem to notice. Like they're more than happy to avoid those places on their own. My heart does a little flip.

The first shop we enter is a little craft boutique with different kits to make jewelry or tie-dye shirts. From the corner of my eye I catch Raphael pull a flyer off the wall and tuck it into his pocket. When I ask him about it, though, he only smirks and changes the subject. Curious.

It doesn't take more than a few minutes for me to find several kits that I just know Dina would love. Perhaps someday we'll get to do them together.

After an hour exploring the aisles, we leave empty-handed and continue down the shop-lined street. Angels bustle about in the late afternoon sun, everyone smiling and happy like they don't have a care in the world. This place is like a little slice of perfection, and I hold tight to the idea that maybe this can truly be the future. Maybe once I graduate, all the drama will float away and leave me in peace.

Raphael, who had gone ahead, skips back toward Theo and me with a shit-eating grin on his face that has my own lips turning up in a smile. "So there's a thing we *have* to do and I need you guys to trust me. Deal?"

"Well, you know I'm in. How about you?" Theo watches me, the smile on his face almost a challenge.

"Alright, I'll bite. What is it?"

"Follow me!" Raphael heads further down the road with Theo and me hot on his heels until we stand in front of an antique photo parlor.

A chuckle escapes me as I look through the front window at the display of photos. There are couples and families, all dressed up in outfits I've definitely never seen before. Further along are a few more pictures of the same angel, her long, flowing hair half tied up with intricate braids. She looks fierce, like a warrior.

Raphael tugs on my arm, pulling me inside with him and Theo. Inside there are even more photos, and I haven't seen a single full-color image yet. Each one has this old look to it, either black and white or slightly tinged with sepia.

A gorgeous woman approaches us, and I can't help but notice how similar she looks to the angel in the window.

"Welcome to our photo parlor. I'm Esther. Are you looking to get some photos done today?"

"Oh, absolutely," Raphael responds eagerly.

"Perfect! Come with me. You'll have a choice of theme, period, and style before we get started. It can be a touch overwhelming, but don't worry. If you find several you like, we can definitely do multiple."

We follow her through the back, stopping at a slate to choose our themes and time periods — Raphael goes a little wild, picking more themes than we can possibly photograph today, but it's easy to get caught up in his enthusiasm. Esther is more than happy to play along, her bubbly personality easy to get along with.

She leads us further down the hall into a wide room packed with clothes. My jaw drops at how much lace and puffy material there is.

"Now we choose the clothes! It's broken down by time period, but since you picked so many, I'd suggest grabbing at least one thing per group and you'll be fine. Masculine outfits on the right, feminine on the left. Feel free to choose anything available on the rack."

"What have you gotten us into?" Theo teases. Raphael only sends him a wicked grin.

"If you find something you'd like our sunshine to wear, grab it. I want to see her in everything." He shoots me a sexy wink that sends an ache of arousal straight to my pussy. The way he said *our sunshine* as if I'm theirs has me damn near fainting with the thrill of it. But can I be theirs? Dina hinted at it before all the demon crap, but had she really been serious?

The guys head off through the clothes, and I try to bring myself back in the moment. It's just words, anyway. It's not like they've made me the marshmallow in their s'more or anything, which I don't even know if I'd want. *Liar.*

"Anything catching your eye?" Esther asks, and I can't figure out if her words have another meaning.

"Everything! Well ... everything except for the ones with the floofy neck. Those look suffocating." I hesitate for a moment before deciding to just ask her the damn question I've had on my mind since she introduced herself. "I think I saw your photos in the front window. You look absolutely stunning, and those braids were incredible."

Her smile deepens, and she lets out a small giggle. "That's actually my grandmother. She didn't make it through the fall of God, unfortunately, but she taught my mother how to braid, who then taught me. I won't be able to get it exactly the same, but I can do that with your hair, if you'd like?"

My eyes flash to hers, shocked at her generous offer. "I'd love that, only if you have time. And I'm so sorry for your loss. Your grandmother sounds like quite the angel."

"Oh, it's no trouble. And doing things like this allows me to feel closer to her again, if only for a short while. Come."

She leads me to a corner with three mirrors and a stool at the center. I sit while she works on my hair, braiding both small and large sections before weaving them through one another until I barely recognize the woman staring back at me.

"Wow."

"The style suits you. Now how about we go find your guys and show them the surprise?" A mischievous glint flashes in her eyes, halting the blush threatening to rise.

We find Raphael and Theo amidst a flurry of clothes. I watch them, enjoying the chance to ogle them from a distance. They're both handsome in their own way, and I wonder if they've ever had to fight over someone. Did they choose their friendship instead of letting anyone get between them?

Esther, likely tired of waiting, makes her presence known. "My apologies for stealing your lady. Did you find everything you were looking for?"

As one, they both turn toward the sound of her voice, but neither gaze lingers on her. It's like they're launched missiles and I'm the target. Raphael's face doesn't hide a single thing. His lust and want are clear as day, and as much as Theo might try, I can see the same on his own.

Blood turns to fire in my veins beneath their heated stares until I almost forget where we are.

Esther only laughs. "Come. It's time to get changed."

Two hours later, and I'm exhausted.

Raphael ended up going way overboard and bought the entire digital collection, and as much as I might hate that he's spending money on me, I can't help but be glad for the memories. I'll keep the photos forever.

Today has been a dream, exactly what we needed after everything that went down at school. So much, in fact, that I'm not quite ready to head back yet. The guys feel the same, and that's how we end up stumbling into a lush green park in the area between the merchant, entertainment, and housing districts.

There's a massive white screen and projector set up with a countdown and the name of some movie I've never heard of. Angels sit on blankets on the grass, and along the edge of the merchant district is a lineup of food trucks and vendors.

"If either of you even thinks of trying to pay for this, I swear."

They share a look, the two of them holding up their hands as if they hadn't been thinking about doing just that. "Good."

We find a tent setup near the food trucks with a mother and daughter inside.

"Do you want a blanket, miss?" the little girl asks with a toothless grin.

"I would love one," I tell her, and watch as her face lights up. She hands me a blanket, but before we can leave, Raphael crouches down in front of her.

"Any chance we can have two, little angel? I don't want my friend to get cold."

She looks to her mother, who nods reassuringly before she passes a second blanket over. I watch as Raphael slips a bill from his pocket and hands it to her, speaking low and soft. She looks ecstatic, and the mom looks like she doesn't want to accept, but now if she doesn't, she'll have one pissed off toddler.

As we walk away, I hear her say, "Mama, can you do my hair like that lady? She looks like a princess warrior."

We grab tacos in a bag from one of the food trucks and a pail of popcorn before finding a cozy spot on the grass. Most of the best areas are taken, but even from our spot near a large oak tree, we can see the big screen perfectly.

With our tacos finished and the popcorn forgotten, the movie starts. Nestled as I am between Theo and Raphael, I can't seem to pay attention to the film. I thought it was about a sick boy whose grandfather reads him a story, but each time I try to follow the plot, the heat of Theo's thigh where it presses against mine distracts me, or the soft caress from Raphael's hand on my back makes me lose track.

A shiver races down my spine as my thoughts run wild with the possibilities. Dina's words play on repeat, reminding me that maybe I don't have to choose. Maybe I can keep these two with me forever.

"Are you cold?" Raphael asks, not bothering to wait for a response before shaking open the blanket and laying it across our laps.

"Thank you." I stumble over the words, my mind reeling even more now that we're all beneath the blanket. It's like we're in our own little paradise here. It feels like we could do anything and no one would know.

Raphael pulls me into the crook of his arm and the three of us lean back against the tree. It takes me a moment to settle as I fight against the fear that Theo might leave. I don't want to make him uncomfortable.

When he doesn't acknowledge it, I do my best to focus on the movie. There's a girl named Princess Buttercup and a masked man trying to save her. *Is this the same movie as before? Where's the little boy and his grandfather?*

Theo shifts beside me, his hand brushing my own where it rests at my side beneath the blanket, and I freeze. His eyes never once leave the screen, though, so maybe he didn't notice. Then his fingers brush my own again.

Feeling emboldened, I turn my hand slightly until it's facing palm up and wait. My heart thuds loudly in my ears as I watch the screen without really seeing anything. Just as I'm about to give up hope, his hand is back.

His movements are hesitant as he places his hand on top of mine, not moving more than that until I intertwine my fingers with his.

As innocent as this all might be, it feels a little dangerous. Would Raphael care that Theo and I are holding hands? Would it bother either of them to know just how much I don't want to choose between them?

Before I can stress about it too much, Raphael runs the tips of his fingers up and down my side until a shiver races through me. There's no way Theo doesn't feel the movement, but nothing in his demeanor gives away that he has. Maybe he's just really into the movie?

Raph sits up a little straighter and presses a kiss to my shoulder before leaning in to whisper, "How good are you at staying quiet, sunshine?"

"What?"

His answering smirk has my body tingling in all the right places. He can't be serious, can he?

He shifts back. "I bet you're not very comfortable against this tree. How about we fix that?"

At his insistence, I move forward until there's enough space for him to sit between me and the tree before he pulls me toward him so that my back is pressed to his chest with his legs on either side of me. He brings the blanket up to cover us again, then curves his arms around my middle, snuggling me close and placing a soft kiss on the nape of my neck.

In the commotion, I lost contact with Theo, and I can't help but feel the loss. Will he reach out again, or has our fleeting moment passed?

I try to focus on the movie, but that only leaves me confused. Who is the creepy guy bringing people into some laboratory inside an old tree and what are they doing to the man strapped down? A thrill goes through me at the idea of being strapped down at Raphael's and Theo's mercy. A fantasy, I'm sure. I would never dare come between their friendship.

Raphael's hands move beneath the blanket, distracting me. He's teasing the waistband of my leggings, dipping a finger underneath and tracing a line there before slipping back out. It's driving me mad. My core clenches with all the thoughts running through my head, but I try not to get carried away. We're in the middle of a park, for Archangel's sake. Theo's sitting right beside us, and I've just been holding his hand.

Truthfully, that last thought doesn't do a thing to dull the growing heat in my lower belly. Images of him and Raphael working me over in secret, right below everyone's noses, have me growing even wetter than before. Fuck. If Raph slips beneath my panties, he'll find me soaked.

Is that an invitation?

Raphael's words seep through my mind, and the eyes I didn't know were shut, pop open. Shit. Did I force my thoughts on him again? I don't bother thinking before I respond. I want him to help me let go. After everything we've been through these past few days, don't I deserve to let loose and be free, just a little? Don't we all?

Yes.

He needs no further prompting before he delves one hand into my leggings, keeping his fingers over the thin fabric of my underwear. I suck in a sharp breath, then immediately wonder if Theo heard it. Instead of looking over like I want to, I drape my arm over Raphael's thigh and let it rest beneath the blanket. If he's paying attention, he'll have noticed, and if he notices ... I don't get to finish the thought before Theo's fingers dance across my hand.

He traces the lines on my palm while Raphael traces the wet seam of my pussy over my panties. Whether they know it or not, they move in sync. Slow, unhurried movements that have my pulse skyrocketing and my eyes darting around the park. No one stares back at us. They only watch the fight scene currently playing out on the screen. I turn my head, eyes locking with Theo's, and it's like everyone else melts away.

Do you like it when he watches us, sweet sunshine?

A whimper threatens to escape but I hold it back, keeping it tucked inside because there is no fucking way I want to ruin this moment. If I weren't so delirious, I might have lied. But at this moment, with both their hands on me, I have to tell the truth.

Yes.

He lets out a low chuckle. Without losing eye contact with Theo, I relax into Raph and let my legs fall open further. He reads my request easily, slipping his fingers beneath the fabric and plunging a single digit inside. I act without thinking and grip Theo's hand while Raphael adds in a second finger.

Pressure builds as he pumps inside me, tilting my entire world on its axis. The park fills with laughter, but the sound is muted, like I'm underwater. I'm oblivious to everything but them. Raphael and Theo. The two angels who have stayed by my side through everything.

My grip on Theo's hand must be punishing, but he doesn't seem to mind. He only rubs his thumb along the top of my hand, his eyes blazing with a heat so potent, I feel as if I might dissolve to ash.

I think he likes to watch us too.

I feel the truth in his words right down to my pulsing core. Theo's enjoying this just as much as I am. Just as much as Raphael is.

Pretend it's him touching you, filling up your perfect pussy.

Inside me, there's a storm building. Electricity buzzes beneath my skin and through the very fabric of my soul, begging to be let out. This. Tonight. It's more than I could have imagined. Raphael's fingers deep inside me. His dirty words playing through my mind. The feel of Theo beside me. Each thing on its own is potent, but together? Together they make a recipe so powerful, I'm afraid I'll never get to experience it again.

Now come for him, little sunshine. Come for us.

He pumps into me until finally the storm emerges and I shatter in his arms with both of their names on my tongue. I don't know if I say them out loud or not. At this point, I don't know anything at all. Nothing except them.

He keeps his fingers inside me long after my orgasm subsides. Theo never pulls away, never breaks eye contact, and in this shared moment with the two of them, it all feels like a dream.

When Raphael finally pulls out, he sucks the taste of me from his fingers. I hear it, more than I see it, and I watch as Theo notices, too. Is that a look of jealousy in his gaze, or am I imagining it?

We stay like that for the rest of the movie. Me, sitting between Raphael's legs with my fingers entwined with Theo's. I can't help but feel utterly cherished. This day was exactly what I needed to unwind and remind myself that life isn't so bad. Whatever these new gold wings mean, as long as I have Theo and Raph at my side, I can get through anything. And hopefully, as the days move forward, we'll get another chance to explore this *thing* between the three of us.

Life is finally looking up.

6

HAYLIEL

The sun shines through my dorm room window, rousing me from sleep.

Waking up without an alarm is one of my all-time favorite things. Even though it's only five minutes before I'm supposed to get up, I feel more rested than if I'd woken up to the blaring noise from my slate.

Last night feels like a dream. I didn't think about the demons or bullies even once. Being with Raph and Theo has that effect. They bring so much light into my life that the darkness can't possibly get to me.

I jump in the shower, singing along to the music playing through the speakers on my slate as I wash my hair. I hated taking the braids out last night, and wish I could have kept them forever. When we'd gotten back on campus, it was far later than we realized, so we went our separate ways. I'd caught Dina in the hallway between our rooms, but her dad called to check up. Again.

She and I desperately need to catch up. I want to tell her about what happened last night and find out what finally convinced her dad not to pull her from school. I'm due to meet her and the guys for breakfast in the main hall, and if I don't hurry, I'll be late.

A small part of me worries that it'll be weird between Raph, Theo, and me, but that's silly. It certainly wasn't weird last night. Not unless weird meant the perfect fucking evening.

After throwing on my uniform, — which includes pants this time with a white button-up top. Instead of the matching blazer, though, I grab the delectable-smelling leather jacket some unknown angel had draped across my shoulders while I was asleep in the library — I toss my slate and flying gear into a little backpack and head out to knock on Dina's door. She doesn't answer, but I can hear her talking to someone. It must be her dad again. I shoot her a text, letting her know I'll save her a seat before making my way toward the main hall.

Stepping through the forest in front of Fallen house is like dunking myself in a tub of cold water. When it's not right in front of you, it's easy to forget the attack, but seeing the damage that the faculty and the Guild are still trying to fix brings reality crashing down on me.

A few students mill about, their gazes trained on me like I'm a magician about to pull one hundred handkerchiefs from my mouth. Just great.

"Good morning, sunshine," Raphael says cheerily, with Theo following behind him. Each of them holds a tray piled high with food and drinks.

Seeing them again makes my heart trip. "Morning! What's going on?"

"The vibe in there is really fucking weird, so we thought it might be a good idea to just avoid that area altogether. Is Dina coming?" Theo asks, his gaze shifting to something behind me. "Never mind."

Dina jogs over, looking more tired than usual. "If I had known being late would result in the food coming to me, I'd have done this weeks ago."

I laugh. "Come with us, milady, to the most fabulous table in this fine establishment. The exclusive arena."

While we walk, I do my best to ignore the stares. This is normal, right? But why does it feel so strange? Maybe because this time, I've actually experienced the change that makes me so different.

Eating in the arena is pretty nice. There aren't many angels around, so I don't feel like I'm under a microscope and can pretend for just a little longer that this is reality.

Dina checks her phone and grimaces. "Shit. I've gotta get to class. See you at lunch?"

"See you!" I call back. "I guess I should go get changed for Wingology. Wish me luck, guys."

Raphael's soft smile shifts into a frown. "There's something going on with that professor. I don't enjoy leaving you alone with him."

I grab his hand, giving it a light squeeze. "Oh, I don't plan on being alone with him, trust me. I'll keep quiet and stick to the back. Maybe he'll forget I'm there." What I don't tell them is that I've considered changing my major entirely, just to avoid him. I don't quite have the mental capacity for that conversation today.

We go our separate ways and I dally while changing into my flying gear. I don't want to be late, but there's no way in hell that I'll be the first person out there, either.

Not that it helps.

I swear this professor has some sort of homing beacon programmed into his brain and I'm the target, because the moment I enter the arena, he's glaring at me. Even though I walked in with a group of other students and never said a peep, it's like he knows where I am.

He waits for us to sit before beginning his speech. "Glad to see you've all survived after such an awful attack last week. Considering recent events, I've decided to restructure our grading and remove next week's midterm. Instead, we'll have several small tests and projects to make up your grade. This will allow less pressure on you, as well as provide us with the opportunity to explore the strange happenings at this very school."

A few students clap their hands, likely excited that we no longer have a midterm to stress about, and while I'm happy, I can't help but find his charity rather odd.

"Now, part of this new grading structure will include informal presentations in front of your peers to discuss what your wings feel like to you. You'll most likely find that each person here has a unique connection with their wings, which is a topic we'll begin to explore over the coming weeks."

The angel beside me, a red-haired girl with freckles all over her face, turns to me. Her skin is pale, almost sickly looking, when she says, "I'd rather have a midterm instead of a presentation."

I'm so taken aback at the fact that someone is talking to me, and not just to throw insults my way. All I manage is a nod and whisper back, "I think I'd have to agree."

"Well, Miss Hayliel, since you're so fond of talking during my class, why don't you make your way down here and start us off," Professor Uriel says, his smile never quite reaching his eyes.

The girl who was just talking to me immediately backs up and shifts further away as if I'm the problem. I want to shout *I was only talking because of you!* But I don't. Instead, I look back to the professor and ask, "I'd prefer some time to prepare." I try, even though it's futile.

"You'll have all the time in the world back at home with your parents if you don't come down here. Whichever you choose is fine by me."

My stomach drops. Every moment of this encounter reminds me so much of that first day. What is it with this guy? Why does he have to pick on me and threaten to send me home? I don't know why I thought things would be any different. Assholes like him don't change.

I walk to the front of the class with my shoulders back and head held high, doing my best to portray a confidence I don't remotely feel. Whispers grow until I'm positive no one is actually trying to hide what they're saying. But one voice is far louder than the others.

Cadriel glares at me, the hatred in his eyes a living, breathing thing. "Can you believe this reject? How has she not been kicked out already? The principal really needs to do something about the absolute trash that's sullying the school's name."

Professor Uriel doesn't say a word. He doesn't tell anyone to be kind or even just to be quiet. All he does is gaze at me while I stand in front of these students and take their verbal blows with as much grace as I can muster. Every interaction with this piece of shit brings him further up our list of suspicious angels. Today is no exception.

But as I stand there, beneath Cadriel's cruel words, I hear something else, something almost *kind.*

"Why is everyone hating on her? Isn't she the reason we're all safe?"

"I heard she killed every single demon on school grounds just by touching their foreheads."

"Whoa. That's next level. If she's a freak, then sign me the fuck up."

Even though what they're saying isn't even remotely true, their words burrow deep inside of me, strengthening my resolve. Ignorant professors and bullies will not beat me down. I won't cower and hide who I am, even if I don't fully understand just who that is yet. Because if it truly was my transformation that killed those demons, then I have a duty to find out everything I can so that if those creatures ever come back, maybe I can protect the school and everyone in it.

Postponing classes means the schedule this week is odd. Professors moved lessons around in order to fit them in before midterms and not overwhelm the students. I like the idea, in theory. What I don't like, however, is that it now means I have to jump from Wingology straight to Chronicles of Silver City.

It's strange walking through campus this time. No one's dubbed me "demon-spawn" yet today, so I have to call that a win, right? I'd enjoy it more if my classmates and fellow students wouldn't stare at me like I held their fate in the palm of my hand. The rumors are getting out of control, and even though these are in my favor, it's still uncomfortable.

Why can't everyone just accept me as I am?

There are a few who do, but unfortunately none of them are in my next class.

I walk through the door, dreading having to deal with the cruel indifference that Professor Sofiel always portrays during class. Everyone stares, but it's the bright, beaming grin from the professor that throws me for a loop.

With her cherry-red lips and wide smile, something about it almost seems menacing. Like her jaw could unhinge at any point and she'd swallow me whole.

"Miss Hayliel, what a joy to see you today. I hope you're faring well after dealing with those pesky demons all on your own."

"Erm ... Hi." What the hell is going on right now?

I rush to my seat, feeling the eyes of the students already here watching me as I go. Fuck. Maybe I want my gray wings back after all. I'm going to have whiplash if more angels pull a total one-eighty like this.

Once Professor Sofiel starts class, I relax and focus. This midterm shouldn't be too difficult. I find the material interesting, and as long as I don't have to listen to anyone drone on about how God would have killed me during his crazed reign, I should pass with flying colors.

A shiver races up my spine, giving me chills. For a second, I worry something awful is about to happen. Maybe the demons are coming back. Maybe I won't be able to get rid of them like I apparently did last time. How am I supposed to do it again when I don't understand what *it* even is?

But it isn't an apocalypse or anything as extreme as that. It's only Seraphina's friend, Temperance, glowering at me from her seat in the middle of class.

Well, at least her hatred of me hasn't changed. Small victories?

"Temperance, is there something more interesting that you'd rather be doing?" the professor asks, causing her to turn around and put on her mask of innocence.

"Nothing interesting, Professor. But it is rather distracting having a mutant angel in class. I'm afraid it will affect my studies." She pouts, and it takes everything I have not to laugh out loud.

If I somehow affect her studies, it'll be her own damn fault. She and her friends are the ones who can't seem to leave me alone. If it were up to me, I'd fit in until I was almost invisible.

Instead of the professor agreeing with her or making some comment at my expense like she's done in the past, her vivid lips turn down in a frown.

"If you can't ignore your surroundings enough to pass my class, then perhaps Silver City University isn't the place for you. Miss Hayliel is an exemplary student. You should make a point to model her behavior. Now, where was I?"

My jaw nearly falls to the floor at her words, and only the very thin line of control I still have is holding it in place. Fucking shit. The professor couldn't have told her anything worse than that.

Do I appreciate she didn't throw me to the wolves? Absolutely. About damn time. But this? Telling her she should model my behavior is going to have serious consequences. *At least it wasn't Seraphina directly, or I might not get to walk out of here.*

Professor Sofiel pauses in her speech to upload something onto our slates, and the angel sitting at the desk in front of me turns around.

She's tall, with short, straight hair, and I'm almost positive I've caught her laughing with the other students at my expense. This time, she wears a smile and says, "Don't worry about Temperance. She's just upset that she can't slay demons at the snap of her fingers like you. That one wouldn't know the first thing about being a savior. I'm Marina. I think what you did is really—"

"Now," Professor Sofiel says, cutting Marina off, "I've just sent a practice test to your slates. Take this time to complete it and see how you do. This is a great way to determine which areas you need to focus on. Please don't waste it."

Thank the Archangels for this small gift. How fickle are angels that Marina now wants to stick up for me? And for what? Contrary to whatever rumors are going around, I can't actually kill demons with the snap of my fingers or a single touch on their forehead. I don't even know if I can bring forth whatever light appeared before. Whatever they think I am, whatever they think I can do, I'm none of those things.

I was wrong to think it would be different now that my wings are gold. I'd rather be the weird, gray-winged freak than whatever the hell this is. It's pure torment.

Focusing on my practice test, I do my best to ignore Marina and the heavy weight of everyone else watching me. To my surprise, I actually do a pretty decent job on the test and jot down a few key areas to focus on. As soon as class ends, I'm out of there. The last thing I need is someone else trying to cozy up to me because of whatever gift they think I possess. And I sure as fuck don't need to get caught in a pissing contest with Seraphina's friends.

Piled up on the floor near the exit to the Tower is a familiar stack of papers. Another newsletter. I'm half tempted to ignore it, unsure I want to read what my classmates are saying about me, but curious too. Does the strange behavior I've witnessed today extend to the *Weekly Observer*?

I cave, grabbing a copy and making a beeline for the bathroom. My friends tell me to ignore these, but I must be a glutton for punishment because I can't. Chances are high that by the time I make it to the cafeteria for lunch, they'll have read it too.

The stalls are empty as I make my way inside the furthest one and lock the door. I lean against the wall, take a deep breath, and start reading.

Gilded in Gold: Is It a Gift or a Curse?
By Harold the Herald

I apologize, dear readers, for my lack of writing
this past week. After the demons attacked our fine
school, I spent time away with my family to heal.
But you can rest assured that not even demons
could stop this column, and I come with many
opinions.

Rumor has it that we have our very own gray-winged angel, Hayliel Gracelin, to thank for subduing the awful creatures and saving us from further injury. But that comment isn't entirely true, for she is no longer gray winged. Several students have come forward to relay their personal story of this change. Marina Mandel witnessed Hayliel's transformation shortly after the attack. "She stood near the well, looking more confused than anything, but there was no denying the shift in wing color. The way the sun glinted off her feathers was almost blinding. We are all in her debt, and I look forward to getting the chance to pay her back."

There is no mistaking the fact that we owe Hayliel Gracelin for ridding our beloved school of those wretched creatures, but is all that shines truly gold, or is something more troubling afoot? Had Professor Uriel been right to assume she had covered her wings in dust? Was Hayliel aware that her wings were gold? And has she known all along that she could rid us of demons? As you can see, I have too many questions and far too few answers. Seraphina Beckett had much to say on the matter. "Isn't this all just a little too perfect? Weirdo outsider wants to fit in ... there are hundreds of stories about this. Couple that with the fact demons showed up on campus, which is something we've never seen before, and only she can dispel them. Does anyone wonder where those rumors even started? It only benefits her to spread them, so of course she'd want them to be impressive and over the top. I stand by my original statement. That lying freak should be expelled."

Strong words from a strong angel. But is she wrong? Could this all be a clever hoax to fit in, or are we truly standing on the precipice of something new?

Whichever it is, I can't wait to find out.

My mind feels like mush. The article isn't exactly bad, definitely not the worst I've seen, and it's not like Seraphina's point of view is new. Honestly, her part just felt rehashed. I wonder when Marina gave her statement to Harold. It had to have been before class, but when did her switch flip from hating me to wanting to be my friend?

Shit. This is all so fucked up.

Crumpling up the paper, I toss it in the trash and glance at myself in the mirror. I look as tired as I feel, but I know exactly what will make me feel better.

My friends.

7

RAPHAEL

"Maybe we should take our lunch and go," Theo says, eyeing the pile of students crowded inside the cafeteria.

I consider his suggestion as I chew on my bottom lip. He's not wrong, but if there's anything I've learned about my sunshine, it's that she's full of surprises. "Let's wait to see what Hayliel thinks."

"What I think about what?"

Theo replies, but I can barely hear what he's saying because I'm lost in the sight of her, drowning beneath her radiant light. It doesn't matter that I saw her just a few hours ago. I already knew she wore her hair down today, flowing freely across her shoulders and over her back.

It's hard to miss the jacket she's wearing today: a black leather thing that absolutely can't be hers. But whose is it, and why is she wearing it?

Before I let myself obsess over it too much, I shift my gaze back to her face. Her usually shining blue eyes hold a little less sparkle today, the gold flecks barely visible. She must not be getting enough sleep. Maybe I can help with that.

"...see how it goes. With you guys here, I don't feel so alone." Hayliel smiles, and I watch as Theo practically melts. He tries to hide it, still worried that our friendship won't withstand wanting the same woman, but I disagree. Other angels, maybe. But not with him, and certainly not with her. This girl has enough room in her heart for both of us. I just have to find out if her mind does, too. If last night was any indication, I think she just might.

"You're never alone, not with us," Theo reassures her, and she reaches out to squeeze his hand.

I take her other one, clasping both of mine on top of her small, dainty hand. "Never. And if this is an invitation for us to bunk in your dorm every night, we accept."

A blush steals across her cheeks, and she laughs but doesn't deny it. *Laugh it off all you want, but you can't hide the spark of heat in your eyes. Oh yes. My pretty little sunshine can definitely take us both.*

We make our way through the cafeteria until we're standing in line to grab food. It feels more like we're the main attraction at the zoo instead of just four students trying to get some grub. But I soon realize they aren't staring at all of us, only one.

Hayliel tries to ignore the stares and politely declines the multiple offers for her to skip ahead in line by students who I'm almost positive were scowling at her not too long ago. By the time we've got everything we need and find a table in the corner, she looks even more exhausted.

Sitting so she isn't facing the crowd, I watch as she slowly comes back to herself. She must sense my staring because she looks over and our eyes meet just as she takes a spoonful of yogurt into her mouth. Well, fuck me. Who knew some creamy white yogurt on a spoon would do things to me?

Dina makes her way to us, pressing a hand to Hayliel's shoulder and asking to save her a seat while she waits in the line that's twice as long as before. It's not like we'd let anyone else sit here, though. Maybe that house leader, Ezekiel, but if I didn't have to see him today, I wouldn't mind. He always manages to upset my girl, and that's just not something that'll fly with me.

The cafeteria is loud with chatter, but I drown it out in favor of listening to Hayliel offer Theo a slice of her pizza when she notices he doesn't have any.

"Nah, but thank you. I'm not really a pizza guy."

"Um. What did you just say? Because it sounded like you said you don't like pizza, but that's crazy talk."

"It's not that I hate it. I'm just particular. And I can't get the image of some random angel biting into a slice on my first evening here and getting the entire layer of toppings draped down his chin." He shudders, likely recalling the smear of sauce and grease along that kid's chin.

Hayliel laughs and holds up her slice. "Well, I haven't been slapped by the angry toppings god. What if I hold it for you and then you can at least try it? I don't know who it was, but maybe that angel just doesn't know how to bite properly. It happens to the best of us."

He glances at me quickly, and I keep my nod as imperceptible as possible despite my want to nod vigorously because shit. This is definitely something I want to see.

"Alright, alright. Pizza me."

She scooches her chair a little closer to him and holds up the pizza. He leans in slowly, his eyes shifting from her face to the slice before he sinks his teeth into it, their gazes locked.

We're in a trance. Me watching them while they watch each other. It's fucking hot.

And when Hayliel lifts a finger, swiping at the sauce on the corner of his lips before bringing it to her mouth where she licks it off ... Holy shit. I might combust on the spot, and it looks like Theo could, too.

Some ass-faced angel approaches us, killing the mood. He sits in the empty seat beside Hayliel with no tray or food in sight. I don't even know if he notices Theo and me here with her, because he only looks at her.

She's ours, I think in his direction, wondering if I can mentally yell it loud enough for him to hear.

"Hi. I hope it's okay that I'm sitting here. I saw you from across the room and knew I had to introduce myself to the gorgeous angel sitting alone in the corner." He moves to brush the hair out of his eyes, even though there's not a single lock out of place. You're not fooling anyone, dickbag.

"Oh, um. Hi. Thank you. I'm not alone, though. My friends—"

"That's right, Samkiel is here now. Maybe we can, you know, be alone together sometime. This Friday?"

The blood boils beneath my skin at his sheer audacity and the uncomfortable look it brings to Hayliel's face. Who the fuck does this guy think he is? I've never even seen this piss-for-brains motherfucker on campus before.

Dina comes back just in time, saving me from making an ass out of myself and shooing him away. I want to. Archangels, I want to. But there's a faint voice hovering on the edges of my subconscious that tells me it's better if Dina does it. I doubt Hayliel wants to be in the middle of a pissing contest between this rando and a guy she hasn't even officially labeled things with.

"Who's this guy?" she asks, looking unimpressed at the obvious tension.

"No idea. Said his name was Samkiel." I try to relax my jaw, but the words come out forced, anyway.

"Right. Well, you're in my seat, Samkiel."

The newcomer hesitates for a moment before giving Dina her seat, but he doesn't leave. Instead, he stands awkwardly on the fringes of our table, staring at Hayliel.

She looks beyond uncomfortable, but she finally says, "Sorry, I'm unavailable."

"Don't worry, I'm flexible. What about Saturday?"

"The day isn't the issue. I'm unavailable to date. Sorry."

Samkiel opens his mouth to speak again when Dina says, "Look, she's already involved with someone else and uninterested. Accept the no and leave."

His face shifts until it looks as if someone's shoved a sour candy in his mouth and forced him to suck. But I barely notice as he continues to stand there. I barely notice the strange look on Hayliel's face as she peers around the table or the way she picks at her food. My mind is stuck on her words. *I'm unavailable to date.* What does that mean? Even Dina said she's already involved with someone, but who? Do I know them? And what about last night?

Samkiel clearly doesn't know how to take a hint because he stands rooted to the spot, a dark cloud hovering over us. "I don't believe you," he says to Hayliel. "You're not really attached. You're just saying that."

I've had enough. Before I can think twice, I stand, slamming my hand down on the table.

"Listen, fuckface. Even if she wasn't already seeing someone, or even multiple someones if she's so inclined, none of that is your business. She said no. She doesn't need any more excuse than that, so why don't you leave before this becomes even more uncomfortable for you."

The cafeteria grows quiet at my outburst, and as I watch him finally leave, I notice Seraphina storming out of the room. Not my damn problem.

I take my seat, muttering an apology for blowing up. I'm not sorry for what I said, though. That asshole needed to understand that whether or not something is true — and I'll admit even I want to know if she's actually dating someone — no is no.

"No apology necessary, Raph. I was about to blow up myself, which I'm sure would have caused even more of a stir. Thanks for always saving me."

"If he didn't do it, I would have. That piece of shit needed it, and maybe a swift kick in the head, too. What the hell even was that?" Dina asks.

"You don't even—" Hayliel doesn't get to finish because two girls show up at the table, holding out a piece of paper.

"By the grace of the Archangels!" one of them whisper shouts.

"Is it really you, Hayliel? We've been looking for you all over campus. Can you sign our newsletters, please?"

"Please, please, please!" the other one parrots.

What the hell?

Hayliel looks just as confused as I am. "Erm ... sure, I guess?"

She scrawls her name across each page, and the two girls pick them up like they're made of glass. "Pinch me," the tallest one says to her friend, who does what she asked. "It's real. The demon slayer herself signed these! Thank you!"

"I think I might faint," the other one says, and then they're running back to a crowded table on the other side of the cafeteria.

"So yeah ... it's been a weird fucking day. I've either been fawned over like you just saw — though the autograph was definitely a first — or hated on like before. I'm half tempted to switch my major just to avoid dealing with Professor Uriel again. And Professor Sofiel basically told one of Seraphina's minions she should be more like me, so I'm sure that won't come back to haunt me later."

Silence falls over us, the only sound coming from Theo's slate vibrating on the table.

"It'll blow over, Hayles," Dina reassures her.

Theo nudges her. "Exactly. I'm sure everyone is just looking for something else to focus on instead of what we all went through. This will be old news in no time."

"And in the meantime, you have us. As a distraction, a getaway, or your executioner. We got you, sunshine." On the off chance she'd been referring to me as the guy she's in a relationship with, I might as well play the part. It's not like cheering her up is something I wouldn't have done anyway.

The smile doesn't quite reach her eyes, but I'm determined to provoke a real one from her. I don't get the chance to pull out all my charm though, because Theo sucks in a breath.

We all turn to him, his eyes shifting frantically as he reads something on his slate.

Hayliel is the first to speak. "What is it?"

Theo looks up, his eyes dark pools of some emotion I can't name. Fear? Worry? "Apparently, SCU wasn't the only place attacked by demons. The article doesn't say where, but the timing matches up to when we were fighting for our lives. Why would they target two places at once?"

"Anyone else have a sense that there's more here than just a coincidence?" I ask, not liking where this is going.

Dina nods. "Is there anything for us to go by to find out where the attack happened?"

"Nothing."

Hayliel's eyebrows pull together as she chews on her bottom lip. "Shit, well at least we have another avenue to explore, right? If we can find the location, maybe we'll be able to connect the dots. I think we should find Ezekiel. Maybe with his ties to the Guild, he's privy to something that we aren't."

I want to protest, tell her we're capable without him and don't need that asshole for anything, but I let my frustration for him go on a long exhale. Maybe she's right. Maybe he'll be able to shed some light on that attack and bring us one step closer to figuring out what the fuck is going on.

So I suck up my pride, reach out to clasp my hand around hers and nod. "We'll track him down this afternoon."

8

HAYLIEL

We couldn't find Zeke anywhere.

He wasn't in his dorm room or the Fallen house. He wasn't in the main hall cafeteria or even with Professor Malik in the weaponry training building. All signs point toward him being off campus, so instead of wasting anymore time searching for him, I decide to leave it for now. I'm supposed to meet Raphael and Theo in front of Power house to continue our research, anyway.

Dina had to duck out, needing to check in with her dad and study for next week's midterms. Something we should probably do as well, but after the weird vibes from everyone today, I'd rather focus my attention on discovering more about myself.

I still haven't flown anywhere on campus, not wanting to take my wings out any more than necessary, and they're starting to itch. Angels are supposed to let their wings free, not keep them locked up. It drives them mad. I'll have to carve out some time soon to let them out somewhere without prying eyes. Maybe Raph can help me.

It would be a whole hell of a lot faster if I'd just deal with the stares and whispers instead of trekking my way across campus, so I'm surprised when I reach the path leading to Power house and don't see any sign of my friends.

A figure drops to the ground in front of me, causing a shriek to rise in my throat that I choke down when I realize who it is.

"We've been looking for you."

"I was off campus, but I've been searching for you, too," Zeke says, looking around. "It's rare I find you alone these days. It's either my lucky day or your worst one, if those Pure boys have come to their senses."

My heart squeezes, but I don't let him see the pain his words cause. "Damn. For a second there, I thought you'd finally had a personality transplant. We have things to discuss, but if you're going to act like a self-righteous dick, then we'll figure it out on our own."

"I'm sorry. I'm trying, really. But—"

As he speaks, the flap of wings from somewhere nearby announces the arrival of the two Pure boys in question. "Trying what?" Raphael asks, face weary.

Ezekiel scowls, taking a step away from me. "Nothing. I have news." He turns to me. "Can we go somewhere private to discuss?"

I nod, not bothering to acknowledge the fact that he wants to talk to me alone. Not today, Satan. "We were all heading to the Power house library, anyway. Let's discuss it there."

The four of us walk in awkward silence. Whatever these guys have against each other, I hope they figure it out soon. This masculine standoff shit is far too uncomfortable for my liking. But even I've learned how hard Zeke can be to get along with. *Except he wasn't always like that with me.*

Students stare as we walk through Power house. With Theo and Raph in front, and Zeke at my back, I almost feel like royalty. But I'm not getting escorted to my inaugural ball, and I'm anything but nobility.

We find a quiet corner and sit, though Zeke hesitates at first before taking the seat at the table across from me, next to Theo. *Still hoping we'd talk in private, huh, big guy?*

To my surprise, it's Theo who breaks the silence. "You said you had news, but so do we. An article went out today about another attack, one at the same time we were under siege. None of us think it's a coincidence, but the article didn't mention where it was, so we can't look into it further."

"Do you know anything that could help?" I ask, trying not to get my hopes up but feeling them inflate regardless.

Zeke straightens, and I almost sense that he's trying to strengthen himself. Against what, though, I'm not sure. When he speaks, I forget trying to decipher it.

"It would seem we've been following a similar lead. I don't have the location, unfortunately, but I was coming to share that it wasn't just another attack. From what I overheard at the Guild, it's possible the attack at SCU was just a diversion, along with the influx of calls and demon sightings in the city that day. A few Guild members mentioned there being a theft, but I wasn't able to gain insight into where it was or what they stole."

"That's quite a diversion for a little theft," Theo wonders out loud.

"Whatever it was must be important," Raphael agrees.

"I agree. But I think somehow, you're at the center of it." Zeke looks at me, eyebrows drawn low.

"Me?" I stutter, my heart rate picking up.

"You can't truly think the way they targeted you was just a coincidence. The way they all pivoted toward you, it was like you called to them on a level that no one else could hear. I can't brush that off as happenstance."

Theo looks like he might agree with Zeke, yet I still can't wrap my head around it all.

"But what does she have to do with whatever they stole?" Theo asks.

"I don't know yet. I'll try to find more at the Guild, but in the meantime maybe I can find something about demon theft in the Fallen library. It's possible this isn't the first time they've coordinated something like this." There's an awkward pause after Zeke's words, and he turns to leave.

I panic. An odd response, sure, but I just don't want him to leave yet. After everything he's put me through, I should hate him. I shouldn't want to spend time with him or hope for a glimpse of the guy I let paint me during that first party. Yet I can't stop those feelings any more than I can change the color of my wings.

"Wait. You're here now. Why not stay and look through the library?"

His back stiffens briefly before he looks over his shoulder at me, gaze panning to the guys. It feels like an eternity before he does anything, and I'm almost positive he's going to walk away.

"Fine. But only because I'm already here."

Theo stays seated while the three of us make our way through the stacks, piling books onto a cart before heading back to our seats. When we return, Theo looks concerned as he scrolls through the comment section of the article he'd read earlier.

Placing my hand on his shoulder, I say, "We'll figure it out, Theo. I know we will."

"I sure hope so, firefly."

Zeke's gaze is on me, heavy and brooding, but I only meet it for a second, offering a smile before diving into my book. Or trying to, anyway. There's too much *noise.* And it's not chatter or the scraping of chairs. It's here, between the four of us. As much as I want all of us to get along, what if too much has happened for us to move forward as friends? Is friendship all that I even want? Fuck. Maybe this is just a lost cause.

That thought is confirmed twenty minutes later when Zeke and Raphael reach for the same book.

Raphael snatches it up before Zeke can, earning an angrily whispered, "Hey!" from Zeke. "You have an entire stack of books to choose from. Why don't you pick from one of those and let me read that one? It's the last of my pile."

"Oh, stop complaining. Here." He hands Zeke a random book from the cart. "We're all here for the same reason. Why don't you flip through this one and I'll let you know when I'm done?"

If Zeke's eyes were angel blades, the glare he shoots Raph would kill him. I'm grateful they aren't. Sparing a glance toward Theo, I find him watching the exchange with me. I wonder what he thinks of all this. Does he want everyone to get along just as much as I do? Or is he on mine and Raphael's side no matter what because of our friendship?

"Fucking Pures," Zeke whispers under his breath, ignoring the book in Raph's hand and grabbing another one altogether.

To my surprise, Raphael doesn't respond, and our little group grows quiet again. Ten more minutes pass until Zeke shuts the book and leans back in his chair, clearly displeased.

"Look, dude. If you need extra time to read, why didn't you just let me read it first?"

"I don't need *extra* time, asshole. This is important. Just because you're willing to skim doesn't mean I am."

Beneath the table, my hands clench into fists. Archangels, they're like a bunch of children. Unable to listen to any more of their shit, I stand. "Excuse me, I need some air."

I feel their eyes on me as I walk away from our little corner of hell without bothering to look back. Whatever my issues are with Zeke, it's clear I'm not the only one. There's animosity in the air, and I wonder if I'm the reason for it. Maybe my want to include Zeke in our group isn't wise.

With my head down, I walk out the front doors of Power house with no real destination in mind. Just being away from all that pent-up tension and frustration is a nice change. There's a soft breeze that flows over my heated skin and cools me down.

I don't know how to handle those three. My own emotions are hard enough to deal with. Add in theirs, and it feels like we'll never get along. But there has to be a way, right?

Without realizing it, I've found my way in front of the nearest statue and I just stare at it, needing a distraction. I wonder which angel was the model for this. Is it even based on someone in particular or just a general sketch the artist had in mind?

"Miss Hayliel. I thought that was you."

Professor Castiel comes up beside me. Just like my first day on campus, he has his white wings out. "Hi! How are you? I meant to say this earlier, but things have been rather hectic. Thank you for what you did for me at the well. I'm not sure I would have handled their scrutiny much longer."

"No thanks needed. I only did what I thought was best."

"Still, I'm grateful. I actually saw you fighting that day. You really know how to handle your own out there."

"A long life has its perks." He chuckles. "From what I hear, though, you do alright yourself."

"Angels do like to talk, don't they?" I reply, avoiding the topic.

"That they do. I wanted to check in with you after everything, but figured you had your hands full. If you ever need anything, I hope you know you can come to me. No questions asked. Besides, my old age has more perks than just strong fighting skills."

If those words came from anyone else, it would probably creep me out. But with his soft, genuine smile, I know he means it.

"I appreciate that, truly. And depending on how I make out on the midterm, I may wind up visiting you for some extra tutoring, too."

"Not a chance. You and Theo are my two best students, though if you tell anyone I said so, I'll deny it."

I mime zipping my lips and throwing away the key.

"I should get going, but don't forget my offer and please extend it to your friends as well. Stay safe, Miss Hayliel."

"You too, Professor."

He flies away from me, leaving me at my spot near the statue, feeling lighter than I had when I first came out. Light enough that I'm comfortable heading back inside and checking in on the guys. *Hopefully they haven't killed each other yet.*

Once I'm inside, I don't go straight to the table, choosing instead to stroll through the stacks in search of something that might help ease the tension. I remember finding an old volume that sounded perfect for Zeke's search, but our pile was already so big that I didn't bother grabbing it. After a few minutes, I find it and head back to a surprisingly quiet table. Raphael must have finished with the book while I was gone, because it's on the table in front of Zeke now and no one is snarling at each other like raging beasts.

"Here. I found this and thought it might hold something about our theft problem." I hand the book to Zeke and sit back in my chair, watching as he pushes the item he'd just fought Raphael over aside.

"Thanks."

"You're welcome."

Silence falls around us, and I know something must have happened while I was gone. Oh, to be a fly on the wall and witness that, but I'm just happy the tension has dissipated.

As I stretch out to lounge in my seat, my foot knocks into something beneath the table. I look up, and Theo is watching me. His eyes are sun-warmed bronze nestled in a bed of grass, and all I want to do is curl up there. He rubs his foot against mine in tiny movements until my worries have melted away and I can finally focus.

"Thank you," I mouth to him, not making a sound for fear of ruining this moment.

He only nods and focuses back on his slate, but his feet stay entwined with mine for the rest of the evening.

9

HAYLIEL

I long for the days when things were normal. Well, okay. Maybe not normal, but they weren't like this.

When I lived at home, at least I had a break. Someplace to truly let loose and relax. Here at SCU, I'm always on guard. Even with my friends, studying like hell for midterms or hopelessly searching for answers, there are always angels around. Watching me. Waiting for me to do something that either proves I'm a savior or the demon-spawned vermin they always thought I was. It's exhausting.

I'm braiding my long, brown hair, wet from the shower, and mentally preparing for another day of midterm prep when there's a knock on the door. My stomach flutters, wondering who it is. Could it be Theo and Raph coming to continue what we started at the park last week? I practically skip to the door, desperate to find out if what I've been dreaming about these past few nights will finally come true.

To my surprise — and the desolation of my vagina — it's not them. Dina stands on the other side of the door, coffee and breakfast in hand.

"Well shit, Hayles. Don't look so damn disappointed." She walks past me, setting her things down on the small table.

"What? I'm not!"

"Oh, you were, but that's alright. I might be too if I had many a suitor to sweep me off my feet. I'm going to need all the details of your little impromptu date, but right now, I just need to get out of here."

A bolt of fear shoots through me as she sits. "Did something happen?"

She lets out a breath. "No, not really. But with midterms, my dad, and everything else going on, I just need a break. Our last girls' day ended early, so I thought maybe we could head to town and just escape it all for a bit. I promise to have you back with plenty of time to study for next week's midterms, and I kind of already let Principal Cael know we'd be stepping out for the day. What do you say?"

I study Dina's face. The strong angel who's been my best friend for years looks anything but strong today. She looks tired, worn down, and in desperate need of a pick-me-up. How can I say no to that?

"Hell yes! Give me a few minutes to get ready, and then we'll head out." I jump into action, pulling on a pair of ripped jeans and a gray tank top before grabbing the oversized leather jacket off the hook on the back of my closet door. It's soft beneath my fingers, and as I slip it on, I'm reminded of that day in the library. I have my own ideas of who left this for me, not that it made any sense. Yet somehow it's become one of my favorite accessories lately.

Stepping out of the closet, I slip on a pair of strappy sandals.

"You ready? We can take these on the road," she calls out, holding on to the bag filled with our breakfast sandwiches.

"Almost!" I duck into the bathroom to brush my teeth, and add a layer of mascara before I'm finally ready to go.

As I get closer to her, my stomach rumbles and we both laugh.

"On second thought, maybe you should eat this now."

"Nah. I won't perish just yet, but you bet your ass I'll be scarfing it down the moment we leave campus." I head toward the door, about to twist the knob, but notice that Dina hasn't followed me.

She's staring at my jacket with an almost knowing look on her face.

"What's wrong?" I ask, wondering if maybe she recognizes the jacket and can shed some light — or confirm — whose it is.

But, of course, she doesn't.

"Hmm? Oh, nothing." But the glint in her eyes gives her away. "Let's go."

"Hayliel!"

I walk around the racks until I spot Dina standing in front of a wall of lingerie.

"Which of your men do you think would like this the most?" She raises her brows up and down, her lips tilted up wickedly.

My cheeks flame despite my attempts to keep the blush at bay as I ponder her question. The piece she holds up is little more than tiny strings of fabric and lace, dyed a deep teal blue that reminds me of the deepest parts of the ocean. I think of Raphael and Theo, of Ezekiel, and honestly, I think they'd all find it hot, but something tells me Zeke would want to tear it off of me the most. Well, if he didn't hate me, that is.

I say as much to Dina, regretting the words as soon as they leave my mouth, because it only proves that I still think of him. After the way he rejected me, that angel shouldn't hold even an ounce of my attention.

"I've said it before, but clearly it begs repeating. He doesn't hate you. At most, he hates himself for how much he wants you. Trust me."

Her words strike a chord deep within me, and I pick them apart while I play with the frilly edges of a silky pink baby-doll top. "It's a nice thought, but it doesn't really make sense. Actions speak louder than words, and he's done nothing but ignore me since finding out about my wings. Why would he do that if he wanted me?"

"If he didn't want you, then why was he so worried about you when the demons attacked? And if he isn't interested in you, then why has he been hanging around when he obviously doesn't care for Raphael and Theo? Think about it, Hayles. That angel has it bad."

I stay silent, not willing to voice my racing thoughts. Trouble. That's what he is. That's all it would cause if he really did like me. At least Raphael and Theo aren't making me choose, or they haven't yet, anyway. With the way Zeke acts around those two, I doubt he'd even want me to stay friends with them if we started dating. This is for the best.

We exit the shop without buying anything and walk down the street until we find this gorgeous boutique. Inside it sports modern decor and rows upon rows of accessories. From hair to wings, this store has it all.

Dina and I spare each other an excited glance, then we split up. Down one aisle I find jewel-toned wing brushes and bedazzled clips. There are shiny wing-tips and feather glitter, the former of which remind me of the man from the Guild who spoke at SCU before the attack. Then along the back wall I spot the most beautiful harness. A dainty rose-gold chain dangles between the model's breasts, flowing underneath and around her back and shoulders. The chain wraps around her neck like a choker, with several more breaking off and appearing almost woven off the side and over her shoulders. I don't know how anyone would get this on, but shit, it's stunning.

There's an image of the model with her white wings out on the back of the pack. The breath stalls in my lungs. It's as if the chain grew to accommodate her wings, draping across the feathers in a delicate pattern that looks almost natural. But is that even possible?

I'm more than tempted to buy it, already picturing myself wearing it at a party or even the beach, where the chain would glitter beneath the light of the sun. Until I see the price tag. As much as I might want it, I'd have to fork over far more of my measly funds than I'm comfortable with.

Maybe some day.

I continue down the aisle until familiar footsteps approach from behind me. Dina has her arms full of accessories in an array of different colors.

"When are you planning to wear all those?" I ask, a chuckle escaping me as I try to count how many items she's holding.

"Hey! No judging or I won't share." She kisses in my direction but can't actually blow it to me because her hands are full. "Plus, I've been hearing rumors around campus that there will be far more parties coming up, and I intend for us to show up for at least a few."

The easy grin falls from my face. "Parties, Dina. Really? I can hardly handle the amount of attention I get already. I'm not entirely sure I'll be able to deal with drunken attention at a party that I'm sure no one actually wants me at."

"Just think about it. Between me and those hunks of yours, it'll be just like we're hanging out but with drinks, and maybe a cool theme. Now, speaking of your yummy boyfriends, I'm going to go pay for this, and then maybe you can spill all the juicy details from your date."

I follow her to the cash register, taking stock of the items she's placing on the counter. There's nipple tape and pasties, wing clips and tips, and even a pallet of glitter in stunning rainbow colors. Then I see it. A familiar rose-gold chain. But there isn't just one package, there's two.

"Dina ..." I begin, unsure how to word the rest of it.

Immediately she notices where my gaze is locked, taking an almost protective stance, like she's afraid I'm going to take it from her pile. "It's nothing. A gift for helping me escape life for just a little bit today. Besides, how else are we supposed to match? We can't be twin baddies with only one chain, Hayles. It's just not possible."

I hesitate, so she continues. "It's only a small gift. One that you deserve and I can easily afford. Please let me get it for you. I promise I won't buy you a single thing more today or even for the rest of the month."

"Make it two months and I'll agree."

"Deal."

The woman working the cash witnessed our disagreement and was waiting patiently for me to agree before scanning the last two items. She rings them through, offering us each a smile. "These are going to look stunning on you! They can be confusing to get on, but just read the guide included with the instructions and you'll be fine. If you're still confused, call us, alright?"

We exit the store, each carrying a bag filled with Dina's new purchases, and make our way toward the nearest coffee shop. The sun shines brightly from above, warming my flesh and making me forget all my troubles. Or it does until an odd sensation runs down my spine like thick molasses.

Across the street, someone stares at us. I can't tell if they're staring at me or Dina, though, so I try to shake it off. Another angel walks past us, their head swiveling around to watch us after they pass. What the hell?

Dina doesn't seem to notice as she chatters on about something. A party? Fuck. I'm being a shitty friend. I take a deep breath and focus on her words, offering a soft sound of agreement so she knows I'm paying attention, but it's not long before another sound breaks my concentration.

Shoes slap the pavement behind us. My heart rate picks up, urging me to run, to get as far as I can from whoever's following us, but that's ridiculous. We're on a busy street lined with shops, so it's not like we're being stalked down an alley.

I peek over my shoulder, trying to catch sight of the pursuer without being obvious. Shit. I really wish I hadn't braided my hair this morning. At least I could have hidden behind it.

"What's gotten into you, Hayles?"

"What? Nothing. I'm listening. You're talking about a party over break."

She throws me a look that tells me she's not buying my shit. I might have been listening enough to figure out what she was talking about, but anything else she'd said was lost to the void. After a second she says, "Yeah, yeah. Come on, we're almost there."

We round the corner and enter a small coffee shop. The nutty scent of freshly ground coffee beans and warm pastries fills my senses. I breathe in deep, wishing I could bottle the aroma and keep it with me. Dina laughs and pulls me forward, moving up the line toward the register. There's another angel in front of us, so she scans the menu written along the wall behind the counter, and before I can do the same, I freeze. Sitting against the window is an angel who looks incredibly familiar. Wasn't he the angel watching us from across the street earlier? How did he get here so fast? Is he following us?

Jolting me out of my fear, Dina drags me to the counter and orders. She hasn't noticed anything off with me yet and honestly, I'd like to keep it that way. I'm freaking out over nothing. Even if it is the same guy, he probably just wants a coffee. *But then why was he staring at you?*

Fuck. When did it get so hot in here? I peel the leather jacket off my overheated limbs and sigh when the cool air touches my damp skin.

"And for you?" the barista asks me.

I shake off my worries and order blindly as I struggle to get back to normal. Dina gives me an odd look, but I only shoot her a smile in return, trying to mask the panic rising inside of me.

Maybe everyone knows what you did during the attack. No. They can't. I haven't confirmed it to anyone outside of my friends, and they wouldn't tell anyone.

Someone calls our names, letting us know our order is ready. I blink a few times and the scene around me changes. The angel sitting near the window is no longer a man but a woman, reading a book and sipping a hot drink. Angels stare, but only the students I recognize from campus. Crisis averted.

I walk toward an empty table, expecting us to sit down and enjoy ourselves, except Dina shakes her head. "Let's go somewhere a little less crowded and enjoy the sunshine before we hole up inside to study."

"You're brilliant, you know that?"

She links her arm through mine with a satisfied look on her face. "Oh, I know."

We don't have to walk too far before we reach an empty bench on the outskirts of the park. The same one I came to with Raphael and Theo, only this area is different. There's a large pond in the center and a family of four are heading toward it with miniature boats in hand. Just how big is this place?

As we settle into our coffees, Dina breaks the silence. "What happened to you back there?"

I pick at the holes in my jeans, unsure how much I should tell her. "The stares got to me. I know they shouldn't at this point. I've been dealing with them all my life, but it's different now. *I'm* different now."

"I don't believe that. You may have gold wings instead of gray, but that doesn't change who you are on the inside. You're still the kind, selfless, passionate angel I've known forever. Who you are isn't defined by your wing color, Hayles. It never has and it never will. The angels who truly matter see it, too. And the ones who can't see you for the incredible woman you are, well, they don't matter. And let's face it. They only focus on others because if they had to look inside themselves, they wouldn't like what they find."

Tears well in my eyes as her words fall on me like rain, soaking into my flesh and bones. My wings may have always made me different, an outcast, but it doesn't change who I am on the inside. I could have turned sour and rotten, become the very freak everyone thought I was, but I didn't. Even when it hurt. And that has to count for something, doesn't it?

"Thank you," I whisper, wiping the tears from my cheeks.

"Always. You're one badass angel, and don't you ever forget it." She pulls me into a one-armed hug, placing a kiss on my temple before pulling away. We sit in silence, finishing our drinks and watching the families play in the park. It's nice not being cooped up inside, surrounded by disappointing old books or study material. That thought makes me think of my men again, and the erotic night we'd had at this very park.

"What are you thinking about that has such a grin on your face, hmm?"

My cheeks heat and I laugh. "Just remembering when I came here with Raph and Theo. Do you remember what you said to me on the Tower, before all hell broke loose? That maybe they weren't testing me at all and might even be willing to, uh, share?"

Fuck, it feels so weird saying this all out loud, even to Dina.

She stops mid sip, then turns her head to meet my gaze. "Yes. But if you tell me something happened, and you've kept it to yourself for days, I'm going to be pissed." She pauses for a moment, and when I stay silent, she continues. "Alright, fine. I'll forgive you, now spill."

"We went to this café and I swear, Dina, they ordered the entire freaking menu. Then we explored this little art store before Raphael took us to this photo parlor, where we dressed up in old outfits and posed for what had to have been a million photos. I'll show you them once we're back on campus."

"While I love everything you've said so far, nothing really screams *they're willing to share me*. What are you leaving out?"

"Have a little patience, babe. I'm getting there." I take a few moments to fidget with my empty coffee cup and find a more comfortable position on the bench, knowing full well that every passing second only fuels her desperation. The look she sends me is filled with annoyance, telling me she knows exactly what I'm doing.

"You're cruel, you know that?"

"You love me for it." I send her my most innocent look and continue my story. "Well, after we finished with the photos, we came here to this park. It was a different section, though, but they had food trucks and popcorn stands set up for a movie night. The three of us shared a blanket, and Raphael grabbed an extra one so we wouldn't be cold."

"Hayliel Gracelin! Please tell me you fucked both of them at an open park movie night."

"No! Well, not exactly. Raph did some wonderful things to my body with Theo sitting close enough that I know he either felt it or heard. Hell, we even held hands while Raphael was getting me off. It was ... everything."

"You lucky bitch." Dina rests her chin in her hand as she gazes off into the distance, lost in reverie. When she finally shifts her eyes back to mine, she says, "So when is part two?"

10

EZEKIEL

B astards!

It's the fourth time in a row that I've had an opening, a chance to escape unseen into the restricted section of the Guild, only for another intern to ruin my chances. Without sneaking into our file room, I'll never know more about that second attack. We need that information.

The digital files are even harder to crack into without proper security clearance. There's no chance I'll sneak onto that server, but I should be able to handle a door. If only I could manage to disappear without raising suspicion.

I log a few more lines from the report Azrael gave me, my frustration rising as I enter the data from yet another investigation I hadn't been part of. *Look on the bright side, at least you have a better shot at the file room this way. Stop complaining.*

The clock on my slate tells me I'm running out of time. Once my shift is over, I'll be shit out of luck until my next one. The longer I go without that information, the more likely it is that someone will get hurt. Not to mention the fact that I have angels counting on me, and as much as I might pretend not to like a certain gold-winged angel and her Pure boyfriends, I don't want to let Hayliel down.

I even made small talk with a few interns today, something I absolutely never do. Maybe I shouldn't have, given the odd expressions on their faces, but I'm desperate.

I wonder who's still hanging around. Only one intern is left in the room with me. His name evades me — Ananiel, I think. He sits a few desks away, his back to me and completely engrossed in whatever task he's working on. I stand silently and take a few steps toward him. Unfortunately, the way to the file room is just past his desk, toward the Lieutenant wing.

When Ananiel makes a sound, this deep, almost thoughtful rumble from his chest, I stop. *Shit!*

I wait a beat before advancing, and when I get a few steps closer, his head falls forward, chin resting on his chest. The idiot is fucking sleeping. I laugh silently, confidence rising in my steps as I hurry out of the room and down the hall.

Luckily, I don't run into anyone by the time I reach the hallway I need to turn down. If I continue straight, I'll make it to the Lieutenant wing, but if I hook a right, I'll find the very room I've been waiting all day to access.

My steps sound loud to my own ears as I approach the door marked *Storage*. I've never come down this way before, even with a lieutenant. Interns might be allowed to tag along on missions and log details, but we sure as hell don't know everything. They keep us in the dark on a lot of shit, but I can understand why. We have to prove ourselves first.

I try the door, but the handle doesn't budge. There's no keyhole like I expected. Instead, on the wall to the right of the door sits a little box with a red light. Fuck. I should have known I'd need a keycard to access it, since that's what all the other sections in this damn fortress have. Looking down, I eye the card attached to the belt loop of my uniform, considering my options.

I could try mine, but that has the potential to land me in hot water. I could try to steal Ananiel's card, but if he woke up, I'd be screwed. There has to be another way.

Heading back down the hall, I turn right toward the Lieutenant wing, not entirely sure what I'm searching for. It's not like I could ask any of them to let me into the file room. The whole point of this is to keep my investigation a secret. For whatever reason, they want to hide the information about that attack, and I want to know why. Does it have anything to do with what happened at SCU? There must be a connection, but why aren't they looking for one?

I pass a few locked doors, the hope that once blossomed in my chest like a delicate flower now fading. Peeking inside the on-duty lieutenant's office, I find it empty, but just as I'm about to turn away and give up, I spot something. A keycard.

Jackpot! No one would suspect a thing if a lieutenant accessed the file room.

On silent feet, I enter the room and grab the card without allowing myself to consider whose it is. Warning sounds ring in my head, but I push them aside and creep toward the door. Voices erupt down the hall, and for a split second, fear immobilizes me. I snap out of it quickly, holding tight to the inner wall while I pretend to look at some award propped up on the bookshelf. My palms turn clammy as the voices get louder, but to my ever-fucking-relief, they keep going.

I wait another beat, then race back to the file room, scanning the card and sneaking inside. The lights flicker on automatically, illuminating the space and causing me to suck in a breath. How the hell am I going to find anything in here? There are seemingly endless rows of filing cabinets and shelves that hold boxes piled on top of each other. If I have any hope of finding what I need, I have to be smart.

I decide to take the room in sections, starting with the first row of cabinets along the wall to my left. Each drawer holds a date, and it doesn't take long for me to realize that the files near the door are the oldest. Heading deeper into the room, I scan the date on the cabinets until I'm almost back to the front of the room and still haven't found what I'm searching for. Shit.

I hurry down the rows of shelving that make up the center of the long room, noting the boxes have similar dates on them, and these appear to be much newer. *Getting warmer.*

There, near the end of an almost empty shelf, is a new box of files. I empty its contents, shuffling through the papers until I find the one I'm looking for, then glance at my slate, noting the time. Fucking shit. I've been gone far longer than I intended to. Whoever's keycard I have will surely notice it's missing soon. I have to hurry.

I flip open the folder and promptly shut it again. This can't be the attack I'm looking for, can it? But when I recheck the date on the front of the folder, I see it is. *By the Archangels.*

Demons attacked one of the Guild armories? But how? Those are locked up tight and protected for a reason. The more I read, the more I worry until it feels like I've swallowed a pail of rocks. From the file, along with some angel blades, there were at least a handful of sun blades reported missing. Our greatest weapon against them, the ones we have so very few of and can't afford to lose. And they've taken some away from us.

Maybe that's why so many angels reported seeing demons. The Guild has several armories throughout Silver City, both real and fake, in order to throw off anyone who may watch us too closely. So how did the demons know which one to attack? And how did they just happen to know which armory would be the least protected? Something doesn't add up.

When I came looking, I never expected *this* would be what they were hiding. It's no wonder they've kept this quiet. If word got out, the entire city would be in a panic, and that's the last thing we need. Though I still don't understand why Azrael kept this from me, of all angels. He has me on fucking desk duty when I could be investigating.

I look through the photos, flipping over runic symbols and empty weapon racks, bypassing the bloody carnage of our slain Guild members until I land on a photo that piques my interest. It's from one of our security cameras at the armory, and whoever it is must not have known it was there. The photo is almost too blurry to make out any details, but the black wings are hard to miss. He's a Fallen. One of his wings looks off, and I don't think it's the grainy photo. A scar, perhaps?

There's no name on the photo or anywhere in the report. Only this picture. Who is he? My first thought is that maybe he's a Guild member who survived, but the report states that everyone on duty at the armory died in the attack. Curious.

I put everything back in its place on the shelf and head toward the exit. I've already spent far too long in here, but this was necessary. We, the Guild, need to know what's happening. We need to be kept in the loop on this if we have any hope of doing our job and protecting Silver City.

I came in here looking for answers, but all I've found are more questions.

The hallway is quiet as I shut the door to the file room and make my way toward the main hall that connects to the Lieutenant wing. I need to get rid of this keycard before someone notices. As I reach the end of the intersection, I peer right and then left. There's a woman coming from the intern bullpen.

She isn't wearing a uniform, but her T-shirt sports the Guild logo. Something about her shoulder-length, merlot-colored hair and jade-green eyes is familiar. Is she an intern, perhaps?

"As if that doesn't look suspicious," she says, looking down the hall I just came from and then back at me. I watch as her gaze travels down my uniform, catching on the keycard in my fist. *Shit.*

"What are you doing over here?"

I wait a beat, then two, before slipping the stolen keycard into my pocket. "I could ask you the same thing."

Her smile grows, but it doesn't soothe the nervous energy racing through me. If she tells anyone that she saw me here, I'm fucked.

"I'm looking for my father. Lieutenant Atlas. I thought maybe he was here."

I try not to let the shock show on my face. Not that it's some big feat to have a father in the Guild — there are a lot of us who do. But with the way Atlas acts with the interns, I just assumed he didn't have any kids. If it's his card I just used, I can't say that I'm unhappy about it because fuck that guy.

Ignoring what I assume is her attempt to brag, I say, "I came to report to my lieutenant, but I must have made a wrong turn. Unfortunately, I haven't seen your father yet today. Good luck."

Without waiting for her to respond, I take a few steps to the right toward the Lieutenant wing, but her voice stops me from going any further.

"Right," she says, clearly not believing me. "Well, I hope you find what you're looking for. If you see my dad, tell him I've been looking for him. And don't worry. I'll keep the rest of this little meeting a secret. For now, anyway."

She's a stranger, so I'm not entirely sure why she'd keep whatever she thinks she knows a secret, but there's not much I can do right now. I need to get this keycard back to its rightful owner, whoever it is. Plus, it's not as if she knows anything about me. There are plenty of Guild members with similar features to my own. Even if she shares where she found me, there's no way it could lead back to me.

Before she gets too far away, she looks over her shoulder and winks. "Nice running into you, Ezekiel."

And just like that, my stomach sinks. But how did she— *Fuck.* My nametag.

I don't respond, just shoot her a weird sort of wave and head toward the on-duty lieutenant's office with my stomach practically dragging on the floor.

Almost there. Then I can get the fuck out of here.

The office is empty, so I hurry inside to place the card back where I found it when footsteps approach from the hall. Shit! There's no time to think, only act. I drop the card to the floor and kick it so that it skitters and lands near the chair. Just as someone else enters the room, I do my best to appear engrossed in the same awards I'd looked at earlier.

"Zeke. Good to see you, though I'm not exactly surprised," Azrael says as he walks further into his office.

My blood turns to stone, but I keep my face neutral. *He can't know. Not unless leaving his card unattended was just a test. Fuck, fuck, fuck!*

"You're not?"

"No. Look, I know you're pissed at me for keeping you on desk duty, and honestly, I'm surprised it took you so long to come bitch me out for it. But just know that it wasn't my decision and I'm still fighting them on it. Fuck, in my eyes, you and the other students who fought so valiantly during that attack deserve medals, not consequences."

His words surprise me. It may not have been the real reason I'm standing here, but I can't lie and say I wasn't curious why he would have benched me. I know Azrael. How could I have thought any differently? "Thank you. I appreciate you sticking up for me."

"You're an asset to the Guild, Ezekiel, and I want you back in the field. Listen, why don't you head home a little early? I'll finish up logging your assigned report and maybe by your next shift, I'll have convinced my superiors to let you off desk duty. Sound good?"

I nod. "If you see Lieutenant Atlas, mind letting him know his daughter was looking for him? I ran into her in the hallway on my way to your office."

"Will do. Now get out of here and enjoy my gift of freedom."

With a smile, I head back to my station to grab my things and head out. Thoughts fly through my mind like a hurricane, pulling me in so many directions that it's hard to focus. I have to tell Hayliel what I found in the file room, and more than that, I have to figure out what it all truly means. What is their goal here?

But there's another thought that won't leave me. I've been second-guessing Azrael and his intentions since the attack, wondering why he didn't answer my call. Why he chained me to the desk and kept things from me as if he was the bad guy. I should have given him more credit. I should have really, truly, given it some thought, and maybe I'd have seen what was so clearly in front of me. He's the exact opposite of devious and manipulating, and how do I thank him? By setting him up.

If it was his keycard I used to sneak into the file room, and if something goes sideways, it'll be him who takes the fall for it.

11

HAYLIEL

The late afternoon sun shines down on me where I sit on the dock. I want to free my wings and feel the heat of it warm my feathers. They've been itching more than usual, and it's not enough that I've started taking them out in my room just to flex them. Out here, though, in the open, I'll keep them tucked beneath my skin. Today hasn't been entirely awful, and I'd really like to keep it that way.

It's a rare moment where I'm alone with my thoughts. Raphael and Theo are supposed to meet up with me soon. Then we'll grab supper and spend the rest of the evening tucked away somewhere. *Maybe where clothes are optional?*

I ignore the voice in my head, even if the bitch is right. As much as I might want a replay of what happened at the park, if I think about it now, I'll only stress. I've got enough to worry about already.

The flap of wings comes moments before the dock shifts beneath me. Right away, I know it's not my two companions, and when the scent of jasmine and leather reaches me on the breeze, I know who it is. Zeke.

Still, I don't bother turning. We've had this weird sort of truce since the attack, and as much as I'm trying not to get my hopes up, I can't stop the pounding of my heart at the knowledge that he's sought me out.

"You're alone." He states it as fact instead of a question.

Has it really been that long since he and I have been alone? I think back, wondering when we might have had a moment together with just the two of us. The incident with my wing sensor, maybe? Heat builds in my low belly as I recall the state he'd been in when I found him. He was shirtless and playful then, similar to how he'd been that first night when we painted each other and spent the night in his room. Oh, how things have changed.

"I'm alone," I reply, parroting his words.

He takes a seat beside me on the dock but doesn't let his feet dangle in the water like mine are. I look at him for the first time in what feels like days. He's wearing his Guild uniform, his hair disheveled, likely a result of his flight back to campus. I wish I were that comfortable in my own skin to fly about wherever and whenever I want.

My lungs stop working when he leans closer, his shoulder brushing my own. By the Archangels, I want to kiss him. But that's silly, isn't it? How can I want him after the awful way he's treated me?

"How'd the midterm go?"

It takes a second before I realize he's asked me a question, but I'm having the hardest time pulling my gaze from his lips.

He smiles like he knows exactly where my thoughts are, then he's moving, brushing the hair off my shoulder and causing my heart to pound. *Shit.*

"Hmm? Oh. Living to fight another day, I think. How's the Guild?"

The heart-stopping grin falls from his face. "I found something. And I get why they've kept it a secret, even if I don't agree."

"Is it that bad?"

"From what I found, the attack here was definitely just a diversion."

"But from what, Zeke? Just spit it out. I can't handle the suspense," I tell him, annoyance clear in my tone, but that only makes the corner of his mouth tilt up slightly.

"I'm getting there, hummingbird. Stop interrupting."

I roll my eyes but stay quiet.

"The second attack was at one of our armories. They killed the Guild members stationed there and took most of the weapons, including the few sun blades we kept locked away at that location."

"Fuck." If they took some of our special blades, we're screwed. We need those to win the war, and as much as that sounds like an exaggeration, a war is exactly what we're in right now. From the look on Zeke's face, he's more than worried. *And he came to tell you right away. If he truly hated you, he wouldn't have done that. Maybe Dina was right after all.*

"It gets worse. The armory locations aren't common knowledge. We have at least a dozen locations, some of which are fake, but they somehow knew which one to target."

I suck in a sharp breath. "There's a mole."

"It would appear that way, yes." He doesn't bother elaborating, choosing instead to just stare at my lips. For a second, I wonder if maybe he's thinking the same things as I am. Would it truly be so bad to let ourselves feel something? To act on the things that we want, consequences be damned.

But then my slate vibrates.

Raphael: We're heading to you, sunshine. Prepare to get wet *winky face*

I know Zeke has read it by the sudden shift in his position. He backs away, no longer crowding my space and making me feel want and need. It's like he's dunked me in frigid waters.

He stands, but I stop him with a question. "Do you have any idea who the mole could be?"

Looking away, he shakes his head. "Not yet. But in the file there was a picture of a Fallen angel with scars along his wings. If I can find him, then maybe he can lead me to the piece-of-shit traitor, and we can finally end this. Share this with your little friends. Maybe they can find a way to be useful."

It takes everything in me not to roll my eyes at him and his obvious distaste for Raphael and Theo, but I ignore it. "I will."

With a nod he takes off, leaving me alone with a million questions crossing my mind and not a single answer to any of them.

The next few days pass in a blur of stress and studying until finally it's the weekend and I can relax. Thanks to Raphael's impressive tutoring skills, I was able to manage both telekinesis and telepathy in tandem. While the other tests I had were difficult, that one had been the one I was most worried about. Before coming here, I had zero experience with our abilities. I was like a newborn baby, trying to take their first steps. But I've made it this far and have no intention of stopping.

Now, the only thing standing in front of me and a well-deserved break is the angelic history midterm. Raphael and Dina finished their tests this week, the lucky assholes, which left only Theo and me with a midterm to study for. Compared to the other exams, it'll be a walk in the park.

Instead of studying, Raphael, Theo, and I are in my room. They're supposed to be helping me pack for my trip to the Fallen district to celebrate The Archangels' Feast, but I wouldn't call what they're doing helpful.

Raphael lounges on my bed, unfolding the clothes I place beside my open bag and making some comment or another about how good it would look on me — or off. When he's done, he hands it to Theo, who's relaxing in the chair he'd pulled over, where he then refolds it and places it neatly inside. Even though he hasn't been the one commenting about my clothes, I've caught him nodding along in agreement more than once.

My blood heats as I think about the night at the park and the fact that the three of us are in my room. Anything could happen.

"I found these in my closet," I say, holding up two hangers, each one with a sweater on it. For the past week or two, Raphael's been offering me his sweater or Theo's at every opportunity. Of course, I take them. There's something inherently more comfortable about wearing their clothes over mine, anyway, but I'm not sure why the sudden push for it.

"Definitely pack those. Then when you wear them, it'll be like we're right there with you."

I grin, liking the sound of that. It's going to be hard enough being away from them now that I've grown accustomed to their presence. Especially since I'll finally have to come clean to my parents about the shift in my wing color.

"Ugh. I hate that we're forced to put our research on hold. It's going to be weird not spending all of my time with the two of you and our heads buried in textbooks."

Raphael stands and walks toward me before pulling me into a hug. "We're going to miss you too, little sunshine, but it's not all lost. The library at my family's estate is pretty extensive. Maybe I'll find something in there that could help us."

"You don't have to do that, Raph. It's a holiday, after all, and you deserve a break."

"It's no skin off my back, believe me. It'll be a gift if I can escape my family, even for a little while."

Theo leans forward, resting his elbows on his knees. "And since I'm not going anywhere, I'll continue searching the libraries here. With the campus nearly empty, maybe I'll be able to get through whatever's available."

I zip up my bag and place it on the floor by the door. "You're both right, of course." I sigh before continuing, "Maybe after my parents get over the shock of my gold wings, they'll remember something from when they were young. Or, maybe if I explore the Fallen district a bit, I'll overhear something useful. There's bound to be rumors going around about the demon attacks, right?"

"That's a terrible idea," Raphael says, looking concerned.

"He's right. It's too dangerous for you to be snooping around like that all on your own."

They're not wrong, but I don't want to be completely useless over the holiday. I have to feel like I'm at least doing *something* to keep our investigation from stalling out. "It was just an idea. At the very least, I'll keep my eyes open for the Fallen angel that Zeke mentioned. And don't worry, I'm not an idiot. I'll be careful, and if I see or hear anything, I'll let you guys know right away."

"Promise us you won't do anything without at least telling us first."

My eyes dart between Raphael and Theo, who look more worried than I would have thought. It's kind of cute. "I promise I won't do anything without telling you two first."

Theo stands, his tall frame looming over me and causing my body to flush hot. "It might be a good idea to loop Ezekiel in on that promise, too. He's a Fallen, after all. Far less suspicious if he shows up than either of us."

I stand there in utter shock. Did he really just suggest I contact Zeke? Not that it's a bad idea — it's actually a damn good one — but I never would have imagined Theo suggesting I do anything with my grumpy-as-fuck house leader. *Curious.*

Raphael looks like he just swallowed something sour, but nods anyway.

"Okay. Good idea." A thought occurs to me, and I struggle to keep the smile off my face. "So should I start a group chat with all of us or ..."

"Yes."

"No."

I laugh. "Don't worry, Raph. I was just kidding. Why don't we get out of here for a little bit? I know you don't have any midterms left, but Theo and I are feeling pretty confident about ours. We only have a few days left before the break. Let's go do something epic before we're separated."

"Now that I can agree with," Raphael says.

"Since we won't be together over the break, why don't we head to the entertainment district and see if there's any early festivities going on?"

Despite the obvious excitement at getting off campus, I can't help but notice the blanket of sadness that hovers over us. It has me wondering if maybe they feel the same pang of loss at being away from me as I do about them.

12

THEO

Our classmates must have had a similar idea because we find several groups making their way, by foot or wings, off campus. A few of them carry a bag, so it's possible they're heading home for the break early, something Raphael could have done, but that's the last place he'd like to be.

I'm sure the principal's inbox must be overflowing with emails from students, following the rules and notifying him of their movements. I get why he did it. I just hope it leads to something.

"Off to meet with your demon brothers, spawn?" someone shouts from the sky. It doesn't take a genius to figure out who it is. Cadriel doesn't have as many followers as he once did in his quest against Hayliel, not since the attack.

She's had to deal with far less hatred since then, but that doesn't mean it's been easy. Somehow, the fawning and obsession are almost as bad as the repulsion. Instead of taking the cruel words personally like she might have a month ago, she only flips him off and keeps walking, her smile never faltering.

I won't let anything dim her light.

Raphael and I don't bother taking our wings out, knowing full well that the beautiful creature between us wants to walk. It's an easy decision not to push her, especially since it means we get more time by her side, but someday I'd like to take her somewhere. A place where she feels secure and safe to fly with us, where she can stretch her wings and have fun without holding back.

We're about halfway to the entertainment district when a Fallen angel soars overhead, circling like an eagle searching for prey before swooping down to land in front of us. If I didn't already know it was Ezekiel, the Assassins' Guild uniform would have given it away.

There's irritation in his gaze, which doesn't really surprise me, but it pisses me off. Particularly when I see the way Hayliel stiffens at his presence. I don't know their history, but it's clear to anyone with a pair of eyes that *something* went down between them. Why else would his cool indifference bother her so much? Whatever it is, neither one seems ready to let go.

I'm not sure how much more of this I can take, but I keep my mouth shut for now, not wanting to ruin the last few days I have with her before the break.

"Theo, can I speak with you?" Other than a quick glance in Hayliel's direction, he barely acknowledges her.

My agitation grows, but I try to tamp it down. *Don't be an ass and make a scene. Not here.* It works, though I'm half tempted to tell him to fuck off, but his request has my curiosity piqued. There's no hiding the fact that Ezekiel dislikes me, so something has to be up for him to seek me out.

I follow him for a few paces, leaving Hayliel behind with a rather pissed off Raphael. *Have restraint, Raph.*

"Are you heading home for the break or staying on campus?"

That's odd. Why the hell would he be worried about where I'll be over break, and how is that important enough to seek me out? I consider asking him just that but choose not to, keeping my reply simple. "Staying on campus."

Ezekiel nods, darting a look over my shoulder that has me wondering if maybe he'll ask me what Hayliel's plans are.

"I'm guessing she told you about the classified information I found at the Guild?"

"She did."

"Good." He releases a sigh, like maybe he doesn't actually want to be here asking for my help, but it's not like I'm forcing him to. When he continues, I still don't fully understand.

"I acquired a few old texts from my father's study and hoped you would help me go through them over the break. Some of them even relate to the wing color search I know you're helping Hayliel with."

Huh? "And you need my help, specifically?"

Zeke folds his arms across his chest, somehow appearing both bored and like he wants to hightail it out of here. "It would appear that way. Unfortunately for us, Professor Uriel was of little help in learning more about a particular passage I found in one of the texts, but he thought that you, of all angels, could help."

What the hell? As if I'd know more than a university professor. What is this slimy angel up to?

I keep those thoughts to myself, though, not wanting to give all my cards away to Ezekiel. Maybe some good can come from this after all.

"I thought it was weird too," he says when I don't respond. "But he seems to think that your Knowledge house residency and proximity to a certain golden-winged angel will prove useful."

"Hmm. Was the passage about golden wings?"

"Not specifically, no."

Curious. Professor Uriel has been a thorn in Hayliel's side since her very first day of classes. Mix that with the weird way he acted after the attack, and I have a hard time believing in his motives. I'd be a fool to let that stand in the way, though. But is getting access to these texts worth spending time with an angel that grimaces every time they see me? It may not be comfortable, but it'll at least give me the opportunity to be alone with him, where maybe I can get him to cut the bullshit act of indifference with Hayliel.

"I can't promise we'll find anything, but I'll help you."

Ezekiel nods. "Duty calls, but I'll be in touch." Then without a single word to Hayliel, he disappears, but not before I catch the long look he sends her way.

As I walk back to share the news with Raphael and Hayliel, I can't stop my mind from churning. This plan with Ezekiel could end horribly. Maybe he'll wind up hating me more after we're done. Maybe he's working with Professor Uriel, and it's a weird trap that I don't see coming. But there's a small chance that maybe, if I can manage it, he'll stop his posturing and Hayliel will finally find some peace.

The park is set up with tents and stalls hosting food vendors, carnival games, and even some recruitment areas for the Guild. Is this what Ezekiel meant by duty calls? For Hayliel's sake, I hope not. If he's here, glaring daggers at her from across the park, she won't have any fun. Thankfully, I haven't seen him yet.

What I do see, though, isn't all that different from the last time we were here. Popcorn litters the grass and angels walk around eating tacos in a bag while their children wear sticky outlines around their toothy grins as they devour candy apples. There's electricity in the air this time, though, and it's not just caused by the complete and total sexual tension between Hayliel, Raphael and me like it was that day.

The Archangels' Feast is a week-long holiday to celebrate the Archangels and their salvation. While it doesn't technically start until next week, families can still give their offerings of thanks to the Archangels early. Somewhere in the park is an altar where angels can leave gifts or say a prayer, but the more prominent families choose to make the trek up to the base of the mountain to show their respect. I know because it's something my grandparents have done every year since before my parents died.

This year I'll get to avoid the ass-kissing. It's not that I have anything against the Archangels, but it's all just show. Before they overthrew God, he was celebrated. And I'm sure someone will eventually take down the Archangels and then whoever claims that victory will be next. It's meaningless.

Hayliel leads us to a stall selling hot apple cider, and she buys each of us a cup. It's hot in my hands and I'm immediately overwhelmed by the scent of cinnamon and sweet, crisp apples.

While we drink, we walk around and take in the sights. In the distance, boats float on the pond, and off to the side of that is some sort of ride that keeps your wings inside but flings you through the air on a cord. I shudder at the thought. Who would want to be trapped like that, unable to save yourself from going *splat* if something goes wrong? Based on the long line of angels waiting for their turn, far more than I would have guessed.

"Whoa," Hayliel whispers as we approach an angel-made alley lined with all sorts of games and prizes. Raphael grabs her hand and leads her toward the first stall with pillars and rings, and we watch as a kid throws his last ring, but it bounces off and falls to the floor. Then he starts to cry. We move on down the line, passing by some with bouncy balls and buckets, or a pyramid of cans and bean bags. Each stall has various prizes secured along the outer frame, tempting passersby to try their luck.

The next stall has what must be the biggest prizes we've seen so far. There are massive stuffed pillows in various colors and shapes, all seeming to represent one of the four Archangels. Raphael must notice the same look of pure awe on Hayliel's face because he pulls her up to the counter.

"Good afternoon and welcome to the toughest challenge you'll face today. Care to try your luck?" Behind him is a wall of moving targets with several worn-looking daggers lined up on the counter.

"She will," Raphael says, before digging into his pocket for a few bills and handing them over.

Hayliel freezes. "What?"

"Come on, don't be nervous, sunshine. Just picture Cadriel's face, and I know you'll hit every single one."

She picks one up, gripping it in her fist, and listens to the man in the booth.

"All you have to do for a prize is throw those five daggers and get three of them to stick. The more of them that stay in the target, the bigger the prize."

Hayliel lines up her shot, brings her hand back, and throws. The blade spins as it moves through the air before smacking into the edge of a moving target. Without wasting time, she grabs another and tries again, but the same thing happens. Her aim isn't terrible, but the handle keeps hitting the target instead of the blade.

She grabs another, and I step forward. "You need more space for the dagger to rotate. That's why the handle keeps hitting instead of the blade. Take a step back and try throwing from there."

"Here?" she asks once she's moved back.

"Exactly. Give it a shot."

She lines up her shot before throwing again, and this time the blade hits the outer rim of the target. But we don't get to celebrate, not when the blade wobbles and falls to the floor.

"Shoot." Picking up her fourth blade, she goes back to the spot from before and lines up her shot. I'm sure lesser angels would have given up once they realized they couldn't win anything, but it doesn't seem to matter much to her. She's just enjoying herself, which is exactly what we wanted from today.

"Throw it a bit harder this time, alright?"

With a throw that even I can admit is impressive as hell, she hits the target with a resounding *thwack*. Her gaze doesn't move from the dagger for several moments before she lets out a whoop of excitement and grabs the final blade.

"I did it!"

I swear, the smile on her face is as bright as the sun when she steps forward to grab the last knife, lines up her shot, and throws it exactly the same way. It hits the target less than an inch from her last shot, but doesn't budge.

"Nice try, miss. Would you like to go again?"

"No, but he would."

I don't realize she's talking about me until Raphael hands the man more money and says, "Why don't you win our girl a prize, Theo? I think that big-ass flame would look perfect in her room."

He winks at me, and when I look at Hayliel, she's watching me with a hopeful expression in her eyes, like she really does want that damn flame.

I pick up a dagger and freeze. Something feels off. Resting it on two of my fingers, I test the weight and find out just how much of a gimmick this is. The handle, though subtle, weighs more than the blade. To someone untrained, this may go unnoticed, but not to me. When a knife is handle-heavy, it usually means you have to throw it by holding on to the blade. That way, when it rotates through the air, the blade will hit the target instead of the hilt.

No wonder this slimy weasel hasn't lost many prizes.

I shoot him a glare and pick up another dagger before stepping back a few paces. There are eight targets, each pulled in different directions. Some go up and down, side to side, while others move in a circular pattern. Once I've chosen which ones seem best, I take aim, making sure to hold the dagger by the blade and throw.

It arcs through the air, spinning horizontally before impaling into the first target. I don't wait before throwing the second one, watching as it hits another moving target. Hayliel's jaw is practically on the floor, and as I grab the last three daggers, I watch as Raph teases her by pushing her jaw closed.

Alright, I may be trying to show off a little, but so what? If I can land all five daggers and they just so happen to also be dead center, then maybe she'll keep looking at me like that. Like I could grab hold of the sun and offer it on a chain to wear around her neck. Even that would pale compared to her.

Pride surges through me as I throw the last three daggers, all of which hit the bullseye. The man in the booth looks annoyed, but I don't even care. Not when Hayliel rushes forward and wraps her arms around my middle.

She feels so tiny against me, but I know I won't break her. This girl has been forged from a flame far greater than I ever realized, hammered and molded into who she is today. An angel with the strength of a thousand suns held within her chest. Yet still, she's soft in all the right places.

I hold on for a second longer than I should, but she doesn't pull away, seeming content to just exist in this moment. At least, until the angel behind the booth clears his throat.

"You won," he says, voice deadpan. "Please select a prize from one of the large items near the front."

I turn to Hayliel, a smile tugging the corner of my lip. "Well? The choice is yours, firefly."

She doesn't respond right away. Instead, she peers around the booth once before nodding. "Auriel's flame, please," she tells the man, then turns to me and says, "Thank you, Theo. I can't wait to snuggle the fuck out of it tonight."

Raphael sidles up beside us, taking the stuffed flame from the carnival worker. "Feel free to think of Theo while you do. I'm sure he won't mind."

Her cheeks pink, but otherwise she doesn't acknowledge it, absentmindedly stroking the soft fabric of the flame. "I had no idea you could throw daggers like that! Have you always had that skill, or?"

I go utterly still as memories flood through me. The reason I learned any of the combat skills I have was out of necessity. A need to defend myself and protect others in the hopes that maybe I'll be able to actually save someone instead of watching on like a sniveling coward. Maybe someday I'll be able to redeem myself.

A hand lands on my shoulder and Raphael's voice finds me through the fog inside my brain. "Theo is an angel of many talents, my sweet sunshine. You may discover even more of them soon."

The pressure of his fingers and the heat of his palm ground me, bringing me back enough that my vision clears, and I can make out the mischievous smirk playing on his lips.

Hayliel looks between the two of us, seeming to grasp that something almost happened even if she doesn't fully understand what. Her hand lands on my shoulder, directly opposite where Raphael's is. "Do you think maybe you can teach me?"

My eyes flash to hers, dreading that I'll find pity there, but instead there's something else. Awe, perhaps. And a touch of heat that travels through my body, scorching the wounds of my past until they don't fester.

"Yes." My voice comes out raw, as if I've gone decades without water. "Everything I have, everything I know, is yours."

A beat passes, the sounds of the crowd fading away until it's only the three of us. I watch as her gaze travels down to my lips and I wonder if she's going to kiss me. Fuck, I wish she would.

"I'm just going to fly this back to campus," Raphael says, snapping the heated moment.

"What?" I ask, caught off guard.

"You don't have to do that, Raph. This was supposed to be a day of fun."

"It *is* fun, and I'll be quick. Don't worry. Just promise me you'll find something exciting to do while I'm gone, okay?"

The look he gives me tells me he's deliberately leaving us alone together. Ever since that night at the park, Raphael's taken it as all the proof he needs that Hayliel would be more than happy to share us, but I'm not so sure. I want it to be true. More than fucking anything. But how can I know she won't have immediate regrets? I'd rather stay their friend than risk losing them both if things go sideways.

Raphael gives Hayliel a quick, searing kiss before he takes off. I can't deny the way it makes me feel to watch them together, but I try to keep the lust off my face when she turns to look at me.

"I think I have the perfect thing to do while Raphael's gone." She holds out her hand and I take it, curious as ever to find out what she has in mind.

She doesn't make me wait to find out, tugging me through the crowded park until we stand at the edge of the pond. On the water are these weird boats with big rubber rings around them. Just as I'm about to ask her what they are, a cold shot of water hits me in the neck.

Hayliel's peals of laughter break through the shock of it and I step back right before another blast of water comes from one of the boats.

She covers her mouth, eyes dancing with laughter.

"Oh. It's on."

We race to the line, which is thankfully short, and grab a boat. The ride operator gives us a spiel about how it works. Push both levers to go forward, pull them both toward you to go backward, and alternate levers front to back in order to turn. And there, on the top of each lever, are the damn water jet buttons. Now this is going to be fun.

We experiment with the levers, familiarizing ourselves with the best positions before steering the boats toward the center of the pond. The entire way there, we throw suspicious glances at each other as we wait to see who will make the first spray move.

I'm planning my first attack when something rams into my boat, jolting me forward enough that the thin strap of the chair rubs against my sides.

Her ensuing laugh is all I need to know that the game is on. Slowly, I turn my boat to face hers and she must be able to tell that I'm about to pounce because she shrieks and pushes the levers on her boat, trying to get away.

"Aww, come on, firefly. Play with me," I taunt, following her with my boat and holding down on the buttons so a stream of water arcs between us. I'm too close for it to hit her, though, so I back off, slowing down until I hear her shocked cry.

She turns sharply, then barrels straight toward me, the arc of her water jets going past my head.

I laugh. "Missed me!"

Her eyes narrow as she presses forward, but I pull my own levers to back up and try to keep the distance between us enough that she can't get me wet. Except she's too damn smart for that.

Her fingers lift and fall, one at a time, over the top of the lever until a few drops of water hit my knees. Instead of keeping the button pressed down, she's only holding it for a second each time before letting go. More water falls onto me, and I can tell she knows because of the triumphant squeal of delight.

Then I hit something on the back of the boat and it jolts me forward. "Hey!" a gruff voice says from behind me. Two more boats slam into the side of me simultaneously, these driven by young angels who have zero intent to back off.

"Get him!" Hayliel shouts, careening for me with her jets hitting me in the chest. And at her command, the two boys press down their own buttons and spray me, too.

I'm helpless to do anything but sputter and laugh. There's no denying that I've been bested. It's clearly evident by my wet clothes.

The ride operator blows a whistle, signaling that it's time for us to head back and let someone else out for a ride. It's only then that the two young angels cease fire, choosing instead to race back to the makeshift dock.

"No hard feelings?" Hayliel asks, her tone worried, like maybe she actually thinks I'll be mad at her for our little game of fun.

"It's only a little water. I'll dry off in no time."

"Good. It's nice to see you're not a sore loser." There's a twinkle in her eye that brings a pang to my chest.

Hayliel is goodness personified. She's a blazing fire in a sea of shadows, keeping the dark at bay. If others could only see her for what she is instead of what they want her to be, maybe she'd believe Raph and me when we tell her how amazing she is. Maybe she'd trust that she's not the bad angel everyone wants her to be. But until then, until the moment she believes it herself, we'll be right there with her, battling the darkness and stoking her flames.

We make it off the boats without trouble, though I couldn't leave without giving her one last spray as she was getting out. Not that I meant to hit her quite so solidly, but I can't deny

I enjoyed it. The soft curls that once surrounded her face are heavy with water and stuck to her skin.

On impulse, I reach up to brush the strands away, intending to pull back the moment I'm done, but I can't. Her skin is magnetic, drawing me in like a force field. My gaze travels down her cheek, her neck, until it rests in the same place my hand is. On her collarbone.

I've never noticed this part on an angel before, but now, staring at the delicate curve of her bone where it leads to the soft flesh of her neck, all I want to do is bend low and place my mouth there. When she doesn't pull away, I wonder if maybe her thoughts are leading to the same spot mine are. And maybe, if I leaned in close and pressed a gentle kiss against her skin, she'd let me.

Before I can do anything, a cold shot of water hits us both as a kid spins in his boat with the water jets on full blast. Probably for the best, anyway. I know Raphael said we could share if she was willing, but we need to talk about it more. I'd be an asshole if I made a move the moment we were left alone together.

"There you guys are! And I see Theo even managed to get you all wet, didn't he, little sunshine? Nice job," Raphael says, grin growing wide.

Hayliel laughs in a surprised kind of way, like she can't believe he just said that, but when she looks at me, her eyes are ablaze with what I can only assume is lust.

We move on through the carnival, passing more food vendors and games, following the flow of traffic toward whatever the angels are gathering for.

"What's going on?" Hayliel asks, raising up on her toes in an attempt to see over the crowd.

It's fucking adorable.

"There's a race through the obstacle course. Winner gets to visit the Archangels' Sanctuary and have a meal with them."

Beside us is a large group of angels that look so much alike they have to be family. Despite the crowd and the sounds of the carnival, their conversation is unmistakable.

"I understand you don't want to race, but this isn't about you, Asmodel. This is about our family honor. We need you to win this. For us."

I share a look with Raphael and Hayliel, who look just as disgusted as I am. Raphael would know just how close that conversation is to my grandparents, but Hayliel wouldn't. She doesn't know much about my life at home, how my parents died and my grandparents took care of me. Or, at least, their version of it. The older generation of angels live by different rules, and I stopped trying to gain their approval a long time ago.

The crowd grows thicker around us as angels head in to watch the show. It's suffocating the way they pile in, shoulder-checking their way to the front without a care in the world. I send Raphael a look that I know he deciphers. This could turn into a riot, and we'll be stuck in the middle.

With a calm smile on his face that I know isn't genuine, he says, "Look. Why don't we head over there?" He points to a large tent a little ways away. No one enters or exits, they're just passing by on their way toward us and the race.

"Yes please," Hayliel says, her eyes wary.

Raphael grabs both of our hands, tugging us toward the tent, and we only have to stop twice to get out of the way of some overzealous idiot before we're free of the crowd.

"This is madness," she says, watching the invigorated angels. "All of this to eat with the Archangels ... but why?"

"You'd be surprised the lengths angels go to earn favor," I tell her, voice solemn.

"This way!" Raph whispers from where he stands just inside the flap of the tent.

"Where is he ..."

We follow him in, and I'm surprised to find it's a tent of offerings. This is where angels can bring their gifts for the Archangels' Feast, and when they're done, they can offer a prayer to one of the four altars.

"Whoa. I've heard of places like these, but I've never been," Hayliel says, her eyes darting around the dimly lit space.

With everyone focused on the race outside, no one is here. The late afternoon light doesn't penetrate the thick fabric of the tent, so the only light we have is from the candles lit throughout the space. A bit of a fire hazard, but I suppose fire doesn't really hurt us, anyway.

I take it all in, feeling the familiar tug of old memories. Even though it's only us here, I keep my voice low and whisper, "My grandparents used to bring me to a place like this every day during the Feast. They told me that our gifts and prayers were the reason our family has such a strong history."

As we walk a little further inside, the room branches off in four directions, two on either side. In the center is an altar depicting the Archangels' signature wings. They have twice as many as we do, and I can't deny the sight is mesmerizing. Piled beside the altar are various foods and homemade treats that must be what others have already dropped off. And behind it, on the other side of the large stone wings, is a prayer bench. If you aren't particularly impressed with one of them over the others, this is where you'd pray.

The silence is hard to get used to. Outside, a crowd gathers to watch a race, but in here ... in here we can pretend that we're somewhere far, far away.

I hear it then, the flap of the entryway opening and voices trickling in with it, and Raphael tugs us into action. We pile into the closest private chambers — the section dedicated to the Archangel Remiel — and secure the flap closed. Our breaths are heavy, mingled together as we wait, but for what? It's not like we were doing anything wrong. What is Raph up to?

Hayliel stands between us, listening to the soft murmurings of whoever joined us. I can't make out their words, but as the seconds tick by, I realize I don't really want to. How can I focus on a stranger's conversation when the angel I want is so close?

Despite the barrier of our clothes, her heat and the pounding of her heart surrounds me as we stand still, fixating on the possibility of someone finding the three of us in here together.

Raphael must sense it too, must feel the ache of want just as surely as I do, because he tilts her head up and kisses her. I can't look away.

Their lips lock, tongues darting out in a dance that looks almost choreographed. As if they've been kissing like this their entire lives. Her breath hitches and she melts into his embrace. She wants this, I realize. And as much as I keep telling myself to leave, to give them privacy, I can't tear my eyes away.

Something shifts in my mind, like someone is tapping on an invisible barrier. I focus on letting them in, and then I hear it. Soft-spoken words through our telepathic bond.

Fuck, you feel so good, sunshine. If I could kiss you like this every day for the rest of my life, I'd be happy.

She lets out a whimper that sounds as loud as a scream, and Raphael brings his hand up around her throat, gripping gently.

Shh. You have to be quiet, little sun, or someone might find us. Then we'll have to stop. You don't want that, do you, baby?

Hayliel doesn't respond, only kisses him harder and pulls his body closer to hers. Her ass grazes my dick as she shifts and I have to bite back a groan. Maybe I really should leave. Maybe—

You like this? Having Theo and me surround you like your own personal fortress? I bet you can feel just how hard Theo is for you, how much he's enjoying this.

A small, soft whimper echoes through our mental bond, causing my dick to twitch. Still, I say nothing. Part of me is worried that if I do, this perfect moment in time will vanish. Their kiss doesn't slow or stop. Instead, it shifts into something more fervent and needy. Watching them is hotter than I've ever imagined, but deep down inside me, I yearn to feel her lips beneath my own.

Do you trust me, sunshine?

Their kiss slows, and for a second I don't think she's going to respond. They're making out in a prayer tent while I watch on like a lurker. What other proof does Raph need that she trusts him? But even as I think it, I can't stop the small sliver of hope that buds in my chest.

I hear her small *Yes* in my mind and wait to see what my best friend has planned, praying that it involves me.

He breaks the kiss, twirling her around and pressing her against him. His hands roam over her body in slow movements, his fingertips barely touching her, and I watch the path they take. She shivers, her hooded eyes locked on mine.

I think it's time you showed Theo just how much you want him, little sun.

He pinches her nipple through the thin material of her tank top and she drops her head back on his chest, her eyes closing briefly. I take the opportunity to look at my friend, needing to know that he's serious. I need to know that this is truly what Raphael wants because as much as I do — and by the Archangels, I want this — I'm not willing to ruin the friendship we have. The risk is too great. If things go sideways, not only do I lose my best friend, but I also lose her. I'd rather live my life without knowing the taste and feel of her if it means not losing the two angels who mean the most to me. And I'd rather not know what I'm missing out on.

Hayliel shifts then, tilting her head to gaze longingly into Raphael's eyes. They don't say a word, at least not out loud, but when her eyes flash back to mine, I know they've agreed on something.

There's another tug in my mind before her warm voice filters through.

Only if you want it too.

Her words open a floodgate inside me. All the need and want I've been suppressing comes loose, threatening to topple me to the fucking ground, but I don't fall.

Instead, I reach for her, pulling her into a kiss I've only been dreaming about for weeks. The spark that travels through me when our lips touch doesn't surprise me, but I don't expect the surge of possessive hunger that flares bright and hot in the pit of my stomach.

She gasps, mouth falling open, and I seize the moment, sweeping my tongue inside to battle with hers. It's all consuming, the need to taste more of her, take more of her. All of her. It's like the world has melted away except for this single point of light in the dark. My firefly.

Raphael's hand travels between us, moving to the juncture of her thighs where he strokes her over the fabric of her shorts, and

I groan through our mental connection. He must touch a spot that feels good because she fists my hair, pulling me deeper into the kiss. By the Archangels, this woman owns me.

How badly do you want to taste her, Theo?

At Raphael's internal words, I break the kiss, trailing my lips down her jaw and into that delicate spot at the curve of her neck. I hover there for a moment, feeling the seconds pass by as if they're hours. Too long not to touch her, taste her. Have her. The moment my lips touch her skin, sucking her flesh into my mouth, I answer. *More than I've wanted anything else.*

Her body shudders between us, breaths coming out in harsh, shallow pants.

Do you hear that, sunshine? Theo's desperate for your sweet pussy. What do you say we put him out of his misery?

13

HAYLIEL

This has to be a dream.

It must be, or else my most secret fantasy has come to life right here in the offering tent. Alright, so maybe it's not my ultimate fantasy, not without a certain house leader missing from the equation, but how can I even think about that right now?

Raphael pulls my shorts down while Theo kisses a path of fire down my body as he settles on his knees in front of me. He's staring up at me, eyes half lidded and glazed, and I have zero doubts that my own are too. My body buzzes, desperate for him to touch me, to taste me like they keep promising he will, but I won't beg. I can't, can I? Once he looks down at the obvious wet spot on my panties, he'll comprehend my begging without my having to say a single word.

Are we really doing this in here?

Would you rather do it out there? Raphael snags my lobe with his teeth and tugs gently before adding, *Think of it like our offering to Remiel. Surely, our divine passion is a far better gift than anything else we might have given.*

Theo is still watching me, his hazel eyes shining like liquid honey. He doesn't touch me, his hands resting at his sides.

If you want to stop, it's alright. But if you want to continue, by all that is holy, firefly, I need you to say the words out loud. Tell me you want this as much as I do.

My core pulses at the sound of his smooth voice in my head. I need this. Him. Them. It's all I want in this moment and nothing will stand in the way of it. Not even my own fears. "Taste me, Theo. Please, I—"

He doesn't hesitate, just leans forward and buries his face in my soaked underwear, kissing me through them. His hands come up to my ass before grabbing the silken fabric there and pulling it down to rest on top of my shorts, which are still wrapped around my ankles, effectively trapping me.

Raphael palms my breasts and murmurs through our bond, *Look at how wet she is for you, Theo. Fuck, she's soaked, aren't you, sunshine?*

I catch the moan in my throat before it escapes, pushing it through our mental connection instead. It's the only affirmation I can manage with Theo's head so close to my aching core.

I wonder if he can see the wetness I feel on my thighs. They've barely touched me and yet I'm already a quivering mess.

Why don't you show us how long you've been wanting a taste, prove how hungry you are. I want to watch her come all over your face.

I feel Theo grin against my thigh, where he kisses a trail up to my aching core and licks the seam of my pussy. While he plays, he frees one of my feet and throws my leg over his shoulder, giving him deeper access. I almost topple over, legs trembling from the feel of Theo's tongue between my legs, but Raphael catches me.

That's it. Let him feast, baby, but remember, you need to be quiet. Theo, do your best to make her scream.

He fucks me with his tongue, going far deeper than I'd expect him to and making my head spin. He doesn't flick my clit like Raphael or even Zeke did. Instead, Theo laps it up like I'm his favorite flavor of ice cream.

I grab on to his curls, pulling him into me until the pressure of his tongue is almost unbearable. It's all too much. The tension between me and Theo has been building for far too long, and now it's time to explode. Here, in this place of worship, I come apart for him. "Theo," I whimper as my orgasm hits and I know I'm only standing because of the two strong angels holding on to me.

But I'm not done. *I need more.*

I don't realize that I've sent that thought through our internal bond until Raphael chuckles behind me. *I think our girl needs to be filled, Theo. Free yourself and lie down on that rug.* He wraps his arms around my torso, one hand dipping between my legs. *How do you feel about going for a little ride, sunshine?*

In a daze, I nod and watch as Theo takes off his pants and reveals his cock. My mouth falls open as it juts out into the air, beckoning me forward, but Raphael holds me back. Theo's dick is beautiful, and quite possibly the thickest fucking cock I've ever seen. The tip glints beneath the flickering light of the candle — pre-cum, most likely, and all I want to do is go lick it up.

Yet as Raphael walks me forward, I realize it's something else. Metal. My eyes flash to Theo's, and he almost looks bashful.

I see you've found his piercing. Go ahead, baby. Make sure he's wet and ready for you.

There's a faint rustling from outside our section of tent. Maybe I should be worried we'll get caught. Maybe I should suggest we go someplace a little more private. But I don't do either of those things. Instead, I drop to my knees beside Theo and reach out for his cock. It's warm and rigid, with two metal balls attached to a curved rod. Gently, I run my thumb over the space where the metal disappears beneath his flesh, and he groans.

Did it hurt when you got this done?

A little.

I let my hand fall to the base of his shaft, trying to wrap my hand around him, but he's too big. Before I can worry about whether he'll fit, I dip down and swirl my tongue over the tip of his cock.

You look so pretty with his cock in your mouth.

Raphael's dirty words spur me on. I dip lower, taking as much of him into my mouth as possible, but it's hard. He's so fucking big, and the piercing only adds to it. Giving up, I drop open-mouthed kisses along the length of his shaft, twirling my tongue over the underside of his head until he gasps. My lips quirk up into a smile and I do it again, in awe of the feeling of such power.

It doesn't last long, though. Not when my greedy cunt pulses with the need to be filled. But will he even fit?

Theo, why don't you show our girl what your fingers can do, hmm?

Raphael hasn't touched me since I came to the rug, and as I lick and suck on Theo's cock, I throw a glance his way. He looks entranced, fixated on the scene in front of him — his best friend and I discovering each other. He undoes the button of his jeans, pulls the zipper down, and lets his hard cock jut free.

Before the worry of him feeling left out can take root, Theo's touching me. My breasts, my stomach, my hips. Trailing over my thighs before finally settling between my legs. He slides a finger through my wetness, little zaps of electricity sparking through me as he strokes my swollen and sensitive clit.

I watch him and he watches me, completely caught up in one another. As he slips a finger inside me, I see the way his eyes roll back, the way he bites his lip. And when they open again and he adds a second finger inside me, pumping into me with slow, delirious movements, I don't miss the feral look in his eyes.

For a second, I can't breathe. He's looking at me like he wants to crawl inside my flesh and live there, and the scary part is … I'd let him.

My body is on fire as he pumps his fingers into me, his thumb hitting my clit with each thrust, and I forget about exploring his cock. He's driving me mad, so close to another orgasm that it almost hurts. His fingers make wet, sloppy sounds as he fucks me with them, adding in a third finger. The stretch is almost too much, but then I feel it. My heart beating against my chest. Ocean waves crashing against the shore. I'm about to come, and there's nothing I can do to stop it.

Don't come yet, sunshine. Straddle him. Let him feel you clench around his cock.

Theo stops moving, eyes darting between me and Raph. I want to be angry, but the thought of having Theo's thick cock inside me while I come is undeniably sexy. It's a need I didn't know I had, but now I can only shift on the rug, bringing one knee over Theo's form and lining his cock up with my entrance.

My desire is so urgent, I can't even muster up the time to take off my damn top. Theo, on the other hand, reaches for the hem of it, his eyes searching for permission. At my nod, he tugs, pulling the tank top up inch by inch until I'm bare before him.

The flutters start up in my belly again as I tease myself with him, coating my slickness over the tip, feeling the metal balls against my flesh. And when I sink down, slowly, slowly, slowly … I swear I see stars. *Holy fuck.* Whether from his size, the piercing, or something else, I have no fucking clue, but I don't really care. It's just too damn good.

There's a deep rumble from Theo's chest as I take all of him, my pussy spasming around his cock and sending little shivers of delight through me. I grind against him, loving the way he feels inside me. He doesn't try to take control, letting me rock back and forth at my own pace until my orgasm rises like a tsunami, ready to crash.

As if he can sense it, knows it's coming, he sits up and sucks my nipple into his mouth. The shift in angle is all I need to throw me over the edge. I try to hold in my scream as pleasure rockets through me, but I don't know if I succeed or not. I'm lost to the pleasure, and just as I think it'll subside, Theo proves me wrong. In one swift move, I'm on my back and he somehow manages to keep his dick firmly planted inside of me.

He pistons his hips, dipping low to kiss me deeply before tugging my bottom lip between his teeth and growling. It travels through his body, vibrating into mine until I'm tossing my head back in ecstasy.

Raphael makes a low noise from where he's leaning against the altar. From this angle, the stone-carved wings behind him look almost like his own, only more ethereal. He has one foot propped up on the cushioned bench sat before the altar, a hand fisting his cock. As he pumps it, the tip glistens with his cum. He looks like a fucking god.

You take his cock so well, sunshine, Raphael says through our connection, his voice strained, giving away just how close he is.

Theo thickens inside me, stretching me. Filling me. And I know he's close. Our eyes lock as his orgasm rolls through him. His cock pulsates, pumping his hot cum inside me and fuck, it feels good.

Reaching up, I pull him down to kiss me. It's passionate and lazy, the two of us completely spent. But something about this moment just feels right. As if we were meant to have this time together in Remiel's prayer chamber all along.

I feel Raphael approach before I see him, cock hard and still in his fist. "I want to see," he whispers, eyes focused on the area where Theo and I are still joined.

Theo's cock is softer now, but it twitches inside my pussy, causing little flutters in my low belly. He pulls out slowly, like he doesn't want to escape the confines of my body as much as I don't want him to, and I immediately feel the loss of him.

Raph groans before dropping to take Theo's place between my legs. He's transfixed on my pussy, and I wonder what he's looking at until it hits me. Theo's cum. It drips from me, and I must be leaving a puddle on the rug, but I can't find it in me to care. Not with how they're both staring.

"Fucking hell," Raphael says, sliding his cock through the mess between my legs before lining himself up with my entrance. "Are you up for this, little sun?"

I swallow, my breaths shallow, and look between him and Theo. Is it possible they want this just as much as I do? Can this even be real? "Gods, yes."

The words are barely out of my mouth before Raphael plunges inside, all the way to the hilt. A moan escapes me, and I slap a hand over my mouth. Shit.

Theo's at my side in an instant, taking my hand away and replacing it with his lips. He kisses me and lavishes my nipples with attention while Raphael fucks me like the world is ending and only our combined orgasm can save it. His fingers move to my clit, gliding over it with mine and Theo's collective wetness before he presses lightly.

My orgasm comes out of nowhere, slamming into me. Before I can make more than a small gasp, Theo's there, stifling the sound with his lips locked on mine. Raphael doesn't last much longer after that, his own climax shuddering through him as hot jets of his cum fill me, mixing with Theo's.

My body vibrates and my mind is absolute mush, so when Raphael dips low to kiss me, I don't hesitate.

"You're ours, sunshine. Do you understand?"

I meet his gaze, then Theo's, before nodding. And I realize for the first time that maybe I really am theirs. But if that's true, it means they're also *mine.*

14

HAYLIEL

"As I live and breathe," Dad says, pulling me into a tight hug. "Mari, guess who's finally arrived?"

There's a clatter of something from inside before Mom rushes out the door and nearly tackles me. A carefree laugh tumbles from my chest as I hug her back, everything slotting back into place for one beautiful second. "I'm so glad you're home! Come inside, tell us everything."

"Now hold on a minute. Let's give the girl a chance to breathe and settle in. We have all week to grill her." He takes my bag, leading me through the door and down a flight of stairs. "It's not as big as your old room, but your mother tried to make it feel like home."

The basement, if I can even call it that, has an open concept design. It's more of a long corridor than a room, but Dad wasn't lying. The handmade quilt from my old room is laid out on the bed. A few of my old posters and picture frames are up too. Memories of a different time in our lives that I'd somehow forgotten about while at SCU. There's only one window, positioned above the bed along the back wall next to what I'm guessing must be a two-piece bathroom.

"This looks perfect, guys. Thank you."

"I know it's a bit small, and I'm sorry that we weren't able to bring most of your large items with us." She wipes away an errant tear, and the sight of it has my heart clenching.

"Hey. None of that, Mom. It doesn't matter where I sleep. What matters is we're together." I press my forehead to hers, taking in the moment of peace. Fuck, I've missed them. I've spent my entire life relying on them for support and they've given it without question. After a few months apart, I'd forgotten how easy it is with them. I can be myself without fear of judgment. *Maybe your old self, but they don't know you anymore.* I push away the niggling reminder that I haven't told them about my wings yet. I'll tell them later this week.

"Who's hungry? We thought we'd do breakfast for dinner. What do you say? Fancy whipping up some pancakes?"

"Hell yeah. The perfect homecoming meal."

We make our way back upstairs and into the tiny galley kitchen, where we mix up pancakes and start frying the bacon. While we cook, Dad presses me on my flight over, not understanding why I'd want to make the trip alone. It doesn't feel like the right moment to tell them about my wings. Although, now that I think about it, putting it off for so long almost ensures there will never be a *good time*. Fuck. They're going to be so upset that I kept this from them.

So instead of being a dutiful daughter and telling them, I avoid, avoid, avoid. Mom washes some berries while Dad and I surreptitiously try to steal a few without her noticing. It fails, of course — I swear she can see everything — but it serves to calm my nerves and reminds me of a time before I started lying to them.

While I empty the last drop of batter into the pan, Dad pulls Mom into his arms and they dance. I watch, reveling in the love I feel radiating off them. I think of Raphael and Theo. They'd teamed up with Dina and bought me a black wing jacket so I'd feel comfortable flying home. Sure, I might need help to put it on, but it hid my golden wings the entire flight here, and for what might be the first time, I actually enjoyed flying. Well worth the ache in my muscles tomorrow.

With a smile on my face, I remove the last pancake from the pan and place it on the pile. "Grub's ready, you lovebirds."

We settle around the table just like any other day before SCU and all the changes I've battled since. It might not be the exact same. The table is smaller and somehow there's way more food than we ever would have had before, but the vibe is the same. *They're* the same. It's comforting as hell to know that with everything going on in my life, they remain unchanged.

My heart swells, knowing that I'm finally home. Sure, it may not be the house I grew up in, but home isn't a place. It's not about the walls or furniture, which street you live on. Home is where the angels you love are, and right now there's nowhere else I'd rather be.

"So, how's school? What are the classes like?" Dad asks before taking a sip of coffee.

"Good, actually! I had my last midterm yesterday and already received my grade this morning. I got ninety-two percent."

"Sweetheart, that's amazing! Are you finding the classes easy, then?"

"Well, not all of them. Some are hard, like angelic powers, and a few of the professors haven't made things very easy for me, but I'm doing alright." I take a swig of juice. "Actually, I was wondering what you guys would think about me showing you what I've learned about our powers. It's nothing wildly complicated yet, but perhaps we could start with telepathy and see how that goes?"

Mom's eyes turn glassy, and I wonder if maybe I should have just kept my mouth shut, but she places a hand on mine and smiles. "We'd be honored, Haylie-bear. Your dad and I always wanted to learn more about our abilities, but, well, they don't make it easy for us, do they?"

"No, Mom. They don't. But I'll teach you everything I can and do up some notes for you to keep practicing when I'm back on campus. Deal?"

She squeezes my hand. "Deal. And speaking of campus, how's Dina? You two must be joined at the hip!"

"She's good! Second-year classes keep her busy, but we usually eat together and try to schedule regular girls' days to catch up. Things have been difficult with her dad though, and for a second there we thought he was going to pull her admission, but that's settled for now at least."

"I never did like her father," Dad says, a scowl present on his lips. "And what about the other students? Is everyone treating you alright?"

"Well, no." I snort. "It doesn't matter where you go, Dad. Silver City is full of assholes. But I've made a few friends and honestly, I'm not sure I'd have made it this far without them. But enough about me! I want to know everything about this place. What's it like living in the Fallen district?"

My parents exchange a glance before Mom says, "It's different. Like with everything, there are pros and cons, but we're just focusing on the pros. We have our own house now and even a backyard."

"It's cheaper, too, so we've got a bit more money every month. That alone is enough to make the rest worth it."

"I'm glad. You guys finally deserve a little grace." Their words tell me one thing, but the odd looks they're throwing each other tell me something else altogether. I don't doubt them, not really, but they're holding something back. What aren't they telling me?

I stand, intending to bring my empty plate to the sink, but Dad stops me. "No, no, no. Sit. Your mother and I will clear the dishes and bring out a little dessert."

I eye the two of them suspiciously, but do as I'm told. Our routine has always been that I clear the dishes after a meal, so it feels weird to just sit here while they clean up around me.

"You remember that pastry you brought us before school started?" Dad asks.

"Mmm, yes! That almond thing."

"Well, your mother's been experimenting, testing out recipes and baking all kinds of things. She's got a real knack for it, you know."

"Mom, that's amazing! Any chance I'll get to try something over break?"

Dad laughs. "Oh, just you wait."

Mom hits Dad with the hand towel before grabbing a glass dish from the freezer and bringing it over. "Maybe I'll have to make enough just for us girls, hmm? Since your father thinks my cooking is such a burden."

"Hey! Don't say that. You'll break my heart, Mari. I'll waste away into nothing but a husk and be forced to travel this world alone and hungry, never to be fulfilled."

I snort. "You must be one hell of a baker, Mom."

She places the glass tray on the table, and my mouth immediately waters. I don't even know what it is, but it's topped with drizzled chocolate and peanuts, so I know it'll be good.

Mom hands me a plate first, then one for herself as she shoots Dad an annoyed look, but I can tell it's all for show. There's no way she'll deny him a slice. And sure enough, she doesn't. Instead, she cuts him a piece that's twice the size of hers or mine.

I cut off a chunk with my fork as I try to figure out what it is. There's a creamy filling with crushed cookies as the base, maybe? "I hope you know how hard it is not to shove this entire bite into my mouth," I tell her. "But what exactly is it?"

"It's called drumstick cake. This is the first batch, so please be honest with how it tastes. I deviated a little from the recipe and I'm not entirely sure if it's going to work or not."

I've never seen Mom look like this before: shy and a little nervous. Especially not about her cooking. Just how much of their lives have I missed while away at school? "Of course, Mom. I'll be honest."

"Ready?" She lifts a fork to her lips, clearly wanting us all to taste it at the same time when we finally notice Dad.

"What?" he mumbles through a mouthful of dessert, the slice on his plate more than half gone.

We both roll our eyes and dive in. It's cold and peanut buttery, with a slight crunch from the base and chopped peanuts. Holy hell, it's delicious!

"Mom! This is incredible." I take another bite. "Addictive even. Now I understand why Dad scarfed his down so quickly. Holy shit!"

She preens and puts another bite into her mouth, savoring the taste. Dad and I have long since finished ours before she's even made it through half of hers. Oops.

I stand, grabbing the empty plates before bringing them to the sink and filling it with hot water. It shouldn't surprise me when Dad shoos me from the kitchen, telling me to go relax, but his words soothe any ache.

"We'll get back into our old routine, I promise. But you just got here. You survived an attack, midterms, and whatever else those kids are throwing at you. Just take today, alright, kiddo?"

"Alright. But tomorrow I'm clearing dishes." I wait for his nod before continuing. "I'm going to go walk off this food, if that's cool?"

"Of course!"

"Just bring your slate," Mom says, joining us in the kitchen. "And don't be out too late. You know the rules."

"I'll be back soon!" I shout, grabbing my bag and slate on the way out the front door.

As promised, I message the group chat, letting them know I'm about to explore a little, but I pause before putting it away. Theo suggested I message Zeke too, but is that even a good idea? His reasoning was sound. It'll look far less suspicious if another Fallen shows up here than it would for a Pure. Sense isn't a part of this, though. He's been so fucking hot and cold lately and I really can't stand for him to ruin my day. With that settled, I tuck my slate away and head right.

It's strange here. The streets feel so familiar, and if it weren't for the filth covering them, I could easily forget that I was in the Fallen district. Well, except for how much smaller everything is. The streets are narrower, and the houses are tiny and cramped together in groups. I'm sure it's nice for my parents to live in a house instead of an apartment, but I'm almost positive our old place had the same square footage, if not more.

No one else is out but me. I walk past crowded house after crowded house, noticing some have their lights on while some don't. It's eerily quiet and lonely on the street. Is it always like this? I trip over something soft, but catch myself before I fall. Do angels avoid these streets at all cost because of how disgusting they are?

I keep going, memorizing the turns I've taken so I can get back to my parents' house. Not that it'll be too hard to find my way. Shit, I can probably follow the tracks my shoes have made in the streets' filth. At least it doesn't smell. Those are small victories, I suppose.

Sounds filter from further up the street, beckoning me forward. I step out into a street lined with buildings that look different from the houses. An angel exits a door, bag in hand, and I realize it's a shop. The more I look, the more I notice the signs announcing produce or bread, even clothes. What the hell?

Are the Fallen expected to shop here, in their own district, instead of in the merchant district? Are they even *allowed* to go elsewhere? What the fuck is happening? Mom and Dad mentioned having more to spend than they ever did before, but the more I see, the more I think it's a gently painted facade. Someone wants to keep the Fallen sequestered, and they're well on their way to accomplishing that goal.

Worry settles heavily in my stomach as I mentally add to the list of things I need to look into. It's getting too fucking long.

Up ahead, a Fallen angel swoops down from the sky, landing hard and walking even more forcefully toward a door on the other side of the street. He doesn't bother putting his wings away, nor does he go inside, but for some reason, I can't look away.

It's only when he starts arguing with someone inside the building that I realize what has me so captivated. In his annoyance, he shifts enough that I can see his wings full on, and it's impossible to miss the featherless line that claws up one side. I wonder what happened to him to stop the feathers growing back. Does it affect his flying?

The longer I stare, the more my thoughts churn. Why can't I look away from this angel? What is it about him that has me so interested?

A commotion starts, and I realize that he's standing at another door, arguing with yet another angel. His distinctly nasal voice is hard to miss, yet I still can't make out what he's saying. I wonder if he was as big of a grump before the accident that harmed his wings or if that's just a product of his misfortune.

Unperturbed, I watch on, fascinated by the scar on his wings. Then everything shifts into focus.

The man lets out a growl of words that I don't catch before turning *in my direction.*

My chest heaves, heart pounding as I duck into a small alley between two shops and try to stay calm. I know why he seemed so familiar and what the small voice in my head was warning me about.

Could this be the angel Zeke saw, the one seen at the armory during the theft? But if it is, what's he doing in the Fallen district, and why is he arguing with those shop owners?

Nothing makes sense and yet, deep down, I just know it's him.

Now what the hell do I do?

15

HAYLIEL

I step through a door marked *staff only* and enter a small café. The angel behind the counter doesn't seem bothered that I've just entered through the wrong door. Not that I'd care if she did. There's absolutely zero chance I would've stayed in that alley and risked being caught snooping.

There are enough problems on my plate right now. I don't need to somehow make it onto the shit list of some psycho angel dude with a superiority complex. Hard pass.

I order a hot apple cider, which the Sinful Café announces as a speciality, to blend in better but keep my eye trained on the scarred angel. He hasn't flown off, which is odd. Does that mean he's not done with whatever it is he's doing in the district?

Though I suppose he could just live here. He's a Fallen, after all. But then what the hell was he doing at the scene of a demonic crime?

I take a seat near the window, pretending to flip through a magazine while I watch him walk down a side street.

Barely a few seconds tick by before I stand, determination making my legs move toward the door. I can't *not* follow him. We have so many fucking questions now and zero answers. I'd be a fool to pass up the chance at finding any. And as afraid as I might be, the thought of being kept in the dark for even a moment longer scares me more.

Plus, it's not like I'm an idiot. I have no intentions of confronting him. Shouting "Hey man! Tell me your name and why you were at the armory during a robbery" is more likely to get me killed than give me any answers. Especially if he kept any of the weapons he stole. But I can be careful, quiet, and at least find out where he's going.

The cider warms me as I nonchalantly head toward the street our scarred friend just went down. If I'm caught, I can just pretend I'm new and exploring. The drink helps too. I'm only a silly schoolgirl, after all.

But the street is empty.

The further down it I go, the less civilization there is. There are no more shops, no angels in sight. Only me and my fear. It's strange, though. I'm not just afraid of him, but of walking away from this with no information. Of letting down my friends, and even myself. How can I be so scared of a corrupt angel, and yet even more afraid that I've let him slip away?

As I approach the end of the street, certain I've lost any chance of learning something helpful, his familiar nasally voice echoes off the buildings.

"It's a fucking disaster is what it is."

The scarred man sounds so fucking close that I almost jump back, but stop myself before I give myself away. There's no doorway for me to step into, only an old tarp covering what might be a rickety shelving unit, and I sure as hell don't think that'll be quiet. Shit.

In my frantic search for a place to hide, I miss the rest of the conversation, and by the time I pay attention again, things have taken a turn.

"You were supposed to be transporting the goods. Instead, I find out you've been blabbing to your friends."

"Come on, Roderick. He's trustworthy. A real loyal angel. You'll see when he gets—" someone says, their gruff voice pleading.

"If I had to guess, you'd trust anything that had two wings and could fly. But this? Nah. What the fuck am I supposed to tell the big boss man, huh? I ain't wanting to look bad, ya know, so here's what we're going to do."

The tip of my shoe finds an old paint can. Even though I barely touch it, the thing skitters into the wall, releasing a dull *plink*. Oh shit.

Silence falls, my heart jackhammering so hard I think I might pass out. I'm so fucking screwed. Do they suspect I'm listening? Are they headed my way? Maybe I shouldn't have come out here alone. Shit, shit, shit.

"If you told anyone else, you little shit, I swear on the corpse of our old god that things will not end well for you." The scarred angel — who I'm guessing must be Roderick — says menacingly, causing my limbs to tremble with the need to flee.

Something crashes to the ground around the corner, and I almost jump out of my skin. What the fuck was that?

I don't have long to wonder before a new voice speaks. It would almost be pleasing, if he wasn't meeting criminals in dark, empty corners of the Fallen district.

"Sorry I'm late, man. I didn't mean to scare you. I come in peace." He laughs, though no one else does.

"You didn't fucking scare us, you idiot. We were about to investigate a noise in the alley."

"Ah, don't bother. It was just these guys." He pauses, but I can't tell why or what he's referring to. Did he bring more angels with him? "See?" he continues, the flap of his wings rustling up garbage to create a cacophony of sound.

"No wings out in front of the boss," the gruff voice from earlier whispers.

"Right. My bad. So, can I see the goods or what?"

Roderick growls, though in his nasally tone it comes off more of a pig squeal than anything menacing. "Hold him."

"Hey!" the new angel shouts as the commotion grows louder.

"What are you doing with that?"

"Cleaning up your fucking mess," Roderick replies.

"Wait. No. Man, you can trust me. You're not seriously going to use that thing on one of your own, are you? I won't say anything! I believe in the cause!"

Everything happens so fast, and within a single moment there's a shriek, followed by this wet, gurgling sound and the thump of what I hope isn't a body. *What the hell have I stumbled into?*

"Get the fuck up," Roderick says. "Take a good fucking look at him. He's lying there because of you. And if you don't want to be responsible for more death, you'll learn to keep your goddamn mouth shut."

There's this pained, half-sobbed groan that hurts my heart, but I still don't really understand what I'm hearing. He's talking as if he just killed an angel, except that's not possible. Not without the blades the demons carry, and why would an angel have one?

But even as I think about it, the angel's words repeat in my mind. *You're not seriously going to use that thing on your own kind, are you?*

I need to get the fuck out of here. Heat curls around my heart, racing down to the tips of my fingers and toes until I'm lightheaded. No, no, no. Not here. If I pass out here, I'm as good as fucking dead.

"It's time you finish your fucking task, don't you think? Those crates won't transport themselves. And you. Follow him.

Make sure he doesn't fuck this up any more than he already has."

Footsteps follow his words before the creaking of a door, and I'm left with my heart in my throat. As much as I want to peek beyond the corner, I don't trust it. This is way more fucking dangerous than I realized. Raphael and Theo are going to be so pissed when they find out. *If I even make it out of here.*

Around the corner, Roderick speaks again, but this time it's soft, almost a caress. "I didn't want to do this, you know. Killing doesn't thrill me. But you threatened everything I've worked for, and I just couldn't risk it. There's too much on the line, and I'll do whatever it takes to protect those I care about. I hope you find peace. One of us should."

Confusion and fear freeze my limbs as I listen on, unsure what to make of his words. He sounds almost apologetic, but can monsters even feel sorry? My mind churns, desperate to find a way out of this mess. The reality of it is that I probably should have left a long time ago, but now I'm too scared to even breathe.

Wings flap beyond the corner I'm hiding behind, and I press in closer to the wall, happy to find the stone cool against my heated flesh. Anyone flying overhead could see me, perched here for all to see. It takes every ounce of strength I have to stay still, breathe normally, and not run for the damn hills.

I don't know how long I stand here, leaning against the wall. I don't even fully understand *why* I stay. With everything that occurred here, I should want to get home as fast as I fucking can and call my friends. And I do want to, but there's a part of me that just can't leave. Not without seeing for myself what lies beyond the wall.

With one final inhale, I step softly around the corner.

On the ground lies an angel with blood pooled beneath his body and splattered around his mouth. *The gurgling.* I pull out my slate, hands shaking as I take a photo. It takes three tries before I finally get one that isn't blurry and the moment I do, I turn and run.

Except I don't get very far.

"You should really be more careful."

I freeze, heart jumping to my throat.

The man on the ground coughs, choking on his own blood. "We possess a lot of powers, but invisibility isn't one of them."

Turning slowly, I take in his words, mouth falling open. "Why didn't you tell them I was there?"

He smiles, teeth red with blood. "You're just"—his breathing stutters—"a kid."

There's a commotion in the building and my eyes flash toward it, certain someone will open those doors any second.

"Go. Before they find you. I'll take your secret with me."

Part of me wishes I could do something for him. And maybe I could get the Guild out here, but there's no saving him, not with a wound from an angel blade. "Thank you. I ... I'm sorry I can't help you."

With one last glance toward him and the door beyond, I turn and bolt.

It feels like it takes forever to get home. Everywhere I look, I see shadows. I see scarred wings and the glint of a knife. So when I finally catch sight of my parents' house, I almost squeal. It looks the same as it did when I left. Red door. Lights on. But it's me that's changed. What I saw tonight sits in my gut, heavy and coiling. How is it that I've stumbled upon something so momentous within such a short period of time? My first visit to the Fallen district and already I have more unanswered questions, more to worry about, and somehow I felt loss. For a stranger. A criminal.

What a mess.

I open the front door quietly, doing my best to get in unseen and avoid my parents. They read me too easily, and right now I'm not sure I can muster the energy to pretend I'm alright.

The house is quiet except for the soft music playing. It calms me, at least, as much as it can, but just like everything else, it doesn't last. Everything from the last hour rushes back, churning inside me with the need to get out.

Is that man still alive, or has he succumbed to his injuries? Maybe I should have reached out to someone earlier. Could I have saved him if I had?

Once I'm safely tucked away in my room, I send Zeke a text.

Hayliel: How can I send in a tip to the Guild?

16

RAPHAEL

How the hell did I survive living with my parents all these years?

I've barely been home for a few hours and I'm already fed up. When I told Hayliel I'd continue our research here, I wasn't joking about it being a gift. If I have to listen to Mom tell me how I should be more like Raduriel, even one more time, I'll projectile vomit.

Will I even make it through the full week here?

My only saving grace is Hayliel. If I can find something to bring back with me, seeing her face as it lights up will soothe everything I might have to deal with here. It'll all be worth it if it helps us find answers.

The family library is pretty large, considering the fact no one ever comes in here. Why collect all this literature if they aren't going to read it? Why decorate the space with beautiful pieces of furniture if they won't sit in them to read? I suppose it's possible they come in here now that their kids are out of the house, but I'd only seen them in here once as a kid, and that was only to show off their collection. The large mahogany staircase in the center of the circular room that spirals up to the second floor brings a bitter smile to my face. When I was young, I remember wishing my parents would let me slide down the railing. They didn't, of course. And by the time I had the chance to try it when they were out of town, the spark of excitement never came.

Shelves of books line the walls and a few decorative pieces of furniture near the entrance. Among the books, my parents also have statues and other artifacts they've collected over the years. Growing up, this area was off limits to us. They didn't want us to ruin any of their collection, and it was only a few years ago that they let us in without direct supervision. That's when they built Raduriel and me our own work space. I shake my head, setting my anger loose. That's the past. But this, what I'm trying to find for Hayliel, is the present. She's my future, and I won't let my family hangups impede that.

I peruse the first floor, picking up a few books that sound promising before heading up the stairs to the second floor. There are more shelves up here, more books to look through, and I find another volume or two.

The private study room I spent half my school years in is open, empty except for the desk that holds so many memories — my parents' unwillingness to help me, Raduriel's enjoyment of the power he held over me as the favorite. Theo came here a few times, but he couldn't stand my brother either. Not when he witnessed how much of an ass he was when I asked for help. He started tutoring me then, sharing the tidbits of information he read about or explaining the process in a new light to help me tackle a problem. He saved me.

Raduriel's door is ajar, which seems odd. I consider leaving it alone and dropping my books down on the desk in front of me, but my limbs have a mind of their own. Despite knowing Raduriel is with my parents, I close the distance on silent feet and push open the door.

His room is lived in. Cozy. It's not just an empty desk in a barren room. His has life. There's art on the walls, a recliner in the corner, and a rug on the floor. He even has a few scribbled notes and an old book left on his desk. Was it always like this?

Instead of leaving, I set the books down, walk around to the chair behind the desk, and sit. If I close my eyes, I can hear his mocking tone and boastful laughter. The way he ridiculed me and always found a way to look better in the eyes of our parents while making me look worse.

But that was then. Now I'm far away, in a school of my own without him, and enough walls built up inside that they can't hurt me anymore. Or so I tell myself.

I shove away the memories and focus on the stack of books in front of me. *Finding something for Hayliel will make this all worth it.*

Each one looks too new to be read, but that doesn't surprise me. Most of the books in this place are more for decoration and clout than anything else.

I grab the first one, *The Anatomy of Wings*, which just so happens to be written by a distant cousin. My parents rarely talk about him. Ever since the growing divide between Pure and Fallen, they've separated themselves as much as possible from all *impure* relatives. As I open the book, I consider reaching out to him. Partly because it would piss off my parents, but mostly because if he knew enough about wings to write a damn book about it, maybe there's more he can tell us.

After looking through the table of contents, my hope plummets. If I wanted to understand the aerodynamics and fibers that make up our wings, this would be the book for me. But other than a chapter near the end about coloring, it's mostly just clinical. So I skip ahead.

> *The color of our wings and their feathers has long since been a topic of discussion among many of our kind. Some believe it to be a depiction of our nature, the type of person we will be, and the actions we'll take. Others believe it's nothing more than happenstance. But I don't think either of those is true. What I believe is far more scientific, with real*

data to back it up. It all comes down to genetics. The tiny atoms that make up the very essence of our souls. DNA from each of our ancestors gets pooled together in a metaphorical bucket, and the predecessors whose genes are most prominent will determine the type of angel you'll become.

The rest of the chapter is a showcase of data points and science to prove his findings, and as interesting as it might be, it isn't what I need.

I flip through the next book, a massive tome on history's greatest angels that might have held good information once upon a time, but now only focuses on the Archangels and their helpers.

Ugh! Will we ever catch a fucking break?

Slamming the book shut, I push it away from me and slump back in the chair. What the hell was I thinking? As if a discovery would fall right into my lap the moment I got here. I'm foolish to believe that.

I massage my temples, hoping I'll find the strength to press on. Instead, all I do is stress and mope. Fuck.

Maybe I just need a distraction.

I eye my brother's desk, wondering if I should search through it. An invasion of privacy, perhaps, but it's not like he even uses this space anymore.

In the first drawer, all I find are pens and several notebooks. I leaf through them, but they're all empty. Untouched. The second drawer holds a single book. *Angelic Secrets to a Higher Power of Living*. Raduriel had been obsessed with it after graduating from SCU. He read somewhere that the Archangel Mikhael could recite every word from inside this old tome, so he began memorizing it, too. Some days I'd listen to him reading out loud, wondering what it was he hoped to gain from all that gibberish, since that's what his words sounded like to me.

Maybe now I'd see what all the fuss was about.

I pick it up, placing it on the desk before moving to close the drawer when I notice something else.

A key.

It's thin and long, and brown with age, but not rusted. Now what could this unlock, I wonder?

The third drawer of Raduriel's desk has a keyhole, but when I try to push the key inside, it doesn't fit. It's unlocked anyway and empty aside from a few scraps of paper.

But I can't find anything else with a keyhole. I even fiddle with the back of the recliner, wondering if maybe there's a hidden compartment, but it's only the inner workings of the chair. Whatever this key is to, it must not be that important if he left it in a drawer and not kept with him. But even as the words pass through my mind, I can't deny the urge to find out for sure.

I look through the upper floor of the library. There's a drawer or two with keyholes, but none that fit the key, and besides, they're all unlocked and empty, anyway. Something inside me screams that whatever lock this key is for, it isn't some already unlocked, empty cabinet.

I try not to get too excited. It's been years since Raduriel moved out of our family estate. The likelihood that whatever this key opens is even still here is slim, but I have to try.

The main floor of the library has even more fucking locks, as if we need a place to hide all our secrets. Instead of testing them all, I take one good pass around the room, paying close attention to each keyhole. Because of how thin this key is, there are only three places it might work, and I get started on the first drawer.

Excitement bubbles through me as the key slides into the hole, but as much as I twist it, nothing engages. Panic threatens to rise, but I shove it down. It's only an old key, and one I found in Raduriel's old things, no less. For all I know, this could only lead me to a stash of notes from our parents or his old test scores. The vain bastard.

There are only two keyholes left. Both are to cabinet doors, though one is made of glass and it's not hard to see there's nothing inside. Well, that makes my decision easy. I try the cabinet along the back wall, except it doesn't work. The damn thing barely goes in at all.

Fuck!

I pull on the key, but it's lodged in the hole. If I break this, I'll never find out what Raduriel was hiding.

Honestly, I'm not sure why it means so much to me. It's not like I'll find a handwritten apology tucked away somewhere.

When I tug again, the door pops open and the key comes out, but my success is short-lived. Another fucking empty cabinet. Slamming the door closed, I lean against the shelf and breathe.

It's not over yet. Maybe what I need is hidden in his room. I suppose it's possible he had a copy of the key made and carries that with him. Not that I've ever seen him with it, but … stranger things have happened. With a determination to find a way inside his room, I make my way back to the stairs, but before I climb them, something tugs at my mind.

The other empty cabinet.

Before I even know what I'm doing, I'm crouched low in front of it, the key pressed to the hole. I don't breathe as I push it inside and turn. Not until the *click*.

My hands shake as I pull open both doors and stare dumbfounded at what's inside.

A bark of laughter escapes as I stare at the very *not* empty cabinet. Glued to the back of the windows is a picture. An exact copy of what I assume it looks like when empty. Someone went to a lot of trouble to keep the contents a secret. But was it Raduriel, or someone else?

Inside are old books, looking far more worn and faded than anything else in this entire library. Some have barely legible titles along the spine, and one doesn't appear to have anything at all. When I pull it out, the once-supple leather is rough against my palm, and the pages are colored with age.

Not only is there nothing on the spine, but even the front and back cover are empty. Curious.

A commotion sounds from somewhere in the distance, startling me. I take the strange, untitled book from the cupboard and lock everything else back up. Until I can search the contents more thoroughly, I need to keep this discovery a secret. No one can know. Especially not fucking Raduriel. He'd be pissed to know that I found his key and whatever he'd been hiding behind the locked doors.

I quickly move my things out of Raduriel's study room and into mine, making sure to leave his as untouched as possible. Only once I'm settled behind my desk, the door to my study room half closed, do I open the blank book.

The leather creaks. How long has it been since someone touched this volume? Decades? Centuries? Has Raduriel even read it?

These thoughts race through my mind as I flip through a few pages, surprised that there isn't a copyright page. Just how old is this book?

Yet, the more pages I flip, the more I realize this isn't some textbook from the archives. It's a journal. Isaac Adams's journal. *The same Isaac whom my middle name comes from?*

The pages are old and dry, the ink faded in spots, but most of what I see is legible. Daily accounts of his life, some with dates from before God was overthrown. My parents never talked much about him, other than to say he wasn't all there. It used to piss me off that they'd given me my middle name based on some lunatic ancestor. Especially because Raduriel's middle name came from our founding father, the angel who set the Adams family on a fruitful path.

But now, flipping through this journal, I think it might not be so bad to have a link to Isaac.

On the next page, the ink is splotched and running. Most of the words are garbled and illegible, but one stands out on the withered page.

Golden.

My heart races as I try to piece together what I can, but the only other words I can decipher are *power* and *fear*. I wince as I read the last word, knowing how much it would hurt Hayliel if she knew these three words were written together. But this damaged, worn-out page could honestly be about fucking anything, and until we can view this original page as it was written, we'll never know.

I flip the page, happy to see this one less damaged, but it's only a recipe. The next is just a list of numbers. Measurements, maybe?

After a few more pages, some filled with drawings and symbols I don't recognize, I finally find something.

If I had not seen it with my own two eyes, I would scarcely believe it.
Golden feathers, shimmering in the first rays of the morning sun.
I felt a magnificent power radiating off him, even from so far away.
Beneath him, the earth lay scorched. Blackened.
Whether he's destined to destroy or protect remains a mystery.
For now.

I reread it three times, and then again once more.

Proof. That's what this is. Evidence that golden-winged angels once existed. Sure, the words might come from the old musings of a madman, but it's something. It's still fucking something.

Frenzy builds within me with the need to tell someone as I search for my slate. I find it still stashed away in my bag and don't waste any time before calling Theo.

It rings twice. Three times. And I'm about to give up when he finally answers.

"Hey, man. You surviving?"

"Barely, but that's not why I'm calling. I think I fucking found something."

There's a beat of silence on the other line before he finally speaks. "Already? You've barely been gone a full day. Are the libraries here just that lame or what?"

"The school doesn't keep copies of old family journals. I found a passage about golden wings in—"

"Is gossiping with your friends what you Pures call helping?" Zeke's voice comes through the speaker loud and clear, and for a second, I can't comprehend what's happening.

Is my best friend actually *hanging out* with that asshole Ezekiel?

Theo responds, and I know it's not a reply to me when he says, "I can just as easily leave, but since I'm guessing you want my help, why don't you just chill and give me a fucking minute?"

Ezekiel mutters something I can't hear, and the anger I felt at learning they were together dissipates.

"Sorry about that. Ezekiel asked for my help with a few demon-related texts he found, and I agreed. Still unsure if it was a mistake or not," Theo says. "Now, what were you saying?"

"My ancestor, Isaac. I found one of his old journals. I'll admit that some of it is nonsensical ramblings, but I found a few mentions of golden wings. One passage even depicts scorched earth. Could you check out the old well sometime? There was so much ash covering the ground after the attack that I didn't notice, but I have a feeling we'll find the grass blackened and burned."

"Absolutely. I'll check on it tomorrow and let you know what I find. Have you told Hayliel?"

"Not yet." Hesitating for just a moment, I add, "I think we should hold off for now, at least until we find a bit more to go on. Some of the entries are a bit *odd*, and I don't want to get her hopes up."

"Agreed, at least for now."

A knock sounds from downstairs, and the lower-level library door opens. "Master Raphael, your presence is required in the dining room."

Sighing, I call out, "I'll be down in a moment." To Theo I say, "Shit. I've got to go disappoint my family, but I'll keep you posted. Don't take any shit from that asshole house leader."

"I won't. Good luck."

The call ends and I'm left muttering to myself. I've finally found something useful, and instead of delving deeper into the journal, I have to go break fucking bread with my family. I'd rather be stuck with Ezekiel.

I put all the books back except for the journal. That one I toss into my bag, along with my slate, and pocket the key.

Isaac Adams might have been considered a lunatic, but even I know angels are judgmental assholes.

Maybe his wild and crazy ramblings are just what we're looking for.

17

THEO

The Knowledge house library is quiet as I relax into the couch with a book.

I'm one of the odd angels who stayed on campus instead of going home for the break, but I'm not alone in that decision. Some of us, those who can choose without causing a war with our families, would just rather stay here. Raphael would have stayed if he could, but I suspect his mother would have shown up on school grounds to drag him back herself. Besides, he'd never hear the end of it and honestly, sometimes it's just easier for him to go along with it than provoke their disappointment. They never know when to stop.

I flip the page of the book I'm reading and settle into the history of a well-documented demon attack from long ago. We won, of course. Another of the demon king's plans foiled. No one knows why he hates us so much, but according to the history books he's been a thorn in our side for most of our existence, so it has to be something big.

Creak.

The library door opens slowly, and I look up at the last person I expected to see today: Ezekiel.

He spots me right away, which makes me think that maybe I should have picked a less obvious spot to work, but I didn't expect anyone to show up.

Instead of saying anything, I focus my attention back on the book in front of me and continue the sentence. Who am I kidding? I can't pay attention to this when his footsteps come closer. What's he even doing here?

He breaks the silence. "Can I sit?"

I wave a hand. "I'm not going to stop you."

He chuckles, dropping into a chair. "Right. Would now be a good time to show you those passages we talked about?"

At his words, I relax a little. "Sure." I'd totally forgotten about his request, which makes sense considering the events that transpired later that day with Hayliel and Raphael.

Ezekiel rummages through his bag before pulling out three texts. One is a thin, soft-covered book, and the other two are thick hardbacks.

"Where did you say you found these again?"

"My father's study." He cracks open the hardback titled *Demonology* and flips a few pages.

The title is familiar, but that doesn't mean anything. With as much as I've researched demons over the years, it's possible I've read it. But it's also possible I haven't. His dad's a lieutenant in the Guild, after all, and it's his actual job to know all that he can about those creatures. Wouldn't surprise me if they had access to books that we didn't.

"Okay, this part here." He points to a section in the middle of the page just as my slate vibrates on the coffee table.

"One second," I say, peering at the screen. It's Raphael.

As I pick it up, he says, "You aren't actually going to answer that now, are you?"

But I don't respond, tapping on the call button. "Hey, man. You surviving?"

"Barely, but that's not why I'm calling. I think I fucking found something."

His words take me by surprise and, for a moment, I'm speechless. So much for losing out on prime research over the break. "Already? You've barely been gone a full day. Are the libraries here just that lame or what?"

"The school doesn't keep copies of old family journals. I found a passage about golden wings in—"

Ezekiel scoffs, his voice ice cold as he says, "Is gossiping with your friends what you Pures call helping?"

Shit. Raphael isn't going to take well to my being with Zeke, but it's not like I sought him out. And the only reason I'm here is for Hayliel and the rest of our friends. We might not like him, but we need him.

Right now, though, all I feel is distaste for the asshole Fallen. Moving the slate away from my mouth, I reply, "You can just as easily leave, but since I'm guessing you want my help, why don't you just chill and give me a fucking minute?"

I take a deep breath, ignoring Ezekiel's mumbled words, and focus back on my best friend. "Sorry about that. Ezekiel asked for my help with a few demon-related texts he found, and I agreed. Still unsure if it was a mistake or not. Now, what were you saying?"

I expect Raphael to sound pissed, but whatever he called to tell me is too good to kill his mood. His excitement is palpable, even through the phone.

"My ancestor, Isaac. I found one of his old journals. I'll admit that some of it is nonsensical ramblings, but I found a few mentions of golden wings. One passage even depicts scorched earth. Could you check out the old well sometime? There was so much ash covering the ground after the attack that I didn't notice, but I have a feeling we'll find the grass blackened and burned."

Was the earth where Hayliel had stood during the attack burned? That day is a jumble of flashes and fear, at least until the end. But by then, I can't remember anything except the way Hayliel looked when she emerged from the shelter of her wings. Scared but strong.

"Absolutely. I'll check on it tomorrow and let you know what I find. Have you told Hayliel?"

"Not yet." Raphael hesitates before adding, "I think we should hold off for now, at least until we find a bit more to go on. Some of the entries are a bit *odd*, and I don't want to get her hopes up."

I nod, my gaze darting to Ezekiel, but he doesn't seem to have heard. "Agreed, at least for now."

There's a commotion on his side of the phone before Raphael sighs then calls out in a weak tone, "I'll be down in a moment." To me he says, "Shit. I've got to go disappoint my family, but I'll keep you posted. Don't take any shit from that asshole house leader."

"I won't. Good luck."

As the call ends, I worry about my friend. He's stuck with a family who fails him at every turn. A mother that always reminds him of his shortcomings. A father without a backbone who never sticks up for his son. And a brother who took every chance to make Raphael feel small and insignificant. Now he has to spend an entire week in their presence without an escape. From experience, I know that when he comes back, it'll take some time to wash away the stench of their disappointment, but between Hayliel and I, hopefully we can push it away sooner.

"Wow. Pures really are ungrateful, huh? A week at home in a mansion with your family where both your parents are alive. It must be so damn hard to be Raphael right now," Ezekiel mocks.

Anger flares in my chest, my eyes hardening as they settle on the piece of shit who doesn't seem to know when to shut the fuck up. "I'd advise you to keep your mouth shut about things you don't understand. Blood doesn't mean jack shit in some situations, and if all you've ever had is the love and support of your family, count yourself fucking lucky."

He opens his mouth to respond, but I cut him off. "While we're on the subject of ungrateful behavior, don't think I haven't noticed your hot and cold bullshit with Hayliel. From what I can see, all she's done is be kind to you, and all you do in return is glare and grumble like a child."

"You might want to take your own advice and shut up about things you don't fucking understand," he says, his jaw clenched.

"Yeah? Well, why don't you spell it out for me then, because from where I sit you're just a butthurt little boy who's pissed off at the world."

"My relationship with Hayliel is none of your damn business."

I chuckle. "If you keep acting like a dickhead, then you won't *have* a relationship with her at all. And you can try to pretend like that wouldn't bother you, but you're not fooling anyone. It's obvious you care about her. Why else would you have rushed to her side when she emerged from her wings or stayed with us after the attack? But your fluctuating dismissive bullshit is affecting her, and she has enough crap to deal with already. So lay off her, angel up, and stop acting like you don't fucking care. You don't have to like me or Raphael, but if you don't start letting Hayliel in, you'll lose her, and something tells me that would hurt far worse."

The anger on his face is gone, replaced with a mixture of remorse and irritation.

It feels so fucking good to finally lay it all out for him. Whether he takes my words to heart and changes, that remains to be seen.

His slate pings, the screen lighting up with a text from the very angel we've been arguing about.

Hayliel.

18

EZEKIEL

I stare at the screen, lost in thought.

Can she sense we've been talking about her? And if she knew the topic of our discussion, would she agree with Theo? It hurts to think about because he's right in some ways. I can't deny that I'm an asshole. I haven't been very nice to her, but it's not like she's a saint either. She brushed me off and constantly rubs her relationship with Theo and Raphael in my face. Maybe someday I'll get over it, but I'm not there yet.

Pulling down on the notification, I read the message.

Hayliel: How can I send in a tip to the Guild?

Huh? I read her words a second time, then a third. Why would she want to send anything to the Guild? And how is it she even *has* something to send in?

"What's wrong?" Theo asks, noticing my frown.

"I don't know yet," is all I reply before pulling up her contact and calling.

She answers on the first ring. "Hey."

"Don't *hey* me after a text like that. Why the fuck do you want to send something in to the Guild?"

I watch as Theo's brows press together at my words and wait for her reply.

"So I went out after supper to walk around the Fallen district, and I'm pretty sure I found the scarred angel from the photo."

"Wait a minute. You mean to tell me you went out, *alone*, in an unknown district and ran into the angel that helped a bunch of demons raid one of the Guild's armories?" The look Theo throws me screams *see? You do care.*

"Well, yes, but it's not—"

"Not what, hummingbird? Stupid? Dangerous? Because I assure you, it's all those things. What the hell were you thinking?"

"I was thinking about finding fucking answers. And I told Raphael and Theo that I was going out for a walk. Besides, it's not like I found him in some shady fucking place. He was at the shops, going door to door arguing with angels."

I glare at Theo, muttering about fucking Pures under my breath. "Damn it all to hell. Telling them doesn't mean shit. If something happened to you, how would they know? Even the Guild's fastest flier would need at least a few minutes to reach the Fallen district. Then they'd need even more time to locate you. What if you'd gotten hurt?"

"I didn't. And I'm not really in the mood for more of your attitude, Zeke, so if you can't help me with the Guild, then I'll just find another way."

I take a deep breath, holding it in for a second before letting it go along with my anger. "No, no. I'll help. You're certain no one saw you?"

"No one saw me."

Theo waves his hand, whispering, "Let me hear."

Rolling my eyes, I ignore him. "Alright. Tell me what happened."

"Well, I followed him a bit and stumbled upon a meeting. There were at least three others there, maybe more, but I was hiding so I couldn't see. Anyway, the guy with the scar is named Roderick. It sounded like he was in charge of whoever was there with him because he was getting angry about some delivery of goods or something. But then he said he had someone to answer to, so I bet he has a superior."

"Fuck. He must have been talking about transporting the shit they stole from the armory. Is that what you wanted to tell the Guild, so they'd look into this Roderick guy?"

"No. Not exactly."

"Hummingbird ..." I grumble

"Listen, so I ... well it just sort of ... look, it's only—"

I sigh. "Spit it out. I can't help you if you don't tell me what's going on."

"There's a dead angel in the Fallen district."

Silence fills the air around me. The only sound audible through the phone is Hayliel's soft breath. I exchange a look with Theo that tells me he heard what she just said, too.

Everyone knows there aren't many ways to kill an angel. We're basically fucking immortal. So if what she's saying is true, that means things have just gone from bad to worse.

I shake my head, and it takes every ounce of control I have not to lash out at her for being so fucking stupid. Instead, I ask the one question I can think of. "Was the angel dead before you got there?"

She doesn't answer right away, and that little sliver of reluctance is all I need to know the answer.

When she continues not to say anything, I ask again, "I need the words, hummingbird. Was the angel dead before you got there?"

"No. I was there when it happened, but I only heard it. Zeke, I'm pretty sure Roderick has an angel blade."

"I don't know what's worse. That Roderick might have one, or that you were close enough to one of those blades that you could've died. Fuck, Hayliel. This is bad."

"I know."

"You're home now?"

"Yes."

"Good. Now, where do I tell Azrael to look for the body?"

"I don't remember the street name. But it was down a street opposite a place called the Sinful Café."

"Alright. I'll let him know. Maybe he'll be able to find something to help us track down the stolen weapons."

"Hayliel said you think there's a mole in the Guild. Do you think it's wise to involve them at all?" Theo adds, reminding me of his presence.

"Theo is with you?" Hayliel asks, sounding surprised.

"Dude, just put her on speaker, for fuck's sake."

I groan but do as he says, clicking the speaker button on my slate. "There. You happy? Yes, Theo and I are bonding over demons and our mutual distaste for one another. As for the mole, it's not Azrael. He's solid, but even so, I won't mention where this tip came from in case he has to tell someone else. We should hold off on telling him Roderick's name, though. If they locate him from something they find on the body, well, that's not on us."

"That's fair," Theo says. "But what do we do about the murdering angel with a blade that could kill any one of us?"

"I have an idea about that, but it might be a little risky," Hayliel says.

"I'm not surprised," I reply blandly. "Let's hear it."

"It's not like he was so hard to find the first time, seeing as I stumbled upon him by accident. He must have a hideout in the district somewhere. If I can find it, maybe we can figure out what his end goal is."

"You're serious," I deadpan, and when she doesn't respond, I add, "One body wasn't enough? You want to risk the next dead angel being you? This is—"

"I'm trying to make it so there aren't any more dead angels at all, and I figured if you tagged along, then maybe we'd actually stand a chance. Maybe I should reconsider the invite."

Her words hit me like a landslide. It's a foolish, stupid idea. One that could get us both killed. But I know her enough to understand that if I say no, she'll just do it alone. Or she'll ask Raphael or Theo to go with her, and somehow that's almost worse.

"Uh, guys," Theo says, "I get Ezekiel is a Guild intern and all that, but you're both students. You don't have medals of valor from battles won, or even experience fending off a deadly blade-wielding rebel. Is this really a good idea?"

Look at that. Something the Pure and I can agree on. Still, I ask, "Do you have a better idea?"

He sighs. "No."

"Perfect," Hayliel says. "Then it's settled. Zeke, how soon can you get here?"

"I'm due at the Guild at first light, but I can come out after that."

Before Hayliel can respond, Theo adds, "And don't you dare think about going exploring before Ezekiel arrives, firefly."

"I won't."

"Promise us."

"I promise. Zeke, I'll message you my parents' address, and I guess I'll see you tomorrow. Have fun bonding. Try not to kill each other." Her laughter cuts off when the line goes dead.

Theo and I share a look of mutual worry and understanding, neither of us liking the plan but realizing that it's our best shot right now. I push one of the thick textbooks toward him and stand.

"I'm going to call Azrael. Why don't you get a head start on the passage in this book? I'll be right back."

Knowledge house is quiet as I exit the library, and I only take a few steps before dialing Azrael's number.

"Zeke, if you're calling to take on more duties, I'm afraid I'll have to say no."

Laughing, I reply, "You know me, Azrael. I can't stay still for too long, but that's actually not why I called."

"Oh really? I'm intrigued. What's up?"

"Someone informed me that there's a dead angel in the Fallen district, near the Sinful Café. They don't want their name involved and asked me to help."

"A dead angel. Are you sure?"

"I believe them, sir. Given the nature of our kind, I thought it best if you handled this discretely, if possible."

"Yes, yes. Good idea. It wouldn't do to start a frenzy. Where exactly will I find it?"

"On the other side of the street from the Sinful Café, you'll find a dead end. The body should be there."

"I'll head there now. And, Zeke, I'm glad that you called me first. It proves I was right to get you out from behind a desk. You've got good instincts that will serve you well within the Guild."

"Thank you, sir. Please keep me posted if there are any developments."

"Of course. We'll chat in the morning."

The call ends, but I don't move as the sudden realization that Hayliel could have died sinks in. She was this close to an angel blade and someone who clearly isn't afraid to use it. Even though she didn't sound it, I know she must have been terrified. How could she not be? Something in my gut tells me she's holding back. Tomorrow. I'll get the rest out of her tomorrow.

Fuck. Maybe Theo is right. It's the last thing I want to admit because, come on. It's *Theo*. But if my actions are adding to her stress when she's already dealing with so much, maybe it's time I re-evaluate. The last thing I want to do is hurt her. That's the whole reason I hate the Pures being near her, isn't it? Fearing they'll discard her like they did me.

Shaking my head, I turn back to the library, to Theo and the passages I hope he can shed some light on. *One thing at a time.*

I find him with all three books opened to the areas I'd marked and his own notebook in front of him, the passages written neatly.

"Sorry, I wanted to look at everything. I hope that's alright."

"It's fine." Twenty minutes ago I'd have been pissed, but now I'm just glad he's interested enough not to wait for me.

"I've actually read these two already," he says, pointing to the two thickest volumes. "But this one is new. If it's alright with you, I'd love to borrow it sometime."

"I've already read it cover to cover twice, so you're welcome to it. Do you have any insight into what those passages mean? Each one hints at something the demons share, but it's not something I've heard of before, and the Guild is pretty good at keeping us informed on all demonic developments."

He's quiet for a moment, studying my face before he finally speaks. "I think it's what they used during the attack on the school. This mental bond where they can communicate or take orders, kind of like telepathy but deeper, somehow. Like they're all connected as demons versus forming that bond like we have to do."

"So if they were in trouble, they could broadcast that to their entire horde for backup."

"Exactly."

Shit. If this is true, how come the Guild doesn't know about it? Suddenly, pieces of the puzzle snap together. The diversion at the school. The strange increase in calls to the Guild. And as soon as everything was in place, all they had to do was speak it through the bond and the entire horde would know.

"There's something else, something I haven't mentioned to anyone because I wanted to be sure." Theo rubs the back of his neck. "I'm trying to trust you, Ezekiel. Please don't make me regret it."

"I won't," I assure him, meaning it.

"I think there's more to what happened to Hayliel at the school than we think. There was a point where all the demons just turned, almost as one, in the same direction. At first I thought they were leaving, having been told their part of the plan was done, but that wasn't it. They all turned to *her*. And I don't think it's a coincidence that she's now got golden wings and a power that can destroy demons."

I look in the direction of the well, remembering that moment as if it were only yesterday. "What are you saying, Theo?" I ask, needing to be sure.

"Either the demon king told the horde to go to the well, which doesn't make any fucking sense, or they could sense whatever she is and knew that if they didn't snuff her out, the war against demons and angels would be changed forever."

19

HAYLIEL

You'd think with all the time to sleep in, that I'd take advantage of it. Catch up on what I missed during the attack, preparing for midterms, all of it. But I can't seem to turn off my brain.

Even while I slept last night, the dreams kept me restless. More nightmares than anything else. The events of yesterday played through on a loop until the words became garbled, and I'm not even sure what's real anymore.

Knowing I'll see Zeke today doesn't help. I told him to meet me here, but now I regret that decision. I should have asked him to meet near the shops or on some random side street instead.

Maybe I'll be able to sneak out before my parents even notice he's here.

Not for the first time, I consider messaging him, but each time I do, something holds me back. Weakness. And weak is exactly what he'll call me if I change my mind about our meeting location, and it's not like he'd be wrong.

To take my mind off it, I spend the morning thinking about Theo and Zeke working together. It's weird to imagine, but it's not without benefits. Maybe if they can get past their shit, things will be a little easier. Archangels know I could use a bit more *easy* in my life.

My stomach rumbles, and I head upstairs. Somehow it's already ten o'clock, and I've wasted hours stuck in a loop of worry and overthinking.

On my way to the kitchen, I stop and stare at the door, wondering what Zeke will think of it. Does his dad live in this district too? Is he used to this area, and the strange Fallen-only shops? I wonder if he sees through their veiled attempts to alienate us from the rest of Silver City. I bet he does.

"Good morning, sleepyhead," Dad calls out from deeper inside the house.

I follow his voice into the kitchen, where Mom is covered in flour and a growing stack of pancakes sits on the counter. "Do I even want to know?" I tease.

"Just a little disagreement. Nothing a little flour battle won't fix."

"Did you sleep okay?" Mom asks, leading me to the table and building me a plate of pancakes, hash browns, bacon, and eggs.

"I did! The room is perfect, Mom. Thank you."

While we eat, my eyes dart between my slate and the front door. I assume Zeke will message me before he heads this way, but what if he doesn't? I need every second to prepare. Fuck, I hate this.

"Is something wrong?" Mom nudges into me softly as I'm clearing the table. "You know you can tell us anything, right?"

"Of course I do. But I'm here with you guys. Everything is perfect."

"Look, sweetheart," Dad starts, shooting a knowing look at Mom. "We overheard you on the phone last night. We know what's going on."

My entire body goes still, fear spiking. "I'm not sure what you mean." I do my best to sound confident, but my voice still wobbles.

Mom takes the plate from me, setting it on the table. "What your dad is *trying* to say is that we think it's great you've invited your boyfriend here. We'll be on our best behavior, I promise."

"Oh. My boyfriend," I repeat, unsure if I should correct them. Which option is worse? Trying to explain why I suddenly need my friend here, or letting them think Zeke is my boyfriend. The fewer questions they ask, the better.

I just hope Zeke sees it the same way.

"We'll clean up here. You go get ready for the day."

"Are you sure?" I ask, eyeing the dusting of flour through-out the kitchen.

"We made the mess, so it's our responsibility to clean it up. Go on, now."

After grabbing the items I need, I make my way to the main-floor bathroom — the only one with a shower. I check my phone once more before stepping beneath the hot spray, but Zeke still hasn't messaged me. He never did say how long his shift was at the Guild, but I don't want him to show up while I'm preoccupied. If he ends up stuck with my parents, who fucking knows what they'll say?

I finish in record time, drying off quickly and getting dressed before braiding my wet hair. By the time I check my phone, I find a message waiting.

Zeke: Just finished my shift. See you in a few.

Sent six minutes ago. Shit! I toss my dirty clothes in the laundry hamper and race from the bathroom. I need shoes, a jacket, my bag and slate, and I need it all before—

Knock, knock, knock.

Grabbing my shoes, I practically jump out the front door, startling Zeke. Maybe if we hurry, we can just leave, get away before they notice.

If only I were so lucky.

"Is that him?" Mom calls.

Panic welling inside me, I do the only thing I can think of in the moment. I drop my shoes, wrap my arms around Zeke, and whisper, "Just go with it, okay?" I don't give him a chance to answer before my mouth presses to his, and fire ignites in my belly.

The kiss is supposed to be chaste, a light touch with no ramifications, but the moment he breaks free of the shock, he wraps me up in his arms and holds me there.

When it ends, all I can do is look at him, this angel who confounds me. And it's only when my parents speak that the spell fades away.

"Hayliel! Bring that boyfriend of yours inside so we can meet him."

I take a deep breath, then mouth the words *I'm sorry* to Zeke before pulling him through the door. He comes willingly, even if he is two paces behind. Maybe I should have told him the plan first, but I worried he wouldn't come at all if he knew. He hates me, and the only reason he's even sticking around now is to find out what the demons, and the angels helping them, are up to.

"Ezekiel, these are my parents. Parents, this is Zeke." I wave my arm between them. "Great, now that that's settled, we'll—"

"Hey, not so fast," Dad says. "I'm Camael. It's nice to meet you."

"And I'm Maribella. You'll have to excuse us. Our Haylie-bear has never brought a boy home before, so we're a little excited," Mom adds, causing my face to flame.

Kill me now.

"Oh, she hasn't?" Zeke asks, throwing me a wink. "Well, then I'm glad to be the first. It's an honor to meet the angels who raised such a wonderful woman."

Mom laughs. "Charming, I see. But you're right, you know. She's pretty amazing. I think this calls for the baby book. Don't you agree, Cam?"

"Archangels, no. We'll be in my room," I tell them before my Mom can go find the damn book, pushing Zeke toward the stairs. As I pass my parents, I whisper, "Best behavior my ass."

Dad laughs and calls out far louder than necessary, "Leave the door open a crack, you two. I don't want any funny business in my house."

I drag a palm down my face, somehow both surprised at how today's gone and also not. Things are never easy, are they?

Zeke looks around the bedroom that may not have been my childhood room, but holds enough trinkets from my past to be damn close. He eyes the family pictures Mom put up on the wall. There's even a few of Dina and me when we were younger. I don't say anything, only watch him as he takes in the brief glimpses of my life with a look of awe, or maybe even reverence, on his face. A far cry from the usual grumpy frown. It's kind of ... nice.

Memories flash through my mind of another night when he seemed happy in my company, one that feels like a million miles away yet was only a few months. If I close my eyes, I can still feel the touch of the brush while he painted my cheeks, the feel of his arms wrapped around me while we flew through the sky, and the taste of his kiss as he brought me to ruin.

"It's cozy," he says, hauling me back from my trip down memory lane. "Nothing like my childhood room."

"Oh, my childhood room was far cozier than this. My parents only moved here recently, when I started school, actually. Another family needed our old apartment, and they were shipped off here."

Our gazes collide, and I feel all the things he isn't saying. Anger for my family. Sadness for me. And maybe even a little regret, but I can't piece together why.

"So what is it I'm supposed to just be going with?" he asks, changing the subject.

I collapse on the edge of the bed, lying back and covering my eyes with my arm. "They overheard us talking last night. Not everything," I add before he can ask, "but enough to know I'd invited someone over. With that, and my apparently strange behavior, they assumed I could only be worried about introducing them to my boyfriend. I didn't really know what else to tell them, so I just sort of went with it. I'm sorry. I should have told you about it first instead of forcing you into a weird situation."

Zeke comes to sit next to me on the bed, far enough away that we aren't touching. "Look, it's fine. I can't exactly be too mad about it after that kiss you offered earlier. Besides, your parents seem pretty great, and I'll get to look through your baby book," he teases.

I sit up, eyes wide with fake outrage. "Don't you dare!"

We're close now, the heat of his thighs reaching my own. And in this moment, the shit we've been going through doesn't seem all that insurmountable. Is it truly possible for us to put aside our past and move forward? Could we be more than just half friends? Fucking hell. I'm a mess. I don't even know what Raphael, Theo, and I are, and here I am trying to complicate things even further.

Mom's voice echoes down from the foot of the stairs. "Cookies are ready! I've left the baby book for now, so you're safe to come up."

"Coming!" I yell back before turning to Zeke. "Are you sure you're okay with this? I'd understand if you're not. You didn't exactly sign up to play boyfriend."

He leans forward, dropping a soft kiss to my forehead, and I wonder if maybe he won't respond at all. But when he does, I almost wish he hadn't. "That's where you're wrong, hummingbird. I chose you first, but you chose them."

His voice is calm as he speaks, as if he's dropping facts from a history book instead of trying to carve my heart up, but it does all the same. I want to ask him about it, dive deep into whatever drives him to believe that I chose anyone at all in the beginning. There's no choice to make if he takes himself out of the running.

A little voice in the back of my head whispers, *Silly little girl. He's right, you know? You did choose. Raphael and Theo shared you in that prayer tent. Remiel saw your choice. And while that* might be true, it doesn't explain the month's worth of Zeke's hatred.

We don't have time to discuss it, heading up instead to sit with my parents. We play the dating couple well while Mom and Dad grill Zeke about his life. I listen on as he tells them about his internship at the Guild, finding myself wholly fascinated and realizing that there's so much I don't know about him.

"Your parents must be so proud of everything you accomplished," Mom says brightly.

In a move so slight I don't think my parents have noticed, Zeke flinches. "Thank you. My dad is, and I'd like to think my mom would be too. She died when I was young, so it's just been Dad and me."

He tries to hide it, but pain seeps from his words in such a rush that Mom is out of her seat and pulling Zeke into a hug.

"I didn't know her, but I can tell you that a parent's love is unstoppable, even in death. Don't forget that."

"I won't," Zeke replies, his usually husky voice turned soft, belying the emotions he's trying to hide.

This angel is like a foreign species, with so many facets to him I wonder if I ever really knew him at all. Some of my anger falls away. We're all dealing with something. Whether it's the loss of a parent, the death of a dream, or something else entirely. And maybe we shouldn't be judging one another without all the facts. Resolve settles in my gut. Zeke and I are going to talk. We'll get to the bottom of whatever this is between us once and for all, and as scared as I am for that conversation, there's a part of me that yearns for it, too.

"We should probably get going," I say, remembering our purpose.

"Oh?" Dad asks, eyeing us suspiciously. "Have a hot date or something?"

I roll my eyes, laughing. "So what if we did, huh?"

"Well, I'd tell you to stay out of trouble and remind you that you're too young to have kids."

"Archangels' blessings, you did not just say that." Heat rises to my cheeks as I tug Zeke toward the front door.

"Have fun!" Mom calls out through a giggle.

Mortification keeps me silent as we take the same path to the shops I took last night. Zeke is quiet too, and part of me wants to know why. Is he as embarrassed as I am? Does he regret coming here at all, despite his sweet words in my room? Fuck, he's probably upset about his mom. I want to ask him about it, plunge into his brain and learn all I can about him and the things he's gone through, but I don't know that he'd let me.

If nothing else comes from this, I pray to the Archangels that we'll at least find answers and make this whole awkward situation worth it.

We finally reach the street with all the shops, and I pull Zeke into the café. He follows along willingly, if not a bit preoccupied, and I wonder if maybe he's having the same thoughts I did when I first stumbled upon this street. Why do the Fallen have their own shopping district, and what does it mean for the future?

I drop my bag on the seat, waiting for him to get seated before I ask, "Chocolate or vanilla?"

He barely takes a second to think about it before he replies, "Both."

A smile curves my lips as I walk up to the register, but something zips over my flesh before I get there. A strange man sits at a table in the corner opposite ours. His clothes look worn and filthy, his fingers stained with color, and he's watching me.

My heart thrashes as I order the café's signature drink: a caffeinated milkshake. The barista throws me a weird look when I ask for half vanilla ice cream and half chocolate, but I don't really care. Angels have been throwing me weird looks for as long as I can remember, and rarely ever about my order preferences.

I snag two straws and head back to Zeke with the large drink in hand, doing my best to ignore the man still watching me.

"I ordered it just like before, babe," I say to Zeke, hoping he'll understand the look in my eyes. "Happy anniversary!"

He stops me from sitting in the seat beside him and tugs me into his lap instead. "This is the only seat you ever need, hummingbird." His lips tip up devilishly as he adds, "Well, I can think of one other place I wouldn't mind you sitting."

Panty. Melting.

His hand rests on my ass and I lean into him, wishing my hair was down to cover the words I desperately need to share with him and also wishing some of this was real and not just a charade. But between being watched and what we're here to do, I can't let myself get distracted.

His free hand moves to my neck, guiding my lips to his. Everything fades away as I let him tug me into the kiss, except it never lands. He shifts me slightly, trailing his nose down the curve of my neck and placing a kiss there instead.

"The guy in the corner. Do you recognize him?"

When I shake my head, it's barely a movement at all. "Oh, no you don't," I say playfully. "I made you wait at least a few dates before *that*."

We drink the shake, acting like we're blissfully in love and ignoring the angel in the corner. I just want him to leave, but it's obvious that he's going to follow our lead. Fuck.

We pack up, holding hands and walking down the street like we really are just a couple out for a stroll. I casually point out the places I saw Roderick arguing with angels, and Zeke makes a spur-of-the-moment decision to cross the road and walk up that side of the street.

Sometime while shopping, our tagalong leaves us, likely getting bored when he realizes we're not a threat, and finally I can breathe a little better. At least for a few seconds, before I realize which street corner we're standing on. The dead end.

My hands are clammy as I think about the man I left lying on the ground. Could I have saved him? Will we find his body there, or has someone already removed it?

Zeke tugs me with him so abruptly, I have to bite my tongue not to make a sound. Then he's pressing me into the wall and I struggle to pull air into my lungs.

His teeth nip at my earlobe, causing shivers to race across my flesh. "Is this the street where you saw the body?" he whispers, keeping his voice low.

"Yes," I reply, trying to ignore the feel of his hard body against mine, and the very obvious bulge I feel pressing against me. There's no denying the thrill of excitement I get from knowing that he wants this too. He may act like he wants nothing to do with me most of the time, but his body can't lie. He's enjoying this just as much as I am.

"Shh," he whispers, gripping my neck as he pulls back until we're finally face-to-face. The heat I find within his green eyes must surely match mine. He trails his gaze down my face, to my lips, and just as I'm positive he'll kiss me, he pulls away.

Focus, Hayliel. You have a job to do, and it's not time to ride his dick.

I count to thirty, trying to cool down my throbbing core and chill the fuck out, but then we're tiptoeing down the street, keeping close to the wall. Until we know what we're walking into, it's best we go unnoticed.

It's weird being back here, but I'm glad to have someone with me this time. Maybe revisiting this place while it's empty will help me replace the memory of that night so I can actually sleep tonight.

Except we're not alone.

Someone paces at the end of the street. Four steps away. Four steps back. He's talking to himself, seeming angry, but I can't make out the words enough to understand why. That nasal voice, though, is hard to forget. Roderick.

Shit.

I mouth the name to Zeke, but he doesn't follow, so I point and make a stabbing motion instead. Well, he certainly can't mistake that.

On the other side of the wall, the pacing stops. Roderick's muttering continues, but now there's a new sound. A distinct tapping that I bet must be from his slate. Who's he talking to, I wonder?

We stand as exposed as I was last night, listening to the man who took the life of an angel because he wasn't part of the plan. I want to laugh at our stupidity. What were we thinking? What was *I* thinking? I guess I assumed he'd be long gone from this place and that maybe we'd find a clue to where he lived so we could break in and snoop. But now, hiding behind the wall from the same angel who appeared in my nightmare last night, I'm not sure what the plan is.

Zeke, on the other hand, has no such worries. He pulls something from his pocket, presses a button, and suddenly he's holding a thick bat. Before I can get his attention to ask him what the fuck he's doing, he creeps closer, moving as silent as a soft breeze.

When he's close enough, he swings the bat so hard he knocks Roderick off his feet, and before he gets back up, Zeke kicks him in the face and knocks him out cold.

"Umm, what the hell was that?" I ask him while staring at Roderick's limp form. He's got a thick nose and bushy eyebrows, but otherwise he just looks like anyone else. If I saw him on the street, I'd never know he was a murdering psycho.

"The way I see it is we need answers, and he's going to give them to us."

"Right," I reply, unsure if this part of the plan was smart or idiotic. I guess we'll find out.

I take in the scene, then look up to the sky and realize we're practically begging someone to come find us. Fuck. Whose dumb idea was it to come here again? Alright, fine. So it was mine. But to actually attack and confront this murderer? Well, that's all Zeke.

"Tell me again how things went last night," he says, placing a pair of cuffs on Roderick. Does he have a tickle trunk in his pants or something? Where does he keep pulling this shit from?

"Roderick was here with a few angels. He wasn't happy about something. One of his minions spilled the beans on their plan or something. Then another guy dropped in from the sky, and that's who Roderick killed. When I left, he was lying there." I point to a spot not too far from where Roderick lay now. "Then they all went into a building, but I'm not sure which one."

"Azrael said he found the body, but we're trying to keep this whole thing under wraps until we know more." Zeke moves from door to door until he finds one unlocked. The door creaks and groans when he opens it, just like it did last night. I go still, wondering if maybe we should have scoped it out a bit more before being as loud as fucking possible and alerting anyone to our presence, but no one comes.

We drag Roderick inside to an empty room where Zeke dumps him unceremoniously into a corner before searching his still form. I ignore him in favor of scoping out the place. He can handle the unconscious murdering angel, and I'll make sure we're not about to get ambushed. Luckily, the rest of the rooms are empty, minus a few unpacked boxes and garbage.

When I look back, Zeke is holding an unfamiliar blade.

"Uh ... is that what I think it is?" I whisper, keeping my voice low like I'll avoid waking the knocked-out piece of shit on the floor.

"Better in our hands than his." He attaches the holster to his jeans before carefully slotting the blade into place and covering it once more with his shirt. He moves so fast that I don't have time to really examine it.

"So, did you have a plan for after you knocked him out cold, or was that it?"

"Not to be rude," he starts, but I know far too well that when someone says that it's usually followed by something dickish. "But it's not like you had a better idea. Now we have the blade in our possession, and when this fucker wakes up, I'll convince him to give me some answers."

"And how exactly do you intend to convince the murdering traitor to spill all his secrets, Zeke? Use some sick torture methods from the Guild?"

"If it comes to that. Look, when he wakes, I want you to stand watch at the door."

"Hell no. I'm not leaving you alone with—"

"I'm a trained Guild intern. I can handle myself. What I can't handle is having this disgusting piece of filth see your face and know who you are."

An exasperated sigh leaves my lips and I start pacing. *What a dick.* This guy shows zero fucking mercy, and Zeke wants to convince him to help us while I sit outside like a prissy little girl? The plan is idiotic, and he's an asshole for asking me to hide.

I don't know how much time has passed before Roderick finally stirs, shifting his bound arms uncomfortably.

"Go, please," Zeke asks quietly, his eyes filled with enough emotion that I can't argue.

I think it's the first time I've seen him look scared. Or maybe not the first time. After the attack at SCU, he watched me like a hawk. Is this why he wants me out of the room? Not because he thinks I can't handle it, but because he wants to *protect* me. Ugh. Why can't he just come right out and tell me how he feels or what he's thinking?

I stand with my back against the wall of the hallway, listening for any sign of a struggle. I'll hide out here like a good little girl, if that's what Zeke wants, but if it sounds like he needs my help, even for a second, I'm going in.

"You've made a big mistake, little boy," Roderick snarls.

"Yeah? Why's that?" Zeke replies, his voice devoid of emotion.

"You're sticking your head in where it doesn't belong. The last angel who did that lost his life. Do you really want to share his fate?"

Zeke laughs. "You realize you're handcuffed and I'm the one standing free, right?"

"Cocky, cocky. Not to worry. I'll be out of here soon, and then we'll see who's laughing."

"While we wait for your daring escape, why don't you explain your involvement in the theft of a Guild armory?"

Roderick sucks in a breath. "There's been a theft at the Guild? This is certainly the first I'm hearing about it," he says, his tone full of false surprise.

"Cut the shit. Where can I find the items you stole?"

"If I did steal anything, and I didn't, I probably wouldn't tell the guy who has me handcuffed, would I? But I might have dropped off a few things of my own in your mama's wet cunt."

There's a *thump* followed by the sound of someone spitting. Good. I hope Zeke made him bleed for that comment.

"Listen," Roderick says, sounding bored. "This has been fun and all, but I grow tired of your childish questions."

Before Zeke can even respond, there's a loud popping sound, followed by the jangling of metal. Things take a turn for the worse after that. There's a scuffle and a few grunts, but I can't figure out who's winning the fight from my stupid place hiding outside the room.

I'll give him another minute to get his shit together and then, after that, I'm going in. I'd rather have this piece of shit see me than lose Zeke.

Who am I kidding? I barely make it another thirty seconds. After a few loud crashes from the other room, I dash around the corner and come to a complete halt.

Zeke has Roderick in a hold. One arm loops around his throat, the opened end of the handcuffs held tight in his grip and pulling Roderick's arm back in an incredibly uncomfortable way. But it's Zeke's other hand that has me stopped in my tracks.

In his fist is the angel blade, the sharp point pressed into Roderick's side. Any sudden movements and that blade will slip between his ribs and end his life. But would Zeke actually do that? Could he kill another angel?

From the way Zeke holds him, Roderick can't see me, but even if he could, I wouldn't be able to move. My limbs are frozen, unable to retreat to the hallway, and terrified to see how this all plays out.

"Answer my questions, and I'll think about letting you live."

"I've already told you everything I—"

"Don't fucking tempt me, Roderick," Zeke grits out, his voice hard and menacing, and somehow the very sound of it has my core tightening with need. *Not the fucking time, vagina.*

"Shit," Roderick mutters, clearly realizing there's no getting out of this. And even if he escapes, Zeke's threat is clear enough. We know his looks, his name, and we'll send the entire Guild after him if we have to.

"How did you get this blade?" Zeke asks, changing tactics.

"My boss gave it to me."

"Who's your boss?"

"I don't know. He's a mistrusting son of a bitch so I haven't met him directly yet."

"Why did you steal weapons from the Guild?" Zeke continues, not letting up on his rapid-fire questions. It's kind of hot to see him this way, all domineering and demanding, as long as I ignore the fact that he's holding such a deadly weapon.

"Fuck," Roderick mumbles, "I don't know that either. Look, I'm on a need-to-know fucking basis, alright? Only fools give away the master fucking plans."

"So what you're saying is you're useless."

"No!" Roderick squeaks in his nasally as fuck voice. "I know where the weapons are. Just don't kill me."

"Where are they?"

"In an old building near the river that divides this area from the rest of Silver City. That's where you'll find the stolen goods."

"If I find out you're lying, don't think for a second that I won't use this," Zeke tells him, shifting the blade slightly. He's convincing, I'll give him that. Even I believe the threat.

"So mistrusting! That's where I was told to bring them. Whether or not you believe me, it's the truth." Roderick's voice comes out weird, every few words broken out by an inhale, like he can't get enough oxygen.

"We'll see about that." Zeke moves fast, hitting Roderick's temple so hard that he slumps to the floor. He puts the wicked blade back in its sheath before securing the cuffs again.

"Come on. We need to go."

20

EZEKIEL

The familiar beat of my heart pounds through my skull as we slowly exit the building. Blood rushes through my veins like water, my heart pumping it faster and faster until I know for certain that Hayliel is safe.

Knocking Roderick out might not have been my smartest move, especially not with Hayliel here. I can play hard and fast with my own life just fine, but not hers. Never hers.

Hayliel stops for a moment, staring at the discarded slate lying on the ground with contemplation lining her gorgeous face. Even with danger looming, she's stunning.

"Leave it," I tell her. "We don't need it to be used to track us down." Hell, I considered taking the device myself, but the risks are too high and far outweigh any potential rewards. Maybe I can tip off Azrael again, and if we're lucky, that asshole will still be tied up and unconscious. Before I do anything, though, I have to think, weigh out the pros and cons of getting him involved again. It might mean having to explain everything to him, and I'm not entirely sure that's a good idea.

Hayliel nods, and we take off down the street. We walk at a manageable pace, not running but not out for a leisurely stroll, either. The last thing we need is to bring any unwanted attention to ourselves.

I take us down another street, changing up the route back to Hayliel's parents' house on the off chance we're being followed. If she notices, I can't tell, but she seems preoccupied. Lost in thought.

Finally, she asks, "How likely do you think it is that there's actually an old building between districts that just so happens to hold the stolen weapons?"

I keep silent, walking us to the next street, and shoot her a sideways glance. "I think it's pretty likely."

"But why? Roderick's a murderer and a criminal. Not exactly the most trustworthy angel. Plus, you were holding him at knifepoint and threatening his life. I wouldn't put it past him to lie or smudge the truth a bit. There could be any number of old buildings near the lake."

Fuck. She always likes to know everything, doesn't she? I let out a sigh, stopping to turn in her direction. "There are several, but there's only one close to the Fallen district."

Instead of responding, she only watches me, her gaze roaming over my face like she's trying to figure me out. She always sees way too fucking much.

To my surprise, she doesn't question me further on it, only nods and continues the brisk walk.

"What should we do with that blade?"

"I've been asking myself that since we left. Part of me feels like I should give it to the Guild right away, along with Roderick's name, but ..."

"The mole," she finishes for me. Sometimes we're so in sync that it terrifies me. Like we share the same mind. Is our bond as strong as the one she has with Raphael? The one I've been doing my best not to think about since learning how deep theirs is and seeing it in action during the attack at SCU. Fuck.

"Exactly. I don't think it's wise to carry this deadly thing around, but I don't want it getting back into their hands. Without knowing who to trust, I can't just hand it over, you know?"

"I know," she says, reaching out to entwine her fingers with mine. "We'll hold on to it for now and see how things play out with Azrael and the body. Maybe we'll learn something about who's on our side and who isn't."

Her skin is soft and warm, soothing the turmoil raging inside me. She's right, of course. Depending on the information that spreads about my tip-off to Azrael, it'll help us determine who our allies are. And something tells me we're going to need as many as we can get.

"If you want to leave, I can cover with my parents. I know this wasn't exactly what you signed up for." She laughs, but her heart isn't in it. And after what we've just gone through, I don't think it's good for her to be alone yet.

"No. That would only make them suspicious, I think. Besides, I want to stay. Your mother promised me a look through that baby book, remember?"

This time when she laughs, her eyes sparkle and dance with genuine amusement. Good. This is what she needs to help move past what happened last night and today with Roderick.

"Do you need any more frosting?" Maribella asks.

"I think we're good, Mom," Hayliel replies, laughing. "Though I think I messed this one up, so Zeke and I should probably eat it, right? Wouldn't do to give such an awfully decorated cookie to the Archangels, now would it?"

"Ha!" Camael sits down at the table across from us. "Well played, daughter of mine. I think I'll be messing up my next one, too."

Since arriving back at the house, Hayliel's parents have kept us busy preparing offerings for the Archangels. I've also learned more about Hayliel in these few hours than I ever thought to. Her old school, and the bullies there. It's no wonder she kept her wings a secret when we first met. I wish I'd have known that earlier. Maybe things could have been different.

Their family traditions cause a dark hole to open in my chest. If Mom was still alive, would we have made a big deal out of this feast thing too? I don't really remember what we did before she passed, and after she died, Dad and I were just so fucking broken. Me for losing a mother, and him for losing the love of his life.

"This is the last batch, and then we'll have everything ready for our offering," Maribella says, taking a seat beside Camael, who's munching on a cookie.

"You ever play crokinole, Zeke?"

"Hmm, I don't think so. Is that even a real word?"

"What?" Hayliel adds, putting the finishing touches on her cookie. The depth and dimension she adds to the Archangel wings just from frosting blows my goddamn mind. "Really?"

"Really. What is it? A card game?"

All three members of the Gracelin family suck in a breath. Uh-oh.

"Code red," Camael whispers, and if I hadn't caught the smile tilting the corner of Hayliel's mouth, I might have been worried.

"Zeke, let's go wash up, and then I'll explain the rules while we put everything together in the backyard. My parents can finish here."

I chuckle. "Why do I have a feeling that I'm not at all prepared for crokinole?"

We wash our hands in silence, each of us watching the other in the mirror as we wipe away the frosting and cookie crumbs.

We've come a long way since our excursion this morning. From holding a criminal hostage to decorating cookies, and now I'm about to play a game with my pretend girlfriend's family. It's surreal.

Hayliel asks me to set up the table and chairs on the deck while she grabs the game board and pieces. The evening air is chilly, so I start a fire in the pit near the table. When I'm finished, I glance toward Hayliel, and all the air in my lungs freezes. Draped across her delicate shoulders is my jacket. The one I placed on her shoulders in the library all those weeks ago. Does she know it's mine?

Before I spiral down that path, Hayliel motions me over and gives me a rundown of the rules. It seems simple, in theory. Flick the little disc and try to get it in the center hole or as close to it as I can. Of course, there are other rules. If the other team's disc is in play, then mine has to hit theirs for it to be a valid move. Easy, peasy.

Except it's fucking *hard*. I've only just managed to get the right pressure in my flick not to shoot the disc straight to the other side of the board, so I've mostly been on defense while my partner, Maribella, gets us points.

We're setting up for one more game — one I know they're only playing to give me a chance to redeem myself — this time with Hayliel on my team, but it means she has to sit across from me. Before she can get up to switch seats with her Mom, I reach over to cup her cheek.

"I love it when you wear my clothes," I tell her. It's a treat to watch her eyes widen when she realizes what I'm saying. *Yes, hummingbird. It's mine. You thought I only hated you, but the truth is so much worse.*

"Archangels' blessing," Maribella coos at us. "Aren't they just the cutest, Camael? I don't think I've ever seen our Haylie-bear so happy."

"Mom," my fake girlfriend whispers to her mom, clearly embarrassed. But if I only get this one day to pretend to have everything I've ever wanted, I'm going to make the most of it. Having Hayliel as my own might not be in the cards for me, but I'm going to soak up every ounce of this pretend relationship, and maybe it'll be enough.

I don't know whether it was the first game as practice, or the rush of joy zinging through me knowing that Hayliel wore my jacket and I apparently make her happier than anyone ever has, but somehow we win the next game.

Maribella and Camael offer for me to sleep on the couch, but I don't think that's such a good idea. The blade is still strapped beneath my shirt, and I really need to figure out what the hell I'm going to do with it. Not to mention the fact that I'm not even sure I could sleep so close to Hayliel and actually stay on the couch. *Temptation is thy name.*

While her parents say goodnight, Hayliel and I head down to her room. where I think we'll finally be able to talk about things in private. Except her idea of private differs from mine.

"We need to call Raphael and Theo."

I sigh. "Do we really though?"

"Yes," she says, taking my hand and leading me to the bed. I envisioned a very different outcome from this act. "I know you don't like them, but they're my friends and they want to figure this shit out just as much as we do. Today, with you, has been incredible, Zeke. Maybe not that whole bit with Roderick, but the rest ... it reminds me of that night before classes started. I like *that* Zeke. I want to spend time with him, and I think others would too. Please don't revert back to Mr. Grumps."

I stare into her eyes as her words hit me like a boulder, straight in the chest. Is this what Theo was trying to tell me? Swallowing past the lump in my throat, I nod. "I'll try."

She puts the phone on speaker, volume low so her parents don't hear, and we sit huddled on the bed while we wait for them to answer.

"Hey, sunshine. Miss me already, do you?" Raphael says in his cocky fucking voice.

"You know I do," Hayliel tells him. "Theo, you there?"

"Hi. Yup. I'm here, firefly. What's going on? How did everything go with Ezekiel?"

"Yeah, how was it? Did that asshole treat you like shit, because if he did—"

"That asshole is on the call too, and no, I didn't treat her like shit. As a matter of fact, her parents loved meeting her *boyfriend* and think they've never seen her happier," I add, smugly.

"Fake boyfriend." Hayliel slaps my arm as noise erupts through the phone. Shit. Right, I was supposed to be on my best behavior. Someone should have told them the fucking same.

"Enough. My parents heard me invite someone and automatically assumed it was my boyfriend. I thought it was easier to just go with it. Zeke and I are fine, but we have some news, and that's why I'm calling. We think we found out where the stolen weapons are stashed."

"Huh?" Raphael asks. "What do you mean, *you think*?"

"I brought Zeke down the path I took when I saw Roderick the first time, and we actually ran into him. Zeke knocked him out. We stole the angel blade and—"

"Back the fuck up," Theo says, shocking Hayliel and me. Not that I've talked to him a lot, but even when he was lecturing me last night, I don't think he ever sounded this pissed off. "You attacked Roderick, knowing he had a fucking blade and a murdering streak? With Hayliel right there in harm's way? What the fuck were you thinking?"

Well, he's definitely pissed, and it looks like it's all directed at me. Sure, it might not have been my finest hour, but I knew what I was doing.

"I took advantage of the opportunity that presented itself and got a mighty fine lead, I might add. Besides, I would never let anything happen to her. You, of all angels, should know that."

The line goes silent, and Hayliel's brows are creased in confusion. Shit. I probably shouldn't have said that last part. Fuck!

"I don't want to argue over who's right or wrong. The fact is, it's done, and Zeke got Roderick to open up a bit. He's kept out of the loop on most things, so he couldn't tell us who his boss is or anything like that, but he told us about an old building near the lake between Pure and Fallen districts."

"Give me a second," Theo says. We hear some shuffling around on his end of the line before he starts tapping away, likely looking up the area on a map. "There are a few buildings this could be, mostly storage buildings or warehouses."

"It's none of those," I say, my chest aching. "Follow the separation between the production and farming districts, then cross the lake. There's a building there that looks more like an old house. That's the one."

"But how do you know that?"

"I just do." The tone of my voice offers no further argument on the subject, and I expect it to start a fight, but no one questions me further.

"Alright. So that's the building. How do we know this isn't a trap? And if we don't know for sure one way or the other, shouldn't the Guild investigate instead of us?"

"Their lives matter just as much as ours do," I say, annoyed.

"That isn't what I'm fucking saying, Ezekiel. They're better equipped than any of us to scout the area and get those weapons back."

Hayliel rubs her fingers up my cheek, over my temple, and across my forehead, soothing me.

I take a deep breath before speaking again, realizing that whatever my personal feelings are on how the Pures see Guild members, they don't matter here. I'm not dealing with purist shits who think the Fallen are a waste of space in Silver City. But damn, is it ever hard to move past.

"Until we know who we can trust, I'd rather we only involve the Guild when absolutely necessary. I think it best if I check it out myself, discreetly."

Hayliel's sigh is so loud it's almost a groan. "Zeke, I'm only going to say this once. You. Are. Not. Going. Alone. I understand that might be hard to accept, but you have friends now, angels on your side, and we are going to do this together. Except we're going to be smart about it and have a solid plan. Does everyone agree?"

"Yes."

"You know it."

"Fine," I grumble, not willing to recognize the warmth growing in my chest. "I'm back at the Guild in a few days, so I'll see what I can find out about how often patrols are in the area, recent call logs, that sort of thing."

There's more shuffling from Theo's end of the line before he adds, "I'll see if I can find any schematics for the building."

"Perfect. Raphael and I will keep on researching as we have been, though I'm limited here in the Fallen district. Let's all agree to keep each other informed and that *no one goes off to investigate anything alone.*" Hayliel stares at me as she speaks, and the scolding tone in her voice makes me want to smile.

Everyone agrees, and we end the call with a promise to catch up later. Then it's only Hayliel and me left, sitting alone on her bed. The moment feels charged somehow, and I wouldn't be surprised to find my hair standing up on end from the electricity coursing through me.

"I should go," I whisper without moving.

"Yeah. You probably should."

It takes every ounce of strength I have to tear my gaze away from hers and stand. My movements are stilted, uncomfortable, but I don't want to do anything to ruin the great day we had — erm, well, a *mostly* great day.

She stands, following me to the door of her bedroom, where I hesitate. Something stops me from going any further, like a whole other being controls my limbs.

"Thanks for today. And for, you know, pretending to be my boyfriend. I can't imagine that was easy for you."

I turn suddenly, finding her closer than expected. Close enough that when she sucks in a breath and releases it just as quickly, I feel it against my lips. "The hardest thing about today wasn't pretending to be your boyfriend or threatening Roderick. It's walking to this door and leaving you, hummingbird."

Gently, I grip her face in both my hands, my eyes glued to her lips, and when her pink tongue darts out to wet them, I'm gone. Swooping down, I press a fervent kiss to her lips, and she doesn't pull away. In fact, she pushes closer, molding her body to mine until it feels like I'm a whole fucking person again.

Kissing Hayliel is like zip-lining down a mountain. That second when you break through the clouds and catch the first glimpse of the world. Suddenly everything makes sense and the issues you thought seemed so big are barely a blip on your radar.

The need to take things further overwhelms me. Why the hell am I leaving when everything I want is right here, lips on mine, and seeming more than willing? Except this isn't a fairy tale, and I sure as fuck am not the hero who gets the girl. I'm just the foolish angel who couldn't see what was right in front of him.

I pull back slowly, trapping my yearning deep inside. As much as it kills me to admit it, she's happy. And even though I don't really know what type of relationships she has with Raphael and Theo, it's crystal clear that what they have is far more than what Hayliel and I have. Somewhere along the way, I stopped wanting to hate her, or even them, for that matter.

Finally, I extract myself from her and step back, putting some much-needed distance between us. Her pupils are blown with lust, and I soak it all in for one more second.

Tracing her cheek with my thumb, I give her one last remark. "If you ever need another fake boyfriend, I'm your angel." And then I'm off. Out the door and flying back to campus with a golden-winged angel firmly on my mind.

By the time I land on my balcony and head into my room, there's a new message on my slate.

Hayliel: Don't hate me, okay?

Dread settles in my gut as I contemplate what she means, but then I see another notification.

Hayliel Gracelin has added you to a chat.

She fucking didn't. There's no way this is a good idea. But when I click the notification, I realize that she absolutely fucking did.

My fake girlfriend just added me to a group chat with her real boyfriends.

This ought to be fun.

21

HAYLIEL

I roll out of bed two days later, feeling less than refreshed.

Sleep eluded me last night as I laid in bed thinking about how I should handle today. We're heading to the mountains to drop off our feast offerings to the Archangels, and that means flying.

Fuck. I should have told my parents about my wings the moment I arrived on their doorstep.

Hauling myself out of bed, I jump into the shower with hopes I'll find answers beneath the hot spray of water. I know I have to tell them. That's non-negotiable. But how can I do it without ruining their entire day?

When I'm dressed, I head upstairs, my feet dragging like I'm walking through sticky caramel. My parents have always accepted me, so why is it I feel this sense of dread, like maybe that's going to change? Gray wings are one thing, but gold? Maybe that's the metaphorical straw that will snap their support.

"Morning! We'll be taking off in fifteen minutes, so make sure you grab something to eat before the flight," Dad tells me when I enter the kitchen. He's sitting at the table, finishing his coffee and muffin while Mom puts the last few touches on our gifts.

Nausea builds in my stomach, but I chew through my banana-nut muffin and pretend that I'm not about to vomit.

"What's wrong, honey?" Mom asks at my side, pushing the hair from my face.

I can't stop the tears from welling behind my eyes or the tremble in my lip. Shit, shit, shit. Why am I so emotional about this?

"Before we go to the mountain, I have something to tell you."

"You know you can tell us anything." Both of my parents eye me with a mixture of worry and excitement, the latter of which I can't quite figure out what they're hoping for. Here goes nothing.

"I haven't been completely honest with you about what happened during the attack," I start, unsure how much to tell them. I can stick to the change in my wings, or I can tell them everything. About the way demons targeted me at school, the light my friends saw when I emerged from the safety of my wings and that it was me who killed those beasts in the end. Which option puts them in less danger?

Neither of them interrupts as they wait for me to continue. Taking a deep breath, I push on.

"My wings sort of transformed in battle, and I think that's what killed the demons."

Utter silence follows my words and brings apprehension to my chest.

"Transformed how, exactly?" Dad asks, before sharing a look with Mom.

"It's easier if I just show you." I stand from the table and move until there's enough room for my wings to break free without knocking anything over, then I take a deep, steadying breath.

On my exhale, I let my wings out.

"My word," Mom says, her eyes wide.

Dad looks equally shocked as he rubs his own before adding, "Mari, are you seeing this?"

I laugh nervously and wait for their disbelief to fade.

"You still weren't hurt during the battle, though, right?" Mom finally asks.

Her question causes my eyes to sting. Of course, she'd care more about the fact that I'm unharmed than anything else. What did I ever do to deserve these two?

"Nothing that didn't heal. I'm just a little more different now, that's all."

"Has anything else changed?" Dad asks, pursing his lips. "I didn't go to a fancy school or anything, but I've never heard of any angel transforming before, let alone killing demons with it. As far as I know, the Guild has the only thing capable of killing them."

"I don't think so. They itch to be let out more, but otherwise I just feel more whole somehow. And maybe I feel a little stronger, but that could just be all the training I've done at school over these last few months."

Mom rushes to me, pulling me into an embrace, and I melt into her arms. "I wish you'd have told us sooner."

Relief floods my system as I squeeze her tightly. "I know. Keeping it a secret was a shitty thing to do. I think I just needed time to come to terms with it on my own first."

"And have you?" Dad asks, coming forward to hug me too.

"Not really." I laugh. "But with us going to the mountains today, I ran out of time. Other than angels at school, I don't think anyone else knows. I've been kind of afraid to be seen with them out in public, so my friends brought me a black wing jacket to wear whenever I fly. It's what I'll be wearing when we go today."

"Those are some really fine friends," Mom says, clutching me for another second before pulling away. "Are you sure you're up for this? Your father can always take our offerings by himself if you aren't. We wouldn't think any less of you."

"I'm sure. To be honest, I'm excited to stretch my wings and fly free with you guys."

"Then let's load up and get on our way!" Dad adds excitedly.

While Dad helps me into the wing jacket, Mom double-checks our bags. They're packed full of every delicious piece of food she made, and if that's not the best offering the Archangels receive, I'll be surprised.

As soon as we're ready, we take off. Sunlight beams down on us as we fly toward the rocky mountain face. We aren't alone in the sky as other families follow the same path to deliver their offerings, too. When I was younger, we used to leave our offer until the last possible day, and it also meant waiting in line for hours with all the other families who had the same idea. Coming early like this guarantees we'll be back home within the hour.

We land on the cliff side and follow the pebble-lined path until we reach an overhang of rock. This place never ceases to amaze me. Nestled within the rock are swirls of a glowing ore I've only ever found here. And in the center of the shaded area stand four statues, one for each of the Archangels: Remiel, Mikhael, Auriel, and Shubael. The sculptures all look the same — carved depictions of their double wings, just like what we saw inside the offering tent — but they each have a sigil etched into the center of their wings to note which Archangel is which.

Dad pricks his finger and leans to press it to Auriel's mark on his statue, but I stop him.

"I know we always gift our offerings to Auriel, but could we gift them to Remiel this year?" Ever since entering that tent with Raphael and Theo, I've felt connected to him in a way I can't really explain. Maybe it's all in my head.

He smiles, then looks at Mom. She nods and says, "Auriel has always gifted us faith in return for our offerings, but maybe it's time for Remiel to help us find our path."

"Why don't you do the honors this year," Dad says, motioning for me to step forward. Excitement zips through me as I take the knife from him to cut the tip of my finger before smearing the blood on Remiel's sigil. I give him a silent prayer, and then we place our offerings on the empty pedestal in the middle of the statues. When everything is on there, we offer a word of thanks and then head home.

Joy buzzes beneath my skin, making me lightheaded as we fly. Today was a good day. My parents know about my wings and I'm *flying* with them out in the open. We've delivered our offerings. And now we can spend the rest of the break doing whatever we want.

When we're finally settled at home, I pull out my slate and bring up my notes on telepathy.

"Mom, Dad, grab whatever you need because your crash course in telepathy starts in five minutes."

A few days later, I drop onto my balcony at Fallen house and press my uncovered wing to the sensor. I feel a mix of disappointment and elation that I'm back at school. The classes, libraries, and opportunities to learn are abundant. Raphael, Theo, Zeke, and the rest of my friends are here. But Mom and

Dad aren't. They're stuck in a district I don't trust, with no clue what's going on beneath their noses.

I drop my bag in the corner and wander to my front door right as someone knocks. When I open it, four angels stare expectantly back at me.

Raphael rushes in first, pulling me into the bathroom before shutting the door and placing an intense kiss to my lips. Desire fills me as I kiss him back, and the rest of the world melts into nothing. He makes me feel out of control in the best possible way. I'm seconds from dropping my pants and having him fuck me right here against the door, but he draws back.

"Fuck, sunshine. I missed you."

"I missed you too, Raph."

I can't tell what it is he sees on my face, but he chuckles darkly and leans in to run his nose up my neck, stopping when his lips meet the shell of my ear. "Keep looking at me like that and I won't care who's on the other side of this door when I take that sweet pussy of yours."

I close my eyes, but not to stop from looking at him. Images rush through my mind of Raphael fucking me in here with Theo and Zeke listening through the door, only long enough for me to come once before they join in. *By the Archangels, I want that.*

Raphael chuckles, nipping at the shell of my ear. "You're safe for now, little sunshine."

When we exit the bathroom, Dina throws me a knowing smile that has my cheeks heating. Theo pulls me into his arms for a hug that steals my breath. He can always tell exactly what I need. When we separate, I find Zeke looking both annoyed and like he might want to pull me into the bathroom himself.

"How's it feel being the Archangels' favorite?" Dina asks as I sit beside her on the bed.

"Pretty damn good," I say, feigning confidence and leaning back, but I miscalculate and almost tumble off the bed.

She catches me and snorts a laugh. "Let's hurry and get the business crap out of the way so I can get to my good news."

"I'll go first," Zeke says, leaning against the wall like he did the last time we were all in Dina's room. "Azrael didn't learn much about the body he found in the Fallen district. He was able to identify him, though he's been tight-lipped with me about it and won't even give me a name. All he'll say is the man had a troubled past and turned his life around, but must have gotten in with the wrong crowd again. He also found out the man's address because he collected a box of belongings to examine. I fucking hate that he's keeping me in the dark, but I'm still pushing for information."

"Can you break into that room again like last time?" Raphael asks, sounding hopeful.

Zeke shakes his head. "No. Turns out, having him keep this off the Guild radar is both a blessing and a curse. We keep the mole in the dark, but now we're at Azrael's mercy for information sharing."

"Please don't take this the wrong way, but I have to ask. You don't find that's at all suspicious?" Theo asks, and he has a point. Keeping everything *unofficial* and not divulging any discoveries with the person who tipped him off is kind of sus.

"I don't. Azrael is like a second father to me. If he's keeping me in the dark, it's only from some misguided attempt to protect me. Not for anything nefarious."

Raphael looks like he wants to argue, but I cut him off. "If you trust him, Zeke, then so do we. But I still hope he can eventually tell you something that might help us."

"I found a few journals locked away in a cabinet that reference gold wings," Raph says, his voice filled with pride.

"You did?"

"I did. But don't get too excited. My ancestor wasn't really all there. I wasn't able to finish reading them all, so I brought them back with me. There was even a passage about a golden-winged angel standing on top of blackened, scorched earth. I couldn't remember if that's how the ground looked near the well after that flash of light, so I asked Theo to check."

"When I went to scope it out, the place had been recently dug up and redone with new seed. We might not have confirmation exactly, but there has to be a reason they tore up the ground, and it very well could be because the grass was burned."

Dina shifts on the bed and looks out the window, even though she can't see much of the campus from up here. "Yeah, it looks like they finished all the renovations over break. It's like nothing ever happened."

"If only that were true," I say with a sigh.

Silence falls over the room as I'm lost in thought. There are so many threads of information, and it's impossible for our little group to follow them all before they disappear. How are we supposed to get to the bottom of something like this?

"Look, I know things seem kind of shitty right now, but we've survived so many things. Attacks, interrogations, hell, even our own families. We need to let loose a little, and I have the perfect thing to help us do just that."

"Go on," I say, and notice Raphael and Theo leaning in closer.

"We're all going to the anything-but-clothes party tonight."

My eyebrows scrunch up in confusion. "The what?"

Instead of Dina, it's Raphael who answers. "Power house is throwing an anything-but-clothes party. Everyone is invited. The only stipulation is that guests must wear something other than clothes."

"And I've already got the perfect idea for our outfits," Dina adds with a satisfied smile. She turns to Zeke, eyebrow raised. "Wipe that look off your face, Ezekiel. When I say we're all going, that means you too."

He rolls his eyes, but I can tell it's all for show. He might have hated the Pures when we first met, but I think his hardshell exterior is beginning to crack.

Striding away from the wall, he heads toward my door, and disappointment settles over me like a cloud.

As if he can read my mind, Theo asks, "Where are you going?"

"Apparently, I have an outfit to make." Zeke throws me one more look before he exits my room.

Dina jumps up from my bed, throwing her fist in the air. "Yes! Alright, you guys go figure out what you're wearing. Hayliel and I have some crafting to do."

22

HAYLIEL

The room is quiet as I sit in Professor Uriel's classroom on Monday afternoon, waiting for him to arrive.

I put the meeting off for as long as possible, choosing to spend time doing literally anything else, like daydreaming about how much fun I had at the anything-but-clothes party. If it were up to me, I'd put this entire thing off indefinitely, but unfortunately that's not an option. Principal Cael messaged me while I was away and asked that I meet with my Wingology professor once I was back and settled. Apparently, he's to be my new point of contact instead of the school counselor that everyone else uses. It's bullshit.

What's even more strange is the fact that this whole thing was Professor Uriel's idea, or at least that's what it sounded like in the email. But he fucking hates me, so what's his angle? Last time I tried to get anything useful out of him turned out to be a waste of time, and I don't doubt that today will be the same. He's already six minutes late. Maybe I should force him to do something uncomfortable in front of a bunch of strangers and see how he likes it.

Just then, he barges through the door in a cloud of cologne. And not the good kind. The acrid scent settles in my throat, making me cough. I eye the door he just shut, wishing he'd left it open so I could get at least a little untainted air. *It's going to be a long day.*

"Right on time, Miss Hayliel," he says, like he hasn't kept me waiting. Asshole.

"Principal Cael said you thought it best to take over the school counselor's duties?" I pose it like a question, wondering — more like hoping — I'd just read the email wrong.

He nods once. "Well, I thought if anyone could help you through such a tremendous change, it would be me, a wing expert. Don't you agree?"

Uh, no. Definitely not. *Please tell me that question is rhetorical.*

I stay silent while he turns a student desk around to face me before dropping into the chair. "Right. Well, let's start with the basics. How are you fitting into your life here at SCU and what would you say your favorite class is?"

Did he really just ask that? He asks how I'm fitting in as if he doesn't fucking know how shitty it's been, even before the demon attack and my sudden change. "Fine," I say, not wanting to get into it. "I'd have to say my favorite classes are History and Angelic Powers. I like combat training as well."

"Good, good." Professor Uriel jots something down in his notebook — an actual physical book, not his slate — and I wonder if he's really taking notes or just making a list of all the ways he plans to ruin the rest of the semester for me.

"And are there any students or professors who have been giving you a hard time? More than the usual school shenanigans, of course." His voice is playful, a grin spreading across his face, but I'm not amused.

I only stare at him in complete shock. I want to laugh in his face, but not because what he said is funny. He knows firsthand what I've been going through because he eggs it on in class and piles on more shit himself. I wonder what his reaction would be if I came right out and told him to look in a fucking mirror because he's at the very top of my *least favorite professors* list.

As for the students, most have backed off since the demon attack — either in fear of what they think I can do or in awe of the same reason. Those that haven't are either backed up by his own shit in class or the Seraphinas of the world, so it wouldn't matter if I shit arrows that could take down the entire demon population. She'd still find a reason to hate me.

Angels aren't just born to be bullies, though. They usually act that way because of something going on at home or elsewhere in their lives. Something that makes them feel small or out of control, so they drag others down to feel better or cause chaos for someone else in order to take control back. It's not right, but I can sympathize enough not to call them out. Whether or not Professor Uriel will do something is beyond me, but I don't want to risk causing more strife for someone who's clearly already struggling.

"For the most part, things have calmed down for me recently," I tell him, finally answering his question. "I have a wonderful support system to rely on which helps."

"Recently, as in since your transformation?" His eyes glint as he watches me, and I don't like the way it makes me feel.

"Yes. Since the attack."

"Interesting. I'm glad you brought this up—" *But I didn't. You did.* "—as I have several questions for you."

Part of me is curious where this will go, given the track record of our conversations so far, but I try to be positive. *Parents, lend me your optimism!*

"I'll try to answer your questions, Professor Uriel, but there isn't much to tell."

"Other than your wings, have you noticed any other changes?"

I sit up straighter, not expecting that question. Have I? I let my mind wander over the past few weeks, trying to pinpoint anything that might be important, but there are too many variables. Am I stronger because of my wings or is that just because I've been working hard? My wings *feel* different beneath my flesh, but that's probably expected after a transformation. Right? Then there's the random hot flashes, but those seem to only happen when I'm paranoid or actually think I might get killed.

To him, I don't say any of this. If he wants to keep tight-lipped when I ask for help, then I sure as shit won't be offering up my answers to him on a silver platter.

"No, not really. I just feel like me." While it's the truth, it's not exactly the whole truth. I feel so much more like myself than I ever have before. But it's not the me from before, it's the me I always could have been but never knew. Something just feels right. Whole. And for the first time in my entire existence, I'm comfortable with who I am.

"Good, good. Please let me know if anything develops. It's completely normal in cases like this for new powers and abilities to manifest, so don't be frightened."

"This has happened in the past, then?" I ask, catching on to his slip.

"Oh, I can't say for certain that this, uh, specific issue has occurred before, just that it's common in big changes."

He's such a shitty liar. Rambling after slipping up is a dead giveaway, but I don't press him on it now. Instead, I mentally toss the information into the odd-behavior bucket with the rest of the shit he's done. I can deal with it later.

"Speaking of, have you and your friends discovered anything of note?"

I wish he'd wipe the creepy smile off his face. It does nothing to soothe my discomfort and only sets me more on edge. The tilt of his lips doesn't meet his eyes. He looks more crazed than happy or comforting. *Fuck, I just want to get out of here.*

"No, unfortunately. Do you have any resources you could lend us that might hold some helpful information?" I press, knowing his answer even before he speaks. But it hits me then that he knows we've been researching. How? Did we tell him, or maybe the principal? I don't think we did, but then how does he know? Dread settles in my gut. Has he been following us?

"I'm afraid not, no. And I truly don't think you'll find anything, either."

His words should disappoint me, and maybe they would if I were someone else, but I've had more professors tell me what a failure I am than I've had new socks. Now, it only spurs me on.

I check the time on my slate and wince. I've been trapped in here for thirty minutes already. How much longer will he keep me here?

"That would be unfortunate," I reply, then stand. "Is that all, Professor?"

"Oh, no. We're only just getting to the good stuff. Sit down, Miss Hayliel."

I drop into my seat, holding back my groan so I don't offend him and make things worse.

"You mentioned students and staff have treated you differently since your, uh, miraculous change. Do you think that has to do with the rumors flying around about your triumph on the battlefield?"

My heart beats louder, pounding so hard that I'm sure he can see the pulse hammering beneath my skin. *He's just searching. He can't know anything when he wasn't even there.*

"Rumors have spread about me since the very first day, if you'll recall, Professor Uriel. And we both know how those affected me then, so if you're asking if I think rumors have an impact on the way angels treat others, then my answer is yes. What I can't answer is the motives behind someone's behavior or actions."

He doesn't take a beat or even a breath before speaking. "So are the rumors true, then? Did you really slay every demon just by touching their foreheads or turn their bodies to ash with a glance?"

There's a knock on the door, but he doesn't rise. He only stares at me, waiting for an answer.

I laugh, realizing he truly believes the rumors. *Of fucking course he does.* "You can't be serious! Don't you hear how ridiculous that all sounds?"

The knock sounds again. This time, the knob shifts as someone tries to open the door. "Excuse me."

When he leaves, it feels like I can finally breathe again, but I know it's not over. He's going to want a straight answer out of me before I leave. The way he's worded the question, it'll be easy enough for me to tell the truth. The rumors, at least the ones he asked about, are false. Exaggerated accounts from angels who want a fairy tale to go with their happy ending. Nothing more.

"I'm not available at the moment. You'll have to come back another time."

"I only need a minute or two," a familiar voice says.

"As I said, right now doesn't work for me," the professor replies, intending to shut the door, but I'm already striding over.

"Theo?" I ask, "What are you doing here?"

"I wanted to ask Professor Uriel a few questions. What are you doing here?"

"He's my new school counselor. But," I say, a genuine smile spreading across my face, "we're pretty much finished, so I'll let you two get to it." While I'm curious about what Theo wants to ask the professor, I've spent way too much time in his company already and just need some air that isn't tainted with his particular brand of cringe.

As I head back to grab my things, Professor Uriel turns to me with utter annoyance on his face. He's not oblivious to the out I just took.

"Miss Hayliel, we were not done. I need to know what else has changed, aside from your wings, so that I may adjust the curriculum if needed."

"Nothing has changed, as I stated. Besides, we'll be meeting regularly, Professor. Whatever questions remain, you can ask them next time." To Theo I say, "I'll wait for you in the hall." Then, with a reassuring squeeze to his arm, I'm free of my interrogation.

I find an empty bench a short walk down the hall and sit to wait for Theo. In the silence of my thoughts, I struggle to decipher Professor Uriel's motives. It's possible he's reconsidered and wants to make amends for the awful treatment he's given me, but I don't really buy that. He mentioned wanting to make sure my classes were still appropriate, so maybe he's telling the truth? Shit. When did I become so cynical?

After the stress of the break, the hot and cold treatment from students at school, and now my utter confusion around the men in my life and their labels, it's no wonder I'm so fucked up. *Get it together, girl.*

I don't know how long I've waited for Theo, but when he comes out, I immediately jump to my feet. We need to get going. To where, I don't particularly care, as long as it's far from the professor and his probing questions.

We walk in silence for a beat until Theo pulls me into an empty classroom. He shuts the door behind us, not bothering to turn on any lights. His sweet coffee scent surrounds me, drawing me closer to him and reminding me of what transpired in the offering tent. We haven't done anything since, but I want to. I'm just so confused. Raphael was more than okay with it, but was it only because he was there? I mean, shit. It's not like Raph and I labeled anything to begin with. *What am I even doing?*

As hard as it is, I draw back and ask him a question to keep my mind off this carnal pull. "Did he actually answer your questions this time, or was it just more of his usual avoid and run away?"

"As if he'd ever answer something outright."

"What were you asking him, anyway?"

"I just couldn't wrap my head around how the Wingology professor at such a prestigious school could be so useless. I had hoped maybe we'd caught him too soon after the attack and maybe his mind just wasn't in it, you know? So when I was here over the break, I found an old textbook in the library with study notes in the margins, and after a quick search on my slate, I learned the book was used a decade ago to teach his class — when Professor Uriel was still teaching. You'd think that whatever was in that book, he'd know, right? But there's an entire chapter on silver-winged angels, yet he never mentioned a single thing to us about it. I thought I'd give him another chance to share his knowledge, just in case it really was chaos from the attack, but nope."

I roll my eyes. "So he just, what, denied knowing any-thing?"

"He told me he didn't bring it up because it wasn't relat-ed. Then he went on about how wing color matters, using Pure and Fallen as a prime example, and told me to stop questioning the faculty. The asshole even looked offended. It doesn't seem to matter how many chances I give him, he always disappoints me."

Leaning my head against the wall, I close my eyes. "Tell me about it."

Theo moves to my side, his arm pressing against mine, but I keep my eyes shut. The news about silver-winged angels should have me excited, but I'm just tired. Tired of the unanswered questions and unending mazes we seem to go through. Why can't things be simple?

"Speaking of, why weren't you meeting with the regular school counselor?" he asks, curiosity clear in his tone.

"Ugh." I run a hand down my face. "Apparently Professor Uriel made a pretty convincing case to Principal Cael about how he would be better suited as my school counselor given the recent turn of events. I got an email over break notifying me about it and totally spaced until today. I'm just glad you arrived when you did and saved me from more of his uncomfortable questions."

"Hey," Theo says, taking my hands in his and making me finally open my eyes. The look he gives me is full of worry. "What do you mean, uncomfortable questions?"

"Just ... weird. I'm probably overthinking everything. Like he wanted to know how I was getting on at school, and if any of the students or professors were giving me a hard time. I almost laughed in his damn face."

"Seriously? Well, you're certainly stronger than I am."

I smile weakly, appreciating his words. "Then he started asking about my wings, wanting to know if anything else had changed besides their color. It wasn't so much the question that bothered me as it was the way he asked it, like my answer would either please him or devastate him. I don't know."

"I'm sorry you had to go through that. If you want one of us to join you next time, all you have to do is let us know. We'd have your back, no question. After how that piece of shit treated you, he's got no right making you uncomfortable."

"I know, Theo. Thank you. I might just take you up on it."

"Why don't we get out of here? Maybe meet up with the rest of our friends and get some food? That always puts a smile on your face."

"The friends, or the food?" I ask, teasing.

"Oh, definitely the food."

He smiles, and I swat his arm playfully before taking his hand and heading out the classroom door.

I drop a message in our group chat — the one I added Zeke to, though his interaction has been abysmal at best — but to my utter surprise, he and Raphael are working together so they can't join us. I had hoped they would attempt to get along, but I certainly never expected *this*. Dina doesn't answer, but that's no shock. She's likely tucked away somewhere with the two special angels she snuck off with during the anything-but-clothes party. Good for her.

We grab some food from the main-hall cafeteria and head to the beach, neither of us in the best head space, but before we make it there, someone calls my name.

"Hayliel! Theo!"

Gagiel approaches us, along with a few angels I haven't seen before.

"Hi!" I say, happy to see him. "How was your break?"

"It wasn't bad. Different in some ways from school, but similar in others." He doesn't elaborate and instead motions to the angels beside him. "Do you remember the friends I told you about, the ones who were taking classes online? Well, they're here! And it's all thanks to you."

I smile, blushing slightly as they look at me with such trust and adoration.

"This is Sidriel," he says, pointing to the petite angel with straight, black hair.

"Hi." She tucks a strand of hair behind her ear and looks away shyly. "My friends call me Sid."

"And these two," Gagiel continues, pointing to the last two angels in their group, "are Tabbris and Yofie." They must be identical twins, with the same reddish-brown curls and stunning green eyes.

I give a little wave, feeling awkward beneath their steady gazes. "It's so nice to meet all of you. I'm really glad you came back to campus! If you ever need anything, Gagiel has my number."

"And mine," Theo adds. "I'm usually with Hayliel anyway, but if you ever need me, I'm there."

"Oh, you must be Theo," Sidriel squeaks out. "You're very handsome."

"Oh. Uh … Thank you," he replies with the cutest blush on his face. Poor guy isn't used to compliments. Maybe I'll have to change that.

"Handsome and beautiful, these two are. Without the sharp stench of asshole." Gagiel's smile is wider than I've ever seen it, and it bleeds through until I can't help but grin right back. "And we wanted you to know that we're at your disposal. Anything we can help with, just call our names and we'll be there quicker than you can say, 'Gagiel, Sidriel, Tabbris, and Yofie, we need you!'"

I laugh. Those words aren't quick to say at all, but I can understand his point. "Thanks. That means a lot."

"Not to be too forward," Sidriel says, stepping closer, "but Gagiel told us about your wings. Gold! If I didn't trust him completely, I might not have believed him. Archangels, your parents must be so proud."

"I only just told them over break, actually. At first they were a little disappointed that it took me so long to tell them. That was followed up by a little bit of shock and a lot of confusion — which is honestly exactly how I still feel about it — but they support me no matter what."

An idea crosses my mind, and I almost hold it in. The old Hayliel would have. She'd have smothered it and figured it out herself. Apparently, this new version of me has learned to trust. "Actually, there is something I could use some help with, if you're game."

"Anything," Tabbris and Yofie say in unison, causing me to laugh.

"Both of my parents are Fallen, so they don't really have access to any resources that could help them develop their powers. Over the break, I gave them a crash course in telepathy, but the results were pretty underwhelming. With everything going on lately, I just want them safe and protected, so if you have any tips or tricks that could help older, inexperienced angels develop their powers, I'd love to hear them."

"That's incredibly sweet of you," Sidriel says, her eyes glassy with a sheen of tears.

Tabbris steps forward, pulling Yofie along too. "We can help. Twins run in our family, and there's always one Pure and one Fallen. We have this notebook at home full of stuff that might help them. Give us some time to scan it and we'll send it over to you, if that's alright?"

"Oh, wow. That's actually perfect. Thank you. I really appreciate it, and if there's any way I can pay you back, just let me know."

Gagiel looks off in the distance, a shudder rolling over him as he notices Cadriel near the arena. "Sorry to run off," Gagiel adds. "We should get going to the cafeteria before it gets too crowded. Care to join us?"

"We're actually heading to the beach, but another time for sure!"

"And remember," Theo chimes in as Gagiel and his friends walk away. "If anyone gives you any trouble, call on us and we'll be there."

"You betcha! Bye!" And then they're off and we're back on our path to the beach.

My heart soars knowing that Gagiel's friends have come back to school. I hate that they were raced out in the first place, but knowing they came back because my friends and I gave them some sort of reassurance or protection feels really fucking good.

Before we reach the sand, Theo stops me with a hand on my arm. "I'm glad your parents weren't too upset about the whole wing thing."

"Me too. They've always worried about me, and you know what? When I reassured them I'm fine, for what may be the first time ever, I might have actually believed it."

He reaches up to cup my cheek, his warm hand soothing away the chill from the ocean breeze. "You're perfect, firefly. We won't ever let you forget it."

There's a beat of silence as we gaze into each other's eyes. Waves crash against the shore, matching the frantic beat of my heart as I take in his hazel eyes and soft lips. The urge to kiss him is strong. He must feel it too, because in the next second his lips are on mine, coaxing them open. His soft tongue twirls against mine, causing little zings of pleasure to shoot straight to my core.

I groan, wanting more, and as he pulls me further against him, I'm left with only two thoughts.

I've kissed three guys in a matter of weeks. What kind of angel does that make me?

Fucking lucky, that's what.

23

RAPHAEL

A loud thud sounds from where Ezekiel sits in his chair beside mine, and I glance over to find him looking sheepishly back at me. *Odd expression for him, but this whole fucking day has been odd.*

"Sorry," he says, fixing the bag of books he brought with him.

Did he just apologize? Alright, I must be in an alternate universe or something, because I don't think I've ever heard the Fallen house leader apologize. It's strange enough having him in my room, but now that he's acting all civil, I don't really know how to handle it. *Oh, the things I'll do for Hayliel.*

"It's fine," I say, because what the fuck else is there?

"Here." He hands me a book with colored tabs sticking out from within the pages. "My dad used to read these to me as a kid, so I thought it might be best if you looked instead of me. I marked a few lines I found interesting."

I read the title, *The Plight Against Demons, Volume 1.* "This is what your father read to you?" I do my best to keep the judgment from my tone, but I must fail because Ezekiel's spine straightens.

"After my mother died, yeah. When she was alive, things were a bit more hopeful."

Shit. I've really gone and done it now. "I'm sorry. I didn't know."

"You wouldn't have. I don't exactly broadcast it. Anyway, I hope there's something helpful in there we can use."

"Me too." We go back to our books, flipping through the pages in silence. I try really hard to focus on each word, each sentence, but things feel *weird*. Ezekiel almost seems chatty. I don't think he's ever dropped a personal fact like that before, especially not willingly, so what's his angle here?

I consider the fact that maybe he's just *trying*. Putting in the effort with me as a gesture to Hayliel. The guy went to the Fallen district to help her out, for fuck's sake. It really does seem like he's pulling out all the stops.

The idea is uncomfortable. He's treated her poorly since the beginning. Making nice with me won't absolve him of any of that. It's her he should be focusing on, even though I'd rather he didn't. Hayliel is the type of angel that must be protected at all costs. She's kind and brave, selfless at times even when she shouldn't be, and I don't trust him not to hurt her again.

I only wish I knew what it was she wanted. It's obvious that it bothers her when he brushes her off, but is it more than that? As much as I don't want her to feel anything for the heartless Fallen beside me, I can't deny that it's a possibility.

Dammit. It won't do me any good to sulk or ponder the unknown right now. Not with so many things already on my plate, so I shove it all aside and throw everything into the book in front of me.

I don't know how much time passes before there's a knock on the door. Ezekiel and I share a look that makes me wonder if he's thinking the same thing as I am. Is it Hayliel? She messaged the group chat earlier and both our slates had gone off with the notification. It's going to be a while before I'm comfortable with the fact that he's in there. She and Theo were on their way to the beach and wanted to let the *group* know in case we wanted to join them. I sure as fuck did, but it's not like I could ditch Ezekiel now. Even if I did, he'd probably just show up, too. Maybe she and Theo brought the food to us instead of to the beach.

At this point, I'll take anyone I can get as long as they can help dispel this weirdness floating around in my room with only the two of us in here.

Except when I open the door, it's not Hayliel or Theo that greets me on the other side. In fact, it might just be the only person I'd rather spend time with less than Zeke. Standing there in all his polished glory is Raduriel.

"Little brother!" he says before pulling me into a hug. Despite my mother always pointing out our differences, we have similar coloring and could even pass for twins, if we tried. Not that I'd ever want to. He doesn't wait for me to invite him inside, just brushes past me. That's when I notice that he's not alone. Another angel follows behind my brother, his reddish-brown hair cut short on the sides and standing tall on the top. The two of them enter my room without even a second thought.

"What are you doing here?" I ask him, shutting my door and trying to school my expression. When I'm sure I've got it under control, I turn around to face them. Raduriel is looking at the photos I have on my dresser, and the other angel — I think his name is Briathos. Some hotshot from the Guild, if I recall — leans against the wall. I wonder what my brother is using him for. It's not like he'd ever *choose* to spend time with a Fallen.

"I'm on campus for business. Apparently, your principal wants to see me. The last time that happened, I received an award and honorary title. Honestly, I've received so many that I kind of forget what they all are, but anyway. I couldn't step on school grounds without checking on my younger brother."

Bullshit. He absolutely could have come to SCU and not visited me at all. I'd have preferred it that way. But if he'd done that, who would he brag to?

"How come you're in here all alone? Mom said you were struggling here, but surely you've made some friends you could hang out with?"

Ezekiel chooses that very moment to clear his throat. All eyes turn to him as he nods.

"Interesting," Raduriel states, looking between the two of us.

Great. Just fucking great. Who knows what story he'll weave when he reports back to Mom and Dad.

Briathos perks up. "Damn, Zeke. Is that you? You're all grown up now."

"Getting there," he replies with a smile. "It's been a while. Are you still working on assignment?"

"Got back last week. I have some downtime, so I'm catching up with old friends. Decided to tag along with Rad here and check out my old stomping grounds. It's great to see you, man."

"You two know each other?" Raduriel asks.

"From the Guild. His dad is a legend," Briathos responds, and I immediately know what's coming next.

Raduriel's eyes light up as he says, "Oh shit, really? Who's your dad?" But I've had enough. I have more important things to do than sit here while my brother decides if my friends are worth his time, solely based on their pedigree. I wouldn't even be surprised if Raduriel tried to worm his way in and steal Zeke's friendship.

Fucking hell. Has it really come to that? Earlier, I'd been dreading this time with Ezekiel and begging for someone to come save me from it. Now, I'm calling him my friend and worrying about whether he'll prefer my brother over me. It's pathetic.

"Look, who his father is doesn't really matter. I appreciate you stopping by, but we're in the middle of something. It might be hard for you and Mom to believe, but I actually have my own shit going on." I regret the words immediately. Outbursts like that are a thing of the past for me. I gave them up a long time ago when I realized it only created fodder for my parents to use against me. *Their emotional boy.*

Raduriel's smile falls slightly, but he's quick to pick it up. He's probably happy that I fucked up.

"Of course." He looks at his watch. "We've got to get going, anyway. Excellence doesn't wait."

"Right," I say, heading toward the door to open it, mocking "Excellence doesn't wait," under my breath.

"Well, it was nice to meet you, Zeke," Raduriel calls to Zeke, who replies with a similar nicety — something I don't think I've ever gotten from him.

In the doorway, my brother and I stand in awkward silence for a moment. It feels like there's so much more I should say, but I can't get the words to pass my lips. Sometimes, when I sit and daydream, I imagine having a brother who supports me. One where everything isn't a competition, and it's us against our parents. But that's only the sad little dream of a sad little boy.

"You know I'm here for you, don't you, Raphael?"

Even though it's a lie, I nod. The smile I give him is strained, but I push on. "Thanks for stopping by," I say before shutting the door.

When they're finally gone, I slump against the door and wish Ezekiel hadn't witnessed that. Hayliel and Theo, or hell, even Dina I'd have been fine with. But not Zeke. He has enough issues with me as it is. This will only add fuel to an already raging fire, and I just can't handle any more.

I head back to the chair I'd occupied before we were interrupted, grab the book I'd been reading, and plop my ass down. Zeke says nothing, but I feel his eyes on me a second longer before he grabs his own book again.

As time passes, so does the tension in my shoulders. Things seem almost normal, and I wonder if something has changed with Zeke or if it's just because of the shitty, awful situation making this seem like a walk in the park. Then I become paranoid. The Ezekiel I know would have put me on the spot with questions and bullshit the moment that door closed, so why is he holding back?

I try to shove it all away and focus on the volume in my hand, reading one of the marked passages about demonic rituals and runes. It's actually kind of fascinating how they draw symbols to enhance or promote certain aspects of themselves, and before long, I'm lost in the book, my prior troubles completely forgotten.

Because things don't always go my way, Ezekiel breaks the silence. "Are things always like that with your brother?"

I don't look up at him, choosing instead to stare at the current page of my book like it holds all the answers. "Like what?"

He's not fooled in the slightest. "Right," he says, clearly not buying my act. We shift back to silence again, but for some reason, it no longer feels comfortable. Part of me wants to answer him, if only to find out why he's asking. If it were any other day, I'd assume he's just going to make some snarky-ass remark like "Well that explains why you're such an insufferable piece of shit," but he's been so strange today that I'm not sure anymore.

A few beats of silence pass again before the need to answer him wins out, and I sigh. "That was pretty much routine with Raduriel. It's worse with my parents, though. I swear sometimes they look at me like I'm not even their child."

"But why? From what I can tell, it's not as if you're a disappointment."

For the first time since my brother left, I glance at Ezekiel. His words are full of conviction, but I can tell he's confused. Is it possible he feels that way on my behalf? No. It can't be. Not for the asshole I know.

I answer him bluntly, having had the answer to his question ingrained in me for years. "Ah, but I am. I'm not *him*."

Silence greets me as his mouth opens and closes before he finally says, "You know that guy he was with? Briathos?"

Now I'm the one confused. Where is he going with this? "Yeah," I reply.

"When I was younger, he mentored with my father, and I hated his fucking guts. He's all my dad ever talked about, and they spent more time together than Dad and I had in a long time. It felt like the only parent I had left was moving on. Finally, one day I just snapped and asked Dad point-blank if he'd rather Briathos was his son instead of me. He stared at me in silence for so long, I thought for sure he was about to say yes."

My stomach drops when he pauses, and I sit here on pins and fucking needles, waiting for him to continue. "Well. Did he?"

Ezekiel smiles. "No. Turns out he had no clue how much it was affecting me because I'd just shut down and bury my emotions instead of talking about them. After I finally opened up to him about it, things changed."

"That's a nice story and all, but there's one obvious difference. My parents actually do want a second Raduriel."

The asshole has the nerve to fucking scoff. "So what if they do? Look, I know you and I haven't always seen eye to eye, and some of that is on me—"

A bark of laughter bubbles up from my throat as I raise an eyebrow at him.

To my surprise, he only smiles before conceding. "Fine. Most of it. But that comes from some pretty fucked-up experiences with Pures and not from you directly. If I'm honest, you actually seem pretty fucking decent compared to a lot of the other assholes I've dealt with before. If your parents can't see that, then they don't deserve your time or emotions. Don't give them room to treat you like shit."

"But they're my family."

"So what? That sure as fuck doesn't give them the right to make you feel inferior or put conditions on their love for you. Even though you didn't ask for it, here's my advice. Talk to them. Your parents and your brother. Tell them that what they're doing is shitty as fuck and you won't stand for it anymore. If that doesn't work, I'd say it's high time you got rid of the shit in your life that doesn't serve you."

His words settle over me. Somehow, they actually fucking make sense. This has to be some alternate reality because shit. Am I seriously going to take advice from this guy? The idea of talking to my family about this is daunting, but Zeke might be right. A parent's love should be unconditional. It shouldn't be on me to *earn* that love. They should give it freely and without question.

But what about my brother's love? Should that also be unconditional? Things weren't always so strained between us. When I was really young, he'd been my best friend. Something changed as I grew up and the more I think about it now, the more I realize just how badly I want to know why we grew apart.

Enough time has passed since Zeke last spoke that it feels awkward to say something now. Instead, I just catch his eye and nod before getting back to the book in my lap.

Who knew the biggest revelation from today would come from the grumpy Fallen house leader?

24

THEO

Water bubbles in the fountain as I walk by, heading toward the weaponry building to work off some of my pent-up energy.

Classes have barely started back up again, and already I'm restless. Every day we don't head to that abandoned building is another day the bad guys have our weapons. It's more time for them to plan exactly how they're going to use them.

Even though I know there's a perfectly good reason we're waiting, it still feels like a waste of time.

Shit. I'm usually far more levelheaded than this.

A familiar figure heads for the arena. Hayliel looks over her shoulder toward the weaponry building, and that's when I see the look on her face.

In a split second, my focus shifts. Training can wait. Finding out what caused that look of pain on Hayliel's face can't.

It takes me a moment to find her in the empty arena, and I have to use the newly formed tethers of our bond to track her down.

"Firefly," I whisper as I approach carefully, trying not to spook her. "What happened?"

She doesn't appear startled by my presence, and I wonder if maybe she could sense I was looking for her.

"It's nothing," she says, wiping her cheeks. It's too dark to tell if she's been crying or not, but that act alone tells me everything. "Cadriel just made a stupid comment."

"What did he say?"

She chews on her bottom lip, staring at the ground before finally saying, "He told me I was just a passing amusement to Raphael, one he'd get sick of soon enough."

"Cadriel is a piece-of-shit asshole and only trying to get under your skin, baby. You know that's not true."

"Well, I told myself that and tried to ignore his taunts about being the rich angels' charity case, but then ..." She looks at me, eyes full of pain. "I stumbled upon Raphael with Seraphina. Fuck. If I close my eyes, I can still see them huddled together. They looked so fucking comfortable with each other, Theo."

I pull her into my arms, holding her tightly and whisper, "Raphael would never do that to you."

She shifts back like I slapped her and snaps, "I know what I saw, Theo."

"I'm sorry. I don't doubt what you saw, firefly. I just think there's more to the story. Have you asked him about it?"

"Fuck no. I hightailed it out of there as fast as I could."

"I think you should talk to him. It's Seraphina, after all. I have more faith in Raphael, even with no details at all, than I ever would in her. Especially when it comes to you. He'd never jeopardize your relationship like that."

Her slate rings, and I watch as she pulls it out and stares at the screen. Raphael's name is there in bold letters, but she doesn't answer it. The screen goes dark for a second before it rings again, and she quickly declines the call before putting it away.

"I don't know, Theo. It was bound to happen eventually, right? Seraphina called it from the beginning. Cadriel said it today. Fuck, even Zeke said something like this would happen. Nobody wants a freak."

Her words cut into me like a thousand angel blades. Does she really believe these things about herself? And screw Ezekiel for adding more doubt in her mind about us. I'm mad at the world on her behalf, and fuck if I'm not disappointed in Raphael and myself for not doing enough to reassure her that this was never a possibility.

"You're the furthest thing from a freak. If more angels were like you, this world we live in probably wouldn't be going to shit right now. As for Raph, I've never seen him more obsessed with anyone. Ever since he met you in the cafeteria, you're all he's talked about."

"I want to believe you, I really do, but we never really made sense, and you know that."

"No, I don't. You two make sense. *We* make sense. What doesn't is the fact that he'd throw this all away for a stuck-up, bitchy angel like Seraphina. Do you know why he's been so open to the idea of you and me?"

"I ... no. I guess I don't."

"Because he saw how happy you were. He'd rather accept sharing you with me and seeing you happy than keep you all to himself. Your happiness is more important to him than anything else, and the last thing he'd ever want to do is hurt you. He's fallen hard for you, firefly. You and only you. Please, at least hear him out."

Her eyes bore into mine, searching them for truth. She must find it because the corner of her lips lift and she pulls me in for a hug.

"You do both make me happy," she admits, pulling back to look at me. "Even if our relationship is a bit abnormal."

I chuckle, my world brightening as the dark clouds of doubt clear from her eyes, and I lean down to press a kiss to her lips. She accepts it without question, kissing me back with fervor until all I want to do is tear her clothes off and worship her.

Both of our slates ping several times and we break apart reluctantly to find unread messages in the group chat.

Ezekiel: I'm checking out that building in a few days. Anything to note with the blueprints?
Raphael: What do you mean *you're* checking out that building? I think you mean we.
Ezekiel: Whatever you say, man.
Ezekiel: So is that a no to the blueprints?
Raphael: Demon Slayers! Assemble! My room, 5 minutes.
Ezekiel: Right. Give me ten.

"Isn't it so cute when they get along?" Hayliel teases.

"Don't you dare jinx it, firefly."

"Think it's okay if I tell Dina to come? She's pretty invested at this point, and I think she'd be pissed if we made plans without her."

"Absolutely. She's part of the Demon Slayer squad," I say, making Hayliel laugh. I could listen to that sound forever. Maybe I should record it and turn the sound into my ringtone. Or is that creepy?

After Hayliel sends the details of our meet to Dina, we head to Power house and arrive on Raphael's balcony in no time. I use my wings to unlock the door and we find him inside with a frantic look on his face.

"Sunshine!" he says when he sees us before rushing to her side. "I have to tell you this now, because I'm certain she's only trying to cause shit between us. Seraphina cornered me in the weaponry building and I tried to get away without literally tossing her aside, which didn't work by the way, but I have no interest in her at all, and in fact I'm falling so fucking hard for you that I couldn't even imagine—"

"Hey," Hayliel says, putting a finger over his lips to stop his rambling. "Breathe."

He nods and sucks in a few deep breaths. "Sorry. I just figured she'd try to start shit, and I wanted to make sure you knew the full story before she could do any damage to our relationship."

A knock sounds at the door, pulling me from the heartfelt moment, and I silently excuse myself to answer it. Before I get there, Raphael calls out to me.

"Theo, that includes you, too. I wouldn't risk the relationship we all have. We're a family."

"I know you wouldn't, Raph," I tell him as Hayliel's eyes well with tears. We *are* a family. Maybe not of blood and bone, but something better. We chose each other, and something about that feels far stronger.

Raphael kisses Hayliel, and I take a moment to just smile and watch. Another knock interrupts my intense stare, reminding me that I was doing something.

Ezekiel and Dina stand on the other side, and as they walk through Raphael's door, it's obvious they can sense the weird vibes in the air.

Dina being Dina doesn't let us get away without mentioning it. "Shit, babe. Can you bottle up some of that sexual tension for me? Because damn!"

While Hayliel laughs, I wait on bated breath to see how the Fallen house leader will take it. When he doesn't say anything, I wonder if maybe our conversation over break really did something.

He settles into a chair with all the comfort of a king sitting on his throne, which reminds me he's been here before. He and Raphael hung out just the other day, and I guess things went well. Good. Now Ezekiel just needs to put everything out in the open with Hayliel and maybe we can all get along the way we were always intended to.

"Alright, so the Guild usually flies a route over the area where that building is located, but when I looked through the logs, something seemed off."

"What was it?" Hayliel asks, dropping into the seat opposite him as Raphael moves to stand behind her. If Zeke notices, I can't tell, but I stay where I am beside Dina against the wall. I don't want to test out his newfound calm just yet.

"The flight paths have changed over the last few years. On its own, that doesn't seem like a big deal at all. But knowing what we do about that building ... isn't it suspicious that those changes result in very little patrol in that area?"

"You think it's the work of the mole?" I ask, not wanting it to be true but fearing it might be.

"The thought might have crossed my mind a time or ten. Even if it is, though, I'm now more positive than ever that we have to investigate."

"You're right," Raphael adds. "We need to see for ourselves. Theo, was there anything interesting to note from the blueprints?"

"The house itself is a bungalow, so all the rooms are on the main floor. There are three bedrooms, one bathroom, an office, and an open concept kitchen and living room. I did find something a little strange, though. One photo showed a rather large barn on the property as well, but I couldn't find any blueprints for it and it didn't exist in any of the other photos."

"That is odd," Zeke adds, his expression thoughtful.

"How are we even going to get off campus?" Hayliel asks. And she's right. We can't exactly tell the principal that we're off to investigate an old house with the hopes of retrieving the items stolen from the Guild.

"We could just lie and tell them we're going to the merchant district," Dina states.

Ezekiel shakes his head. "That won't work. All absences are reported to the Guild and spot checked. From what I could find, someone thinks a student was involved in the attack, so they're going to great lengths to discover who it was."

Dina's mouth drops open as she stares at Zeke, and I'm just as surprised. They think a student was involved? But why? If they were trying to cancel midterms, an attack seems a bit overkill, but I can't think of any other reason why they might do something like that.

"Why don't I just go? I'm exempt from checking in with the principal and if things go sideways, I'm the only one of us really trained. That way, no one else has to risk anything. Whatever I find, I'll report back. Besides, for all we know Roderick could have emptied the place as soon as he woke up."

"I think the fuck not," Raphael growls at the same time as I say, "Not a chance."

Hayliel watches Zeke before shaking her head too. "We all go or none of us go."

"Well, what about this?" Dina says, chewing on her lip. "A compromise. I'll stay back and cover for you. Maybe create a diversion, so no one is watching when you leave. With the way my dad's been acting, I think it's best I hang back on this one, anyway."

"Are you sure?" Hayliel asks, looking sad.

"I'm sure. And that way, if anyone ever suspects you went off campus, I can be your alibi. We were just studying in the Fallen library. It's not like anyone else ever goes there. But I need your word that you'll be careful and not do anything foolish."

"I will," Hayliel tells her.

Dina moves her gaze from me to Raphael before settling on Zeke as she says, "And I need your word that you'll protect her at all costs."

"We will," we all say in unison, which might just be the first time we've ever all agreed wholeheartedly on something.

25

HAYLIEL

The night air tastes sweet, despite the sour note to our plans. Maybe it's just the fact that I'm flying free with my friends, my heart racing with excitement instead of the fear or worry I should have. I owe it all to the fantastic jacket they gave me, which hides my wing color from anyone who might be watching.

Among the clouds, it feels like nothing can touch us.

"You look good up here, sunshine," Raphael calls over the wind, making my stomach flutter.

Zeke had threatened to fuck me in the sky all those months ago, but the asshole never made good on his threat. Something tells me that Raphael and Theo would be more than happy to oblige. *Yeah, but you want the house leader too*, the little voice in my head quips. Just like always, I ignore it.

"You look good beside me," I tell him, meaning every word.

"There it is," Theo and Zeke whisper at the same time, pointing toward a charming old house. Beside it sits a large, red barn, which must be the one Theo said wasn't noted anywhere. There are no lights on or signs of movement from what we can tell, but we make our descent slowly, anyway.

We land near a large oak tree and wait. None of us trust the angel who directed us to this building, but it's not like he gave us a time to show up, and we're on his schedule. It's been long enough that hopefully he's forgotten all about Zeke and the information shared with him. Who am I kidding, the likelihood that Roderick gets amnesia and forgets that Zeke stole his weapon, threatened his life, and forced him to spill his secrets is slim to fucking none.

Cicadas sing their mating call around us, but otherwise things are quiet.

Raphael waves everyone to him and holds out his hands. Theo and I each take one and hold our free hand out to Zeke, who doesn't really look like he cares for whatever Raphael has planned, but still he grabs on.

Just wanted to make sure we all had a strong enough bond to speak telepathically, in case things go sideways and we need to communicate.

I grin at him, my handsome unofficial boyfriend with such bright ideas. Zeke looks pleased too, much to my surprise. Or, at least as pleased as he can look right now. Whenever I catch him glancing toward that old house, something dark settles over his face.

Let's move a little closer, Zeke says through our bond before turning and heading toward the house. The rest of us follow along, being careful not to make too much noise in case there really are others here.

We make our way around the back of the house toward the front door, keeping an eye out for any window we can peek through, but most of them are boarded up. Strange.

By the time we make it to the front door, I'm starting to wonder if maybe this was all a ruse. I turn to say as much when I notice Theo and Zeke huddled together.

Zeke's expression is haunted, and Theo is talking to him softly.

"Just breathe. Feel the earth beneath your feet and listen to the sound of my voice. You're safe."

I want to ask what's going on, see if I can help, but the moment doesn't feel right. So instead, I just watch on until Zeke snaps at Theo.

"I don't need your fucking assistance," he says, the words coming out on heavy breaths that tug on my heart.

Theo keeps quiet, holding his hands up in surrender and stepping away. I don't miss the look he shoots a rather angry-looking Raphael either. Is Zeke having a panic attack?

The question tilts my entire world on its axis. My strong Guild intern house leader always seems so unbreakable. Seeing him like this, vulnerable and in pain, makes me want to fix everything that's wrong with the world, if only to bring him peace.

I approach him slowly, unsure if it's the right move, but knowing I need to ease some of his pain.

"Zeke," I whisper, pulling him into a hug. "I'm here. Whatever you're fighting, I'm right here beside you."

He takes in a shaky breath but doesn't say a word, just lets me hold him and sooth away as much of the panic as possible. Finally, he wraps his arms around me and hugs back. We stay like that for a while, not bothering to care that we're in the open and could be spotted by anyone.

"This is where my mom died," he admits. The words carve into my heart, slashing it open until I feel his pain as my own.

The monotone, lifeless lilt to his voice cuts me deeper as he continues, "Demons took her and held her captive in this very house before they killed her. To this day, Dad and I don't understand what it is they wanted from her as a hostage. We only wish we could have given it to them and saved her life."

"I'm so fucking sorry, Zeke." My words feel insignificant against the gravity of his loss.

"Shit. I'm an idiot. I thought I could handle coming here, but clearly I'm just a weak-ass little bitch who can't handle their feelings. What the hell was I thinking?"

He turns away from me, fists clenched at his sides, but I don't let him suffer alone.

"Hey," I say, wrapping my arms around him from behind. "Suppressing your feelings doesn't make you strong. The fact that you're still standing here, still considering walking into that house in search of answers, shows me you're one of the strongest angels I know, because I don't think I could do it." It's on the tip of my tongue to suggest that he stay out here and keep watch for anyone approaching, but I know better. He'd refuse.

His chest moves as he breathes in deeply, holding it for a second before letting it go along with some of the tension in his shoulders.

"You can do this," I promise him. "And if we come across something that's too much for you, just say the word. We'll get through this together."

"Together," he repeats, covering my hands with his.

He takes one more deep breath before he turns and pulls me into him to place a kiss on my hair. "Thank you."

"Always."

Raphael and Theo say nothing as we head back toward them, and when Zeke apologizes to Theo, he shakes his head in response. "There's nothing to apologize for, man. We've got your back."

An odd sense of comradeship settles over the four of us. We might be about to enter some random discarded house where our enemies could ambush us at any moment, but none of that can penetrate this feeling of rightness. We're finally all getting along, and holy hell, does it feel good.

With a spring in my step, I walk toward the front door of the old house, fully intending to just waltz right in. Alright, so maybe I'm riding the high of my newfound family and stuck in a world where clouds are made of marshmallows and houses are just chocolate-covered wafers, but who cares? Demons can't attack me there.

Instead, the door is locked, and as much as I want to just break it down, Raphael stops me. "It's not exactly subtle if we tear the door off its hinges, sunshine," he says with a laugh.

"Good point."

I expect Zeke to come to the rescue with some fancy-ass tool from the Guild, but it's Theo who steps past me and crouches down in front of the lock. Zeke watches on in disbelief, but shines the light from his slate toward him, anyway. In seconds, he's turning the knob and opening the door like what he did isn't the coolest fucking thing.

"You've got to teach me that," I whisper, my body all tingly from watching this hunky, nerdy angel of mine.

"You know, if you weren't a Pure, I'd ask you to intern for the Guild," Zeke adds with a wry smile on his lips. "Well, as long as you fight as good as you pick locks, but at least that can be trained."

Theo throws Zeke a cocky grin. "Trust me. I'd give you a run for your money, intern."

As I watch the exchange, I want to squeal with excitement. But shit. Aren't we supposed to be quiet? Dammit. And we're out here yacking like a gaggle of old ladies.

We head inside slowly, with Zeke taking the lead, followed by Raphael, then me, and Theo taking up the rear. Inside, it's dark without the light of the moon, so we all take out our slates and turn on the flashlights to illuminate the space.

I suck in a breath as the full extent of the room is revealed to us. Near the door is a dark mark branded into the wood, so worn that I can't tell what it used to be. The rest of the house is just as dirty, but I bet it was beautiful once. Homey. Now it's covered in dust and grime, with garbage thrown across the floor. A shell of what it once must have been. The walls are bare, except for sad discolorations that speak of a family long since removed. I wonder who used to live here. Are they still alive somewhere? Do they ever think of this place?

We search the entire house, going from room to room, opening cabinets and drawers, hoping we'll stumble across *anything* that could help us, but it's empty. The only thing we know now is that whoever's been staying here loves Cheetos. I've walked by at least five empty snack bags.

At the last room, the one I assume was once an office, Zeke stays in the hall, looking in at the far wall with such pain in his eyes. I can't imagine what he's feeling right now, being in this place that holds such haunting memories. As much as I want to ask him why this room is so familiar, I don't. I only go to him and push some of my strength and support toward him through our bond. I feel Raphael and Theo doing the same, and can't help the little tug on my heart at the gesture.

"They can handle this room," I tell him and tug on his hand. "We need to figure out what to do next."

He follows me without arguing, and I hope he can sense that I'm not pulling him away out of pity or because I don't think he can handle it. It's because I know he can, but no one should have to go through that. Fuck, he shouldn't even be here at all, in the house where his mother was murdered. It's not fair.

"Why the fuck did Roderick send us here?" Zeke asks with a sigh.

"You and I both know he can't be trusted, but don't give up hope yet. There's still the barn to look through, and that building looks far newer than this one."

He slams his boot into the old chair, shoving it backward and sending up a plume of dust. He tugs on his hair in frustration. "This is bullshit."

"Zeke," I say, shining my light toward the chair he just moved.

Raphael and Theo join us, but my focus is on the symbol stamped on the floor.

"Zeke," I try again, my whisper turning frantic. "Didn't I find you researching runes in the library?"

This gets his attention. "Yeah. Why do you—"

His words cut off as he finally looks toward me where I'm crouched on the floor.

"That's a protection rune," he says, tracing the dark lines with his finger, but as he gets to the tip, he has to push the couch out of the way to continue. "This isn't right."

"What do you mean?" Theo asks.

"Whoever drew this rune didn't connect these two pieces here, so it's nothing more than a mark on the floor."

"What about the one near the door?"

"Show me."

I lead everyone to the entrance and show them the faded dark spot on the wall where Zeke once again traces it with his finger. "It's too faded."

"I think it was supposed to be a truth rune. See this curve here." Theo points to a faint line that curves down.

I watch on in disbelief, because damn. I'd never even heard of runes before I caught Zeke looking at them, but I shouldn't be surprised that Theo knows. He's like an encyclopedia of information.

"We'll get into how you know about runes later," Zeke tells Theo, looking both pensive and intrigued. "But for now, this building holds nothing more for us than terrible memories and more questions."

"My dad always used to say barns were full of secrets. Maybe it'll be the same here."

All three of us turn to look at Raphael in confusion.

"Your dad said that?" I ask, confused.

Zeke laughs. "Aren't you super rich? Why the hell would your father know anything about barns?"

"Yes, but he's only rich because he married my mother. He worked on his father's farm for years before they met."

His words answer a question that I've been dying to ask but haven't wanted to pry. This must be why his father never stands up for him. Fear of losing his wife's money and status. Somehow, that only pisses me off more. Raphael is too good an angel to have parents who treat him how they do. How can they not realize how great their son is?

I shake away those sad thoughts and follow the guys from the house. We split up into pairs. Raphael and Theo head around one side of the barn while Zeke and I go the other way. We're quiet as we listen for any sound coming from inside, but unless this barn is insulated as fuck, we're alone.

The front has two large wooden doors, and I noticed another door at the back. There's only one window above the door, but when Zeke flies up to peek inside, he can't see past the dark tint. *Looks like we're going in blind.*

There's no lock to be found, only a sliding set of doors with latches to keep them shut when the wind blows. Curious. Why was the house locked but not the barn?

We all exchange one last look before Zeke unhooks the latch. When he pushes the door, it releases a wicked groan that has all the hairs on my neck standing up. None of us move as we wait for some terrible disaster to occur, and when a minute passes without a sound, I almost let out a whoop of excitement.

As soon as we're inside, Zeke closes the door and we're thrown into darkness. If I couldn't feel the protective ring of bodies around me, I'd probably be hyperventilating.

Inside the barn, it's eerily quiet. Mixed with the utter darkness, it's almost suffocating. Theo taps on his slate until the flashlight turns on and we get our first glimpse of the barn. Just like the house, this place is dirty, but where the house had furniture inside, the barn only has large, wooden crates. My pulse quickens as I look inside the closest one, positive that we've finally found what we're looking for. Except there are no weapons or gear inside. It's completely empty.

"That can't be right," Zeke whispers, voicing what we're all thinking.

We use the flashlights on our slates to check the rest of the boxes, but all nine of them are empty or filled with hay.

How fucking naive can we be that we thought everything would be here, as if we weren't taking the word of a murdering criminal? I can't believe we've been this foolish. Was this entire thing just a ploy to keep us distracted and focused on something else?

The guys are arguing in hushed tones when my ears pick up a sound, but with the four of us in this dark barn, it takes me a moment to figure out that it's not coming from either of us.

"Did you hear that?"

Immediately, all three of them go quiet. Listening.

The noise I heard before comes again, this time followed by the unmistakable sound of someone's voice. Dread pools in my stomach as another voice speaks over the first one, and with each word, it sounds like they're getting closer. In my panic, I can't make out what they're saying, but they don't sound too thrilled.

What the hell are we going to do?

I look at my friends, hoping they'll have a plan, but the expressions on their faces tell me all I need to know. We're about to get caught and boy, are we fucking screwed.

"How many times do I have to tell you to latch this door? For demon's sake. I ask very little of you, and the least you can do is your fucking job," an unfamiliar voice says, in a deep, polished timber.

Hide! Theo shouts through our bond and snaps me into action.

I dart behind the nearest crate and turn the flashlight off on my slate just as the barn door slides open. There's a shuffling as one, two, three, fuck, maybe more visitors enter the building.

I look around me, unable to make out my friends until I spot a slight glow near the back. Shit! Whoever that is must not have been able to get the light turned off in time, so they just hid it inside their sweater. This is all too damn risky.

The deep, glossy voice comes again. "And as for your whining, I don't give a human's ass whether you like working with me or not, as long as you hold up your end of the bargain."

"Yes, Boss," someone else replies, sounding way too close for my comfort, but my ears perk up anyway at the mention of a boss. I wonder if Zeke picked up on it, too. Could this be who Roderick reports to?

Is everyone hidden? Raphael asks through the bond, and we all agree telepathically.

Did anyone happen to check the back door? Zeke's husky voice echoes through my head with what could possibly be the best question in the history of questions.

Unfortunately, we were all too preoccupied with searching the crates. We never even considered checking the door. How the hell are we going to get out of this one?

Can anyone see without getting caught? I'd love to know who this apparent boss is. I push my question through the bond, hoping for at least a better answer than the last one.

As the guys answer, telling me we're shit out of luck on that front, the boss man says, "You three go get a room presentable for our next guest."

Next guest? Theo's question burns through my mind, fear settling in my gut. They don't mean us, do they?

A commotion starts from somewhere outside, and it almost sounds like they might be having a fucking party or something. What the hell is going on here?

A prickle of awareness slides down my spine, and I turn, searching through the darkness. I spot the little patch of light beneath fabric and realize that whoever it is looks to be moving.

What are you doing? I ask, not even sure who I'm referring to at this point.

It's Zeke that replies as he moves again. *As long as this noise keeps up, I can make it to the door and stay partially behind these crates. It might be our best chance to escape.*

Fucking hell, Raphael replies, annoyance clear even through our bond. I can't exactly blame him. If Zeke's plan goes sideways, we're all screwed. But we will be anyway if we don't find a way out of here.

Watch your light. I can see it through your sweater, I tell him.

Got it, hummingbird. Thanks.

"So. How many have you procured so far?" the strong voice of the boss asks.

"Enough," someone replies, and I'm left hoping they'll divulge what exactly it is they're collecting.

"Cut the bullshit. I wouldn't have made a deal with demons if I could create these blades on my own. Give me a number."

What the hell? An angel and a demon, working together? This is really fucking bad.

"You might call the shots up here, but I don't report to you. In fact, I've been explicitly told not to provide you a number, so my answer remains the same," the guy, who must be a demon, says.

The barn feels too stuffy, overflowing with tension between these two clearly powerful men, and I wonder if maybe they'll just start fighting each other. That might be nice.

Instead of the epic showdown I hope for, the boss only says, "Fine. For now, anyway. Besides, I've learned to be a little more picky about who I gift them to."

"And what is it you plan to do with that Roderick fellow? He almost ruined the entire operation with his stunt in the Fallen encampment."

I've almost got it, Zeke says through our bond. *If you can, try to move toward the back, but be careful.*

I walk slowly, trying to remember how the crates were positioned so that I don't accidentally stumble into one. My heart races, speeding up as I keep my focus split between my own movements and the conversation happening near the front of the barn.

"Oh, I've not forgotten. If you must know, I've already put something in motion and will be sending an extraction team his way shortly. Then he'll be brought here and taught a lesson that very few angels have ever truly learned."

"How do you know he'll show up?"

"As far as he knows, he's to wait for me outside the Fallen district, closest to the Guild. He wouldn't pass up the opportunity to meet me in person."

"And you aren't worried about your so-called protectors?"

I wait, holding my breath for the answer, but it doesn't come.

Something silent must have passed between them because the demon says, "Fine. Then let my team do it."

I expect the other guy to refuse, but he doesn't. The only thing he requests is that Roderick be brought back here coherent and alive.

I almost let out a yelp of surprise when I bump into someone, my stomach coming all the way up into my throat until I realize who it is.

Fuck, Theo. You scared me.

We're almost out, firefly. He holds me for the briefest second, and I practically melt into him.

"My king wants to know if you've gathered any further information about the powerful creature who took out too many of my brothers."

A shiver goes down my spine. He isn't talking about me, is he?

"This again? My heavens, your *king* is rather obsessive. No. I have nothing definitive, but when I do, I'll pass it along."

"He's getting rather … antsy, so I suggest you look a little harder."

I hear a vibration and for a moment I panic, thinking it's from one of us.

"All in due time. Now, duty calls," the angel in charge says, sounding more tired than he was earlier. "I'll be in touch." And then, after a few steps and the flap of wings, the barn is silent.

"Get rid of these crates, then take a group to grab the insolent angel."

"On it, commander," whoever the demon is talking to replies, but I can't focus on any of that because holy fucking shit. He's going to get rid of the crates, but where will we hide then?

Uh, Zeke? I don't mean to pressure you, but we're running out of time.

Just about … There. Go. Quickly, but for the love of the Archangels, be fucking quiet.

Theo and I scurry to the door with who I'm hoping is Raphael close behind us. It's only partially held open, but the light of the moon filters into the barn like a damn beacon. Please, please, please don't let anyone still inside notice.

Just as Raphael makes it through the door, the wind picks up, tearing it from his hand and slamming it into the wall.

There's not a chance in fucking hell that will go unnoticed.

26

HAYLIEL

Run! Raphael calls through the bond as we take off in a sprint away from the barn.

Stay to the ground. No one flies, do you hear me? Zeke shouts, but he doesn't have to warn us. We were all on campus that day, and we heard enough in that barn to know there weren't just angels nearby.

There's a racket coming from behind me, but I don't bother turning back to see what it is, not when I'm running downhill and the slightest misstep could cost me.

Tall grass at the foot of the hill beckons us onward, so close I can almost smell the damp, earthy scents already. Zeke reaches it first, but he doesn't dive into the reedy throng like I expect him to. Instead, he holds the reeds open for Raphael and me.

I breathe in deep, out of breath, but not from exertion. It would take a whole hell of a lot more than that to tire us, but the fear of getting caught steals the very air from my lungs.

We're safe.

Except, when I look around, I don't see Theo anywhere.

Where's Theo? I ask through the bond, terror seizing my every thought.

I move back to the entrance of the tall grass and find Theo crouched low near the stump of a tree, trying to take in deep breaths but seeming unable to. Shouts come from the house or the barn, I can't tell, but I have a feeling they know someone's been snooping around where they shouldn't have.

Raphael, is this like what happened at the assembly?

I think so, but this looks worse. I'm going to go help, he says only seconds before he bolts from the tall grass, but Zeke stops him. I watch on in horror, wondering if these two idiots are about to throw punches at a time when we really don't need a fucking dick measuring contest.

Stay with Hayliel. Protect her with your damn life if you have to. Keep to the grass and head up the river. Theo and I will join you there.

Raphael only stares at Zeke, and I wonder if maybe he'll say no. That's his best friend out there, and until recently, Zeke hasn't been very warm and welcoming to either of them.

It should be me, Raphael grits out mentally.

I know it should, but if they spot us, I have a better chance at protecting the both of us.

If the two of you can't agree, then I'll fucking go get him myself, I add, annoyed. We don't have time for infighting right now. Shit or get off the fucking pot.

Like hell you will, Zeke replies at the same time Raphael says, *Not a fucking chance.*

They exchange a weird manly nod before Raphael pulls me deeper into the tall grass and Zeke makes his move toward the open expanse of land and Theo's waiting form.

Inside the tall stalks of grass, sounds are muffled beneath the swish of their movements on the wind. I try to hear beyond it, to listen for any sign that Zeke and Theo are in trouble, because as much as I want to do as I'm told, I won't leave them. And deep down, I know Raph won't either.

We make it as close to the river as we can while still hidden in the safety of the grass, but we head up the river like Zeke told us to. Raphael stops and pulls me into his arms.

"They'll be with us soon, sunshine. I promise," he whispers, placing a kiss on the top of my head.

I stay there, tucked in his arms and play his words on repeat, trying to get the images of angry demons and a panic-stricken Theo out of my mind.

When we finally pull apart and continue walking, we keep our hands clasped tight, each of us pulling strength from the other.

We don't get very far before there's a commotion from beyond the grass, loud enough to be heard but too faint to make out exactly what it is. I squeeze Raph's hand, and he squeezes back.

"We both have to put our faith in your house leader now. And as hard as this is for me to admit, he hasn't let us down in a situation like this yet."

"You're right. We'll have faith together," I tell him as we push on.

Seconds turn into minutes, but we keep walking. Inside the grass, I can pretend I'm somewhere else. Somewhere without demons and changing wings. The rainforest, maybe. I read a book about that place once. Maybe it's like this.

All of a sudden there's a flap of wings, followed by a gravelly voice that's way too fucking close for my liking. We drop to the ground, crouching low and staying completely still. After a few minutes, whoever it is flies away, but we stay unmoving. For all we know, this could be the fake-out leave just to catch us in action.

I release a breath and notice Raphael do the same, but our reprieve doesn't last long. A rustling comes from the grass behind us, the sound almost musical, and if I wasn't almost shitting my pants with fear of it being a demon, I might have enjoyed the sound.

Raphael and I are preparing for an attack when a figure comes into view.

I want to shout in relief, but I don't. I don't even move, just let Theo come to me, with Zeke following close behind.

Wrapping my arms around him feels like heaven, and I can't stop a tear from escaping me as I grab his face and haul him in for a kiss. It's messy and inappropriate, given our current situation, but fuck, I'm just glad he's alright.

I turn to Zeke then, hugging him as well while whispering, "Thank you for bringing him back to us." I have every intention of pulling away, but some ethereal force pushes me forward to place a kiss on the edge of his lips. It's nothing like the one I just gave Theo or the ones Zeke and I have shared before, but for now, it's enough.

We walk on in silence, with Theo and me holding hands. It's foolish really, but I'm not quite ready to let go of him yet. If we keep going down this path, encounters like these might become a regular thing. We have to find a way to help keep Theo grounded in those moments.

When we feel there's enough distance between us and the barn, we stop walking. So much information has been shared over the last few hours and it feels like I haven't had a single second to process it all.

"I should have asked this before, but is anyone hurt?" Zeke asks, looking between the three of us.

We all shake our heads, feeling lucky that the demons didn't investigate too thoroughly. Were they fools, or did they simply not care? Or maybe they had orders from whoever was in charge not to pursue anyone that stumbled upon their operation. We'll never truly know.

"Please tell me we're all on the same page here, and that Roderick guy set you up," Raphael says, looking pissed off. It's like he stole the words directly from my mind because I've been cursing Roderick since being in that barn.

"Oh, he set us up alright," Zeke replies, shrugging. "He likely assumed we'd die there and it would clear up one more of his problems. Unfortunately for him, we survived and have even more information than we did before."

I nod, glad at least that we're leaving that interaction with *something*. "Do we really believe that angels and demons are working together, though? With everything we've been taught, the idea seems a little far-fetched."

Demons are portrayed as evil creatures, ones we should avoid at all costs. So what would possess an angel to seek them out or, better yet, what would possess a demon to agree to any sort of deal with their sworn enemy? What would either side gain?

"Far-fetched or not, it kind of makes sense with every-thing that's happened lately," Theo adds.

Zeke nods once before elaborating. "Take the armory, for example. There's no way demons would have known anything about the Guild schedule or their secret buildings. Most of that information is highly classified, which means even if they were watching us, the likelihood of them stumbling upon it is pret-ty slim. However, if they had someone on the inside, demons could take every weapon we have, including our sun blades, and really put us at their mercy."

Fuck. They have a point. But it still doesn't make sense. "That's what I don't understand. Why arm demons not only with the weapon that can kill us, but also with the only thing we have that can destroy them? It's suicidal. Plus, from the conversation we just overheard, apparently whoever's working with the demons wants access to *more* of those angel blades? It doesn't add up."

"There must be something we're missing. Do we think the powerful creature they spoke of was referring to her?" Theo asks the question that's been racing through my mind since I heard them talking.

Raphael runs a hand through his blond hair. "I can't remember another recent instance where an angel killed a bunch of demons, so I'm thinking yes."

"Shit. Nice to know they haven't figured out anything definitive, I guess," I say, not really finding anything *nice* about any of this.

Zeke looks at me, then the others. "We'll just have to be more careful in case they start looking a little harder."

"We might have left that place with more information, but it feels like we're back to square one." Raphael takes out his slate, looks through the notifications and then puts it away. "Dina is asking for an update. Should I tell her we're coming back to campus?"

"Not yet. It doesn't feel right to just give up yet." I run through the options in my mind, but none of them are good. We're just students, for fuck's sake. And the information we have seems far more serious than we're capable of handling. "There has to be someone we can talk to about this. Someone who can do more than we can. Is there anyone you trust at the Guild?"

"Azrael and my dad would never get involved in something like this, but with the way Azrael is withholding information, I'm hesitant to bring this to him. We're *this* close to figuring it out, and I'm done being kept in the dark. Besides, if we ever do have to bring it to the Guild, I want something more concrete than 'Hey, there's this angel who's working for this guy who's teamed up with angels. Oh, and he's probably locked up or even dead now, so good luck.'"

"You have a point. So what do we know?" Theo asks, taking out his slate and stylus to take notes. Fuck, even in this situation, he's adorable.

I think about it for a moment before stating the obvious. "We know there's a group of angels working with demons and collecting angel blades."

"And we know that Roderick's involved, but he reports to someone who I'd bet was the *boss* in the barn with us," Zeke adds, sparking my memory.

"That's right! He said his boss gave him the blade. I bet losing it is what got him in trouble. Serves him right for sending us to our deaths," I say, though I don't exactly mean it. I might hate the guy, but did I wish for him to be tortured and killed? Fuck. Maybe I do.

"Well, there's a way we can find out."

I'm lost in thought, so it takes me a moment before I realize what Zeke just said. Before I can ask him to elaborate, Raphael beats me to it.

"What do you mean?"

"Roderick wasn't very forthcoming before. It's possible that he really doesn't have any information, but he also never had a reason to tell us shit. This time, we have leverage."

Confused, I ask, "Leverage?" But it's Theo who answers me.

"An information trade. His knowledge for ours. And given what we know could possibly save his life, he'd be foolish not to take us up on it."

"Hold the fuck up," Raphael says, disbelief lacing his tone. "Are you suggesting we try to find Roderick again? And get information from him, again. Information that almost got us killed the first time, I might add."

"That's exactly what I'm suggesting. If he doesn't want to play our game, then we leave him to his fate and we can get serious about talking to the Guild. Like Theo said. He'd be foolish to refuse."

"Well, we've certainly had more idiotic ideas," I say dryly.

Raphael sighs, like he thinks this plan is way too dangerous, but doesn't want to argue further. "What's the plan, then? Head toward the Fallen district and hope we stumble upon him out in the open?"

"We split up," Theo says, looking between us. "Raphael will be with me, and Zeke will go with you."

"But," I start, not liking the idea of us getting separated. And even though my protest was only for our group being apart, I don't miss the pained expression on Zeke's face at my obvious distaste for the plan.

"As much as I hate to admit it, it makes the most sense, sunshine. He's Guild trained, and until one of us can prove that we're better at protecting you than he is, you'll be safest with him."

"It wasn't that. I just don't like our group separating. But you're right. We can cover more ground that way."

"Now, we have to act fast," Theo says, his voice grim. "If we don't, we'll wind up in the middle of whatever Roderick's boss has planned for him."

A shiver runs down my spine at the thought, and I shake my arms to dispel it.

"Alright, so is everyone set on the plan?" Zeke asks, his gaze flashing between the three of us. "Find Roderick. Get answers. And head back to the university stat."

"We'll use the bond if anything goes wrong." I'm not entirely sure who I'm trying to reassure, them or myself, but it feels good knowing we all have this connection to fall back on. If we make it out of here, I'll have to really consider the extent of my feelings and decide what it means.

I give Theo and Raphael a hug before we go our separate ways. From our spot in the tall grass, I can see the bright lights and plumes of smoke from the factory district, which means it's almost a straight flight to our right to the area where Roderick should be. We could walk there, but that would be way more suspicious than flying.

The four of us take off, flying low to the ground, but when Raphael and Theo land, we keep going. If we're going to split up, we might as well start on opposite ends and meet in the middle.

Trees and bushes, old rocks and flowers zip by beneath us until we finally stop. I didn't spot a single living being on the flight over here, and something about that makes me nervous. Where are all the little nocturnal critters?

Zeke and I land a few feet apart and walk back into the area we just came from. Neither of us says a word. Our only focus is on finding Roderick. Excitement bubbles beneath my skin at the possibility of learning more. Part of me is terrified of what we'll discover, if we'll even learn anything at all, but mostly I'm just eager to uncover more of our enemy's plan.

As more time passes without running into Roderick, that excitement turns into disappointment. Has this all been for nothing? A wasted night of dashed hopes and more questions?

Snap.

My head swivels toward the sound. Zeke looks in the same direction, but there's nothing but old trees and dirt. Probably just an animal stepping on a dead branch. Except, I haven't seen any animals.

I'm stepping toward Zeke and the direction of the snapping twig when I'm yanked into a hard body and a warm hand presses over my mouth, silencing me.

The sharp, cold edge of steel presses against my neck, and a scream crawls up my throat, begging to escape. The position reminds me of the one Zeke held Roderick in not too long ago, and panic wells within me. If this is the same sort of blade, then things just got really fucking bad.

The angel holding me chuckles, causing the hair on my arms to stand on end. I want to call out to Zeke, to tell him to get the others and head back to campus, but I'm frozen, trapped in fear of what might be my last few moments before death.

"Well, well, well," a familiar nasally voice says from behind me. "Fancy meeting you here."

27

HAYLIEL

At the sound of Roderick's voice, Zeke turns.

I watch as an array of emotions flashes across his face. Disbelief. Horror. Anger.

Roderick only laughs. "Brought a little treat for me this time, did you?" He removes the hand covering my mouth and trails it down my cheek almost tenderly, causing a shudder to rock my entire body. "But I'm afraid she's not really my type."

"Let her go," Zeke replies darkly. Through our mental bond, he says, *Try to stay calm, hummingbird. We'll get you out of this mess, I promise.*

Hope rushes through me, but it's dashed away when Roderick speaks.

"Now that wouldn't be very fun, would it?" He moves his grip, pulling my head back uncomfortably and exposing my throat. There's a small prick of pain before a thin line of warmth trickles down my neck. I just hope Zeke doesn't notice. If this is how I die, I'd rather he not witness it. "Do you like the way I'm holding her? When I saw you both stumbling about in the dark, I thought it would be fitting. You held me in a similar position not too long ago, if you'll recall."

"Yeah, and then you sent me off to my death. Thanks for that, by the way."

"Ah. So you went! I'm a little disappointed to find you here and looking so *alive*. Did you take this pretty little thing with you? I bet she'd make a damn fine bargaining chip with my less civilized friends."

Anger blooms in my chest, bubbling up until I can't hold it down any longer. "You murdering son of a bitch," I bite out, my fear of dying floating away somewhere beneath the sea of red behind my eyes.

He chuckles and says, "I just play the card I'm dealt, sweet thing. And I bet if you knew anything about loss, you'd have made the same choices."

I want to respond and tell him I would never, ever, take someone's life. That he can spout whatever bullshit he wants about loss, but killing another angel just spreads the loss around and I have no interest in that. But before I get the chance, Zeke speaks again.

"The items weren't there, you know. All we found were empty crates and trash. Until your boss showed up with his, how did you put it? Less civilized friends. Aren't you supposed to be meeting him soon?"

I can't see Roderick, but his body stiffens and the humor he had just moments ago vanishes.

"Your first time meeting him too, I think he said. Aren't you a lucky angel. Finally getting to meet the man in charge."

Zeke's taunting him, but I can't figure out why. Isn't pissing off the guy who currently holds me at knifepoint kind of a dumb move? If the weapon he's holding is as deadly as I think it is, then I'd rather we stop provoking him.

What are you up to, Zeke? I push the thought toward him, but he doesn't respond.

"What are you saying?" Roderick finally caves and asks.

"We came here to offer an exchange. Your information for ours. And trust me, you need us far more than we need you. But the longer you keep her in harm's way, the less inclined I feel to help you."

"You're lying. There's nothing you could possibly know that would *help* me. You just want to protect your precious little toy."

"Maybe I am. Maybe I'm not. Are you really willing to risk your life on it?" Zeke sounds so fucking convincing, which is most likely why Roderick stays quiet. Probably trying to decide if it's worth trusting us or not.

In a flash, someone barrels into us from behind and I'm thrown forward. Instead of landing in a pile on the ground, though, I wind up a few feet away, crashing into a tree. My wrist bends uncomfortably as I land, and there's a sharp pain beneath my right ear, but otherwise I'm alive. What the fuck just happened?

Raphael is beside me in a second, hauling me into his arms before setting me on a patch of moss. "Shit, sunshine. How the hell did you get over here?"

"I have no idea. How did you know where to find us?"

"That house leader of yours used the bond to call for help." He presses a kiss to my forehead before adding, "Stay here. I've got to go help tame a beast."

He rushes back to help Theo and Zeke where they fight to restrain Roderick, but I'm lost in a trance. Did Zeke really go to Raphael and Theo for help? My brain is working on information overload, and I can't help but wonder if these small shifts in trust will change things for our group once we're out of here.

Roderick fights back far more viciously than he did when we surprised him the first time, but he's no match for three very tired, very angry angels. By the time I've checked myself over and taken a few steady breaths, they have him pinned.

I join them, tripping on the fallen dagger that Roderick threatened me with earlier. It's nothing but a regular blade, wholly unable to kill me.

"Are you alright, sunshine?" Raph asks, pulling one of Roderick's arms awkwardly around a tree while Theo does the same with the other.

I nod and smile. "Thanks for coming to my rescue. It wasn't an angel blade after all, thank the Archangels."

Roderick struggles to get free, but it's futile. *Not with my guys holding you down*, I think with a smirk.

Your guys, huh? Raphael teases through our bond, causing my cheeks to heat. Ah, shit.

Um, I, uh, just meant—

"Quit it with whatever disgustingly mushy mental conversation you're having and get to the fucking point. You want me to listen? Well, I'm listening."

Annoyed, I step toward him and scowl. "We have information that could literally help you *survive*, but seeing as you're a murderer, I'm starting to wonder if we should even bother. And do you know why, despite every cell in my body telling me not to, we're offering this to you, Roderick?"

I take another step, feeling the tension rise higher around us.

"Because while I don't give a flying fuck if you live, the information you can give us might just be enough to save the lives of other angels. So if saving your life also means saving countless others, I'll do it."

Silence follows my speech, which kind of bums me out a bit because it was a damn fine one. But something shifts in the air, pulling my attention.

"Do you feel that?" Theo asks, looking around.

"Fuck! We're running out of time." In lightning speed, Zeke stands in front of Roderick, one hand fisted in his shirt as he lowers his voice to a deadly decibel. "What does your boss want?"

Roderick must have at least a little self-preservation because he doesn't waste a second before answering. "He never shared his final plans with me. I just know he has several angels in high places that help him skirt around red tape."

"Who?" Raphael asks, his grip firm on Roderick's arm.

"I don't know for certain."

Zeke turns, cursing and kicking the roots of a tree.

"I think I've narrowed one of them down. The mayor. I think he's working with the mayor. I don't know for certain or who the others are. Now I've held up my part of the deal. It's time for you to make good on yours."

"The Guild," Theo says, looking toward the mountain where Guild headquarters are.

"No," Roderick dismisses, but his voice lacks conviction.

"That's why he wasn't scared to meet you here," I add softly.

Zeke sighs. "And I bet whoever he's working with is the mole we've been looking for."

"Shit! If you're right, then we're all fucked. Now tell me what you know that could save my life."

"Guys ..."

At the sound of Raphael's voice, I turn to look in the same direction he is, and my blood turns to ice. The sky is lighter now, with dawn approaching quickly, but that's not the only thing heading our way.

Along the skyline, I count at least eight demons flying toward us.

28

HAYLIEL

"Tell me quickly and then let me fucking go. We made a deal," Roderick demands, his eyes wide.

"This meeting with your boss was a trap," Zeke tells him, not bothering to dance around it. "He sent in a squad to bring you back to that house so he could teach you 'a lesson that very few angels have ever truly learned.' Whatever that means."

Roderick lets out a crazed laugh that pierces through the panicked fog. "It seems our trade was all for nothing then. The only place you'll be taking that information is to your grave."

"We have to go," Theo says, his tone brooking no argument. We're beneath a thick canopy of trees, so it's not likely that they've seen us yet, but as much as that might help us now, it won't last forever.

"A deal is a deal," Zeke tells Roderick before nodding to Theo and Raphael for them to let go of his arms.

I brace myself for an attack from the angel we just freed, but it never comes. All he does is stare at the demons like his fate is sealed.

When Zeke turns to me, he notices the blade in my hand and immediately pulls the pack off his back. It takes him no time to reveal five pristine daggers that glint beneath the growing dawn. "Here. Just in case."

"These would have been helpful at the barn," Raphael grumbles, but I'm just glad we all have some way to protect ourselves should things go sideways.

I hesitate for a moment before approaching Roderick and holding the dagger out to him, hilt first.

Apprehension fills his gaze, but he snatches it from my grasp and backs away slowly. I might not agree with the things that he's done, but I'm not heartless. Whatever lesson they intend to teach him will come in pain and blood. At least this way he can fight back.

"Let's go. We can lose them in the farming district," Theo says. The four of us run in that direction, only to stop a few feet later when we exit a group of trees and notice a second group of demons headed our way.

I count them, adding another seven to the group coming from the opposite direction. We're fucked. Royally, undeniably fucked.

We move back under the cover of trees, hoping they haven't spotted us yet. "Please tell me someone has a plan," I say, my stomach sinking to the ground.

"The Guild," Zeke says. "I doubt everyone is working with them. I'm proof enough of that."

He's right. Even if most of the angels working for the Guild are traitors, we'll force them to make a choice. Either they stand by our side and fight off the demons or stand with them and let the entire city know where their true loyalty lies. I just hope it won't come to that.

"Sounds good enough to me," Raphael adds before we take off in a sprint.

We keep to the ground, not willing to risk anything by flying. There's still a chance they don't know where we are, so we weave through the thick trunks of trees, hopping over roots until we reach the end of our coverage.

"Can anyone see how close they are?" Raphael asks as he looks up at the sky, attempting to see through the foliage.

When Theo and Zeke shake their heads, the weight in my stomach grows heavier. I look around, wondering where Roderick went off to. "Maybe they've found Roderick already and won't even know we're here."

"I like your attitude, sunshine. Everyone ready to run their hearts out?"

We count down like we're about to enter the most important race of our lives, and maybe we are.

"Three. Two. One."

The sky is even lighter as we dash across the open field and toward Guild headquarters. Wind rushes through the loose tendrils of my hair, boosting my belief that we'll make it.

An angry growl comes from somewhere behind me. My heart almost pounds straight out of my chest as I push myself harder, faster. The growling grows closer, joined by the flapping of wings.

No, no, no! We're still too far from the Guild.

Beneath my feet, the ground rumbles as demon after demon lands. I stumble, nearly tripping over my feet, and even though I catch myself, it costs me precious time. Something slams into me from behind and I'm thrown forward, skittering over the hard dirt.

Hayliel! my men call out through the bond, and I feel them surge toward me as I stagger to my feet. They make it to me before any other creature, and it's then I realize that the four of us are in way over our heads. We're about to put everything we know about combat to the test.

Demons converge on us from all directions, swiping with their claws. That they aren't all using angel blades hasn't gone unnoticed. A small victory, I suppose.

I wish we had time to collect ourselves, even if only for a moment. To plan, to act, to say all the things I've been too afraid to say.

But we don't get a moment, and without a sun blade, we're screwed. I wish I knew more about what turned those demons to ash in the last attack. Had it really been me? Was it only my transformation that brought it on, or is it something I can do at will? Fuck. Some savior I am.

We stick together, standing back-to-back as the creatures circle us like starving wolves. None of us know what they want. Is it our deaths, or do they have orders to bring us back with Roderick to learn the same lesson as him? Neither option sounds appealing to me.

So far, I've counted fifteen of the beasts. Against our little party of four, I don't like those odds. The snarling creatures form a circle around us, and I expect them to attack all at once, but they don't. They come at us in pairs, taking turns and seeming almost gleeful. What are they doing?

The four of us move as a team, ebbing and flowing like the ocean. In any other situation, I might be in awe of our synchronization, but I can't focus on that now. I deflect a blow from a particularly large demon and stagger back into Theo. "Sorry," I tell him, noticing the blown out pupils of his eyes, but I don't get the chance to make sure he's okay because another demon swings a claw-tipped hand toward him.

"Look out!"

I act without thinking, letting my heart and mind move for me. Theo is mine. All of these guys are. And no one will take them from me.

Rage and fear pump through my veins like blood as I slice my knife clear through the demon's arm, severing its hand completely. It falls to the ground with a *thud*. The beast pulls back with a snarl, black blood pouring from the stump.

I feel my men's eyes on me, their shock just as obvious as mine. I shouldn't have been able to cut through skin and bone that easily.

Somewhere to my left, a demon releases a piercing shriek that has me covering my ears and wondering if he's blown my eardrums. Then the demons change tactics. It's like they'd only been playing with us before, but now that I've drawn blood, they're no longer having fun.

The demon whose hand I just cut off rushes me, but I tuck and roll out of the way before he can make contact. *Ha! Sucker!*

While that move might have saved me in the moment, it put a little more distance between me and my men. They come at us harder now, ganging up on us, and it's clear what they're trying to do. They want to separate us. Get us alone and take us out. We can't let that happen.

This is nothing like the battle at school, and it's clear now as I struggle to avoid the death blows coming my way that they'd been holding back before. For whatever reason, during the attack at the school, their goal hadn't been to maim us. Now I fear we aren't so lucky.

Fifteen demons against four angels. How are we going to make it out of this one?

As the fight moves on, the space between me and my men grows. If these assholes wanted to get us alone, they're succeeding. Shit! I try to check on them, to at least make sure everyone is standing, but the beasts don't give me a chance.

"Were you snooping around where you shouldn't be, little angel?" a demon says from behind me. I whirl around, ready to fight, but the creature only stands there. He's covered in scars, but there's something about them that almost seems purposeful. Rows of them, all neatly lined up on his chest.

I don't respond, unsure where his line of questioning is going and, frankly, not really caring. As long as I have this reprieve from the fight, I might as well use it to my advantage and edge back toward my friends. The last thing I want is to become another notch on his flesh.

He puts his hands behind his back, tucking them beneath his wings. "I didn't believe it at first. Doors and locks aren't really important where I'm from, so it's not hard to assume one of us forgot."

I shuffle back a step, then another, cautious not to make it too obvious. An alarm goes off in my head, telling me to hurry and get back to them. But is it for their safety or mine? I'm alone with this chatty demon and, for some reason, that terrifies me.

"But then I heard something else." His hands drop to his sides, and our eyes lock. "A mention of *power*. We can feel it, you know? Even smell it, if it's potent enough. It's part of how our kind survives."

"Why are you telling me all this?" I ask, confused, but not wanting him to stop.

He grins wickedly, his sharp teeth glinting beneath the pre-dawn light. "Does all that power make you dense, little angel? I'm telling you because I can. Besides, it's not like the information will leave this lovely field."

I barely have time to process his words before another demon joins us. He approaches me, sharpening his claws together gleefully before he lunges. I move a second too late and pain tears through my leg where his claws slashed me.

The pain fuels my adrenaline and spurs me into action. I may not have a sun blade, but I can incapacitate these assholes enough to get my friends and me to safety. And I vow to myself right here and now that when we get out of here, I'll do whatever it takes to access the power that angels and demons alike seem to think I possess.

I manage to bury my blade in the asshole's skull, but it doesn't matter. I get rid of one and two more show up in his place. They don't give me a moment to collect myself or catch my breath, forcing me to fight for what feels like my very life, despite them not holding the one weapon that could kill us. *It will be worse if they haul you back to their boss.*

Pain ricochets up my arm, and I look at a demon fucking *biting* me. I yank my arm from between his teeth and tear the skin even more. Blood runs down to my hand, dripping from my fingers onto the ground beneath my feet, but still the creatures don't stop.

They come at me, again and again, and for every cut I make on them, they make two more on me. It's futile, our survival. We aren't equipped to make it out of this alive, either in weapon or skill.

A loud whooshing sound fills the space around me, making my heart race with fear. If more demons show up, we're more than fucked. But the creatures I'm fighting seem just as confused by the sound as I am.

A spear shoots through a demon's head a few feet away, and then the angel who threw it drops from the sky and pulls it back out. More angels show up, all of them wearing the Guild uniform and all of them fighting at our side.

The tide shifts in our favor as our backup makes this a proper fight. One we now have a chance of winning. The demons I'd been fighting fall back, looking to who I assume is their leader — the scar-covered creature who threatened my life and watched on as his dogs tried to tear me apart — for confirmation. I don't hear any words, but I can tell something transpired between them because they quickly disperse. They must understand that trained Guild members are clearly the bigger threat.

With a rare moment of freedom, I search for my friends and clench the wound on my arm to staunch the bleeding. Parts of it have healed already, but not fast enough.

Not too far from me, I spot a Guild member with metal-tipped wings exchanging blows with a demon whose horns are the biggest I've ever seen. This must be a lieutenant, and I wonder if maybe it's Azrael, but with his back to me I can't quite tell.

Beyond them, Zeke is fighting two demons at once and looking far too relaxed while doing so. Raphael and Theo are nearby, fighting their own demons. As if sensing my gaze, Theo looks up at me and I can read so many things in his eyes. Fear. Pain. Loss. But he does his best to bury it and get us out of here. With Raphael there to pull him back if need be, I know they'll be fine.

We aren't out of the woods yet, but my confidence is renewed and hope spurs me into action. Taking one final moment to assess my route, I consider sticking to the outskirts of battle and circling back to my friends, but that's too risky. My best chance is to stay close to the trained Guild members, and what's better than a lieutenant?

I run straight through the battle, toward the men who hold far more of me than I ever thought I'd give. I'm desperate to be near them and see this battle to the end.

But want and hope never did have much of a place in combat.

I don't make it very far before something rams into my side and sends me careening through the air, where I land in a heap on the ground. Stars float around me as I try to get my bearings and stand. The ringing in my ears is all I can hear as I look around at the battlefield. Angels and demons fight, but why is it taking so long with the Guild here? And how come it feels like there are far more than fifteen demons?

Something tickles my hair and I whirl around to find the scarred demon watching me gleefully yet saying nothing.

I dig deep within myself, searching for the strength I need to clear away the stars from my fall, but when I find it, it's too late.

Two more demons now stand at my side, all three of them wearing smug smiles. I feel for the dagger but find it no longer gripped in my hand.

Shit. It's there. Lying on the ground between me and the scarred leader. If I have any chance of getting out of this circle of death, I need a weapon.

But in my cloudy state, he's faster than me.

I never make it to the blade.

He rushes forward and wraps his arm around me in a way that could almost be considered an embrace. Except I don't feel safe or loved.

I only feel pain.

It erupts in my shoulder, my side, my back. My lungs struggle to draw in oxygen, and I fear my lungs might give out. A burning heat weaves its way through my veins until it feels like I've swallowed the sun. Something ignites deep in my chest until all I am is fiery pain.

"Dead little angels don't have power, do they?" the scarred demon whispers in my ear before he drops me, and I sink to my knees.

My chin falls down, and I catch sight of something sticking out of my shoulder.

A blade.

Is this what hurt me?

As the excruciating pain builds within me, I only stare at it. The intricately detailed handle holds me in a trance. Along the hilt are runes, and sitting at the very top is a gorgeous black orb swirling with red.

How can something so beautiful cause so much pain?

29

THEO

I block an attack from the left, then whirl around to avoid incoming claws from the right. My blade buries into the chest of my attacker, but even though he's down for now, he's not dead.

Having the Guild show up and fight at our side is a fucking blessing. With our measly weapons, we wouldn't have lasted much longer. I mean, shit, Raph and I are already wounded. Ezekiel looks as calm as ever, but he can't hide the blood seeping through his shirt. Hayliel, my bright firefly, fights like a warrior. Her strength and determination fuel my own, and when I saw a demon fucking *biting* her, I almost lost it. None of us are getting out of this unscathed.

It could be worse, though. They fight us with claws and teeth and brute strength. All things that can harm us, sure. But they can't kill us. And none of the demons seem to hold the angel blade that can carve us from this world.

Sounds of the snarling beasts threaten to take me under, to paralyze me and send me back in the past, but I fight against it. I've already had to rely on my friends far more than I care to admit tonight, and I don't want to make it any worse.

If only it were that easy.

A female voice shouts in pain from behind me, and suddenly I'm tumbling back in time. I turn toward the noise, but my vision turns fuzzy. The view before me of a Guild member and a demon locked in combat shifts. I no longer stand on an open field. Below me is the asphalt in the skate park. And a few feet away from me is my old friend, bleeding out beneath the angry demon stabbing her to death.

I blink and it's gone, shifted back into the field.

Everything is blurry, but I can still see the demon approaching with lustful hatred in its eyes.

I should move. Bring up my weapon. Something! But my limbs no longer want to cooperate. Regardless of how hard I try, my body won't listen, so I do the only thing I can do. Prepare myself for pain.

Zeke rushing toward my attacker, taking its focus off me, penetrates the fog of my vision. Then the calming voice of the man who's saved me from myself far too many times.

"Come back to us," he says, turning me around to face him. His hands are warm against mine, grimy with a mixture of black and red blood, but warm.

"Raph," I croak out, willing my mind to get it together.

"I'm here. We aren't in that skatepark. We're in an open field close to Guild headquarters, remember? It's not exactly safe, but we need you for a little longer, Theo. The Guild is here to help, but we need you too."

With my eyes closed, I breathe in and out, letting his touch ground me. Sounds become sharper, and when I open my eyes, the world is no longer fuzzy.

Around us, demons take to the sky, flying off in all different directions and carrying their injured with them.

"They're leaving."

Ezekiel is talking nearby, but my mind is still too fucked up to make out what he's saying.

"They must have finally realized they had no shot at winning," Raphael adds, still assessing me closely. His eyes travel over my wounds, just like I'm doing for him.

But nothing makes sense. Everything that I know about these creatures leads me to believe that they don't give up. And despite the Guild being here, not a single demon actually died a true death. That doesn't really scream defeat.

I think of the last time they acted weird. At the school, they toyed with us more than they tried to hurt us. Then they all converged on one being and, because of how things played out, we don't actually know what their intentions were.

My gaze travels past Raphael, roaming over the crowd of Guild members until I see her. My firefly.

She's on her knees, gazing down at something protruding from her shoulder. Is that ...

I stand on wobbly legs, rushing toward her and damn near face-planting in my need to get to her. If only these damn limbs of mine wouldn't shake.

Just as she's about to fall backward, I catch her.

"Hey. You're okay. I've got you," I say, and feel Raphael's presence beside me.

Her breathing is ragged, choppy, and when her eyes flash to mine, they're far too glassy. Then, without a word, her head lolls to the side and panic threatens to consume me.

No, no, no, no, no. *Wake up, firefly.* I push the words through our bond, but it's like I'm shouting into a void. Like she's not even there.

"We need a healer!" Raphael calls out, dropping to his knees and pressing his palm into the wound on her side, trying to stop the bleeding. Just how many fucking times was she stabbed?

"I'm going to pull this out," I say when Ezekiel comes over, hauling a Guild member with a healer badge on her uniform.

She shakes her head. "Leave it. It's the only thing stopping the flow of blood. Let me heal her other wounds first."

I fucking hate leaving it there, but I do as I'm told. What the fuck do I know about saving anyone? By the Archangels, I was going to remove the damn thing and that probably would have caused her more pain.

The healer takes Raphael's spot and places her hands over the wound on Hayliel's side, concentration etched into her features. We aren't taught healing in first year, so I know shit about how to help her.

Not that it matters, anyway, when I can't seem to take my eyes off the blade in her shoulder. It's not one of ours, I know that for certain. The odd runic markings on the hilt aren't familiar, and the gem embedded in the pommel makes me shudder.

The healer won't be able to help. Zeke's voice sounds like agony personified, and I realize he's just standing there.

Anger flows through me as I look up at him. *If all you're going to do is be a negative Neil, then why don't you fuck off?*

Raphael places a bloodied hand on my back, giving me some of his strength. *Why won't she be able to help?*

But before Zeke can reply, the Guild healer grunts. "Why isn't it working?" She looks away from the wound to us and then the blade I almost took out, and her face pales.

The blade, it's ...

"I'm sorry," the healer says, unable to meet our eyes. "With this type of wound, there's nothing more I can do."

"What do you mean there's nothing more you can do? For the love of the Archangels, we're damn near indestructible." I can't keep the fury from my tone, but even as the words pass my lips, the pieces slot together in my mind.

I look from the healer to Raphael, and finally to Zeke. Without me even having to ask the question, he nods, turning my entire world upside down.

There's only one thing that can kill us, and I'm staring right at it.

That's no regular weapon sticking out of Hayliel's shoulder. It's an angel blade.

Noise fills my mind as reality sinks in, shattering my heart into a billion tiny pieces.

Hayliel is dying, and there's nothing any of us can do to stop it.

Find out what happens next in book 3, Wings of Strife.

Acknowledgements

I'm so proud of this book, and I hope you found joy within the pages despite the teeny, tiny cliffhanger.

Thank you to my editor, proofreader, formatter, and cover and graphic designers for putting up with me and helping make this one hell of a book.

To all the friends who have kept me sane these last few months, I'm so grateful the book world brought us together. I adore you! And finally, thank you to all the readers who took a chance on me. Without you, this wouldn't be possible.

About the Author

Victoria is a Canadian girl with a love for travel, music, books, games, and mayonnaise. She spends her mornings writing before work, and hopes to one day write full time. Friends say she gives the best hugs and you can usually find her laughing at her own lame jokes.

Facebook Group: /victoriasvillainousqueens

Facebook: /victoria.pauley.506

Instagram: @victoriapauley.author

TikTok: @victoriapauleyauthor

Linktree: /victoriapauley

Website: victoriapauley.com

Also By Victoria Pauley

Standalones

Caged *(MF Gang Romance)*

A Night of Indulgence and Sloth *(MFM, Office,*
Dark Romance)

Series and Duets

<u>Silver City University</u>

(RH/Why-Choose, Academy, Paranormal Ro-
mance)

Wings of Deception

Wings of Torment

Wings of Strife

<u>Creating Destiny Duet</u>
(Double MF Fantasy Romance, Greek Mytholo-
gy)
Guided by the Stars
Fighting for the Stars

www.ingramcontent.com/pod-product-compliance
Lightning Source LLC
Chambersburg PA
CBHW061102210726
48294CB00001B/256